The porch was dark. Maggie was halfway to the door when she realized someone was leaning against the wall next to it, hidden in the shadows.

The breath caught in her throat. She gasped and wrapped her arms around the case that cradled the Angel violin.

He moved into view standing squarely in front of the door. His hair fell to his shoulders and he wore a suit.

"Do not be afraid." He spoke with a British accent. He had a strong, pleasant voice, but what was he doing lurking outside her house at midnight?

Maggie could scream, but who would hear her? The neighborhood's seclusion no longer seemed to be anything but a menace.

She took a step backward, wondering if she could beat the man to her car.

"Please, Maggie, I will not hurt you."

There was just enough light to see him smile. He had very white teeth.

"You have come for the violin," she said.

By Michael Romkey
Published by Ballantine Books:

I, VAMPIRE
THE VAMPIRE PAPERS
THE VAMPIRE PRINCESS
THE VAMPIRE VIRUS
VAMPIRE HUNTER
THE LONDON VAMPIRE PANIC
THE VAMPIRE'S VIOLIN

THE VAMPIRE'S VIOLIN

MICHAEL ROMKEY

BALLANTINE BOOKS • NEW YORK

The Vampire's Violin is a work of fiction. Names, places,
and incidents either are a product of the author's
imagination or are used fictitiously.

A Del Rey® Book
Published by The Random House Ballantine
Publishing Group
Copyright © 2003 by Michael Romkey

www.delreydigital.com

ISBN 0-345-45208-9

Manufactured in the United States of America

First Edition: April 2003

OPM 10 9 8 7 6 5 4 3 2 1

For my family: Carol, Ryan, Matthew, and Drew. With special thanks to Joanie Johnson, who has forgotten more about playing the violin than I will ever know.

ALLEGRO

Anno domini 1744

1

THE BELL IN the old Roman tower in the northwest corner of the Monastero di Chiaravalle began to toll at midnight. The golden tone flowed out over the sleeping *campagna,* caressing the vineyards and olive groves with its deep, hypnotic sound. The duke in his castle, the peasants in the village, the sheep in the fields, the foxes in their dens—they had listened to the Compline bell all their lives. If they noticed it at all that night, it was as a reminder that they were watched over by a power that never slept.

The monks, simply clad in unbleached woolen robes and sandals, stirred from their cells, moving quietly through torchlit gallerias and into the central courtyard. They stood with hands folded, not speaking, obedient to the brotherhood's vow of silence. The abbot moved to the front of the group in the courtyard, walking quickly despite his great age, his tonsured hair shining like a silver halo in the moonlight. The monks began to chant Gregorian plainsong as the bell fell silent. They followed the abbot in twos toward the chapel, the Latin verses reverberating against stone walls and rising up to heaven.

* * *

Bishop Georgio Falcone knew he would not be missed, one brother more or less among many. And even if he were, no one, not even the abbot, would question his absence.

In Florence, Bishop Falcone lived in a palazzo as splendid as any prince's, the walls hung with paintings and rich tapestries, secretaries and emissaries scurrying through the hallways attending to his business, responding to his summonses. On retreat at the monastery, Bishop Falcone lived the simple life of a Cistercian brother. He slept on a hard bed in a monk's cell equipped only with a wooden chair and a desk. He wore the humble robe of a brother, the gold-and-ruby bishop's ring the only outward sign of high office.

Bishop Falcone waited until the brothers were in the chapel before setting off across the courtyard, his destination a doorway set into an arch in the church's north wall. The door opened onto a landing at the head of a downward spiral of stone stairs. Beyond the weak circle of light thrown by his single candle, there was only the impression of a cavernous darkness falling sharply away, a yawning passageway plunging into the earth's musty womb.

Keeping close to the wall on the treacherous stone stairs, Bishop Falcone began to descend into the Monastero di Chiaravalle's crypt.

When he was a young man and new to the priesthood, Falcone thought his vocation would protect him from sin. He had been very naïve then. Time taught him that there was no escape from the devil's tricks. You could resist evil in its usual forms, but just when you mastered it, temptation took on another shape, subtle and infinitely seductive in its new form. Even if you were constantly vigilant, sin could work its way into your heart, a worm boring into a rose, its presence unsuspected until it was too late.

"Credo in unum Deum, Patrem omnipotentem, factorem coeli et terrae, visibilium omnium et invisibilium . . ."

The brothers' voices floated down from the chapel as Bishop Falcone's sandal-clad feet felt their way down stairs rubbed smooth and slippery by centuries of use. The monastery had been built on the ruins of a Roman villa, and the catacombs beneath it had been used for Mass in the early days of the church, during the Persecution, before the Church's ultimate triumph over paganism and sin.

The candle began to gutter. Bishop Falcone stopped, cupping his hand around the flame, willing it to live, not wanting to be caught in perfect darkness halfway between one world and the next.

"Et in unum Dominum Jesum Christum, Filium Dei unigentum. Et ex Patre natum ante omnia saecula. Deum de Deo, lumen de lumine, Deum verum de Deo vero . . ."

The flame grew brighter, seeming to draw strength out of the music. Falcone's smile was bitter. He, too, was sensitive to music. If he had not taken vows, he would have become a musician and composer, like Corelli and Vivaldi. But Satan had turned that against him, using Falcone's love of music as a weapon to destroy his soul.

Cupping the flame, Falcone continued down into the crypt, each step as an admission of his descent into worldly temptation that had brought him to this place, in shame and penance.

"*Genitum, non factum, consubstantialem Patri: per quem omnia facta sunt. Qui propter nos homines, et propter nostram salutem descendit de coelis. Et incarnatus de Spiritu sancto ex Maria Virgine: Et homo factus est. Crucufixus etiam pro nobis: sub Pontio Pilato passus et sepultus est . . ."*

At the bottom of the stairs was a small chapel with a ceiling vaulted in the old Roman style. The air was chilly and damp, like a cave, and smelled of decay, gray cobwebs hanging in drooping loops from the ceiling. Four passageways led off into the catacombs, where the corpses of dead monks reposed on biers carved into the living rock. Each of the walls framed an alcove piled high with the skulls of monks whose bones, unstrung by death, had been removed from the catacombs to make room for newer arrivals.

There was a simple altar in one corner, the wooden cross blackened with age. Bishop Falcone lit the altar candles, but their combined light threw only a simulacrum of illumination in the chamber, the dim light serving mainly to draw more darkness from the crypt's far-reaching catacombs. The shadows loomed and danced in the flickering light. It was almost as if the darkness were a conscious, breathing entity fed on the rotting bodies of monks, hungry now for Bishop Falcone's soul.

"*Et resurrexit tertia die, secundum Scripturas. Et ascendit in coelum: sedet ad dexteram Patris. Et iterum venturus est cum gloria judicare vivos et mortuos: cujus regni non erit finis . . ."*

Bishop Falcone knelt down, the rough stone poking

painfully into his knees. Making the sign of the cross, he began to pray.

"Free me, Lord, from my earthly lust. Drive from me the unholy desire consuming my heart."

"Et in Spiritum sanctum, Dominum et vivificantem: qui ex Patre Filioque procedit."

Footsteps came up slowly behind Falcone, stopping only a few feet behind.

"Replace the burning desire in my soul with your cleansing fire, Lord."

There was a slithering sound behind the bishop, like rats scuttling across the dusty floor. Falcone made the sign of the cross and slipped the robe off his shoulders. He nodded his head, acknowledging he was ready for what was to come. The cat-o'-nine-tails split the air with a serpentine hiss cut short with a loud slap when the whip struck the bare skin of Bishop Falcone's fleshy back. The blow bent Falcone over until his face nearly touched the floor before him.

"Qui cum Patre et Filio simul adoratur et conglorificatur: qui locutus est per Prophetus . . ."

The bishop pushed himself upright with one hand. His skin burned, the pain spreading out across his back, pulsing with each quickened beat of his heart. He drew in a slow, ragged breath.

"Et unum sanctam catholicam et apostolicam Ecclesiam . . ."

"Again," Falcone commanded.

The whip scourged him a second time, tearing into the welts raised by the first blow. Blood trickled down his back.

"Confiteor unum baptisma in remissionem peccatorum. Et expecto resurrectionem mortuorum . . ."

"Again . . ."

The third blow nearly knocked him sideways.

Falcone had never truly wanted anything—not advancement in the Church, not a woman, not power and influence, not even the red cap of a cardinal—as much as he had lusted for the succubus haunting his nights and days. The desire never left his thoughts for more than a few minutes when he was awake, and it commanded his dreams when he slept. It even polluted his mind when he celebrated the Mass, a hungry wanting that would lead to his damnation, unless he could drive it out of his body and soul.

"Again!"

Falcone squeezed his eyes closed, anticipating the blow that pitched him forward. He lost consciousness for a few moments, his cheek pressed against the cool, dusty stone of the crypt floor. It came to him then, as it always did when his guard was down—a sound so sweet that an angel might have been singing to him in the secret language of heaven, soothing and caressing him, tenderly lifting his bleeding body and broken spirit. Falcone awoke then to the pain of his bleeding back, and to the greater spiritual pain that came when he realized he was not hearing the voice of an angel in his mind, but of the demon that had taken possession of his soul.

The bishop pushed away the brother's arm that solicitously helped him sit upright. "The whip," Falcone said, his voice weak. "Scourge me again, Brother, for I am not yet cleansed."

From the sanctuary far above the crypt, the last line of the Credo chanted in plainsong floated down to them as the brother slowly lifted the whip.

"Et vitam venturi saeculi. Amen."

The promise of the world to come seemed very far away to Bishop Falcone. He was enslaved mind, body, and heart, like a Hindu hashish eater who lived only to float lost in his intoxicated dreams. If it killed him, Bishop Falcone would be freed from his lust—his lust for a *violin*! On his last visit to Florence, he had been bewitched by the enchanted singing of one of Archangelo Serafino's magical violins. If he couldn't overcome the all-consuming obsession to possess one of the Angel violins, as they were called, he would lose his soul, for it was a mortal sin to love anything above God.

"Amen," the monk standing behind Bishop Falcone said.

And then, again, the sharp rush of the falling whip.

2

THE BLIND OLD man's fingers felt the air until they located the stack of quarter-sawed spruce boards. He picked up the first, held it to his ear, rapped it with his knuckles.

"Bello," he said.

Yet evidently the quality was not sufficiently *bello*. He shook his head and put the board aside. He picked up another and repeated the process. This piece of spruce was set aside, too. He was halfway through the stack of wood before he found one that satisfied him.

"Silvio!"

The journeyman put down the clamp he was using to fasten the maple rib of a new violin to the frame.

"Yes, *Padróne?*"

"Listen to this one. Can you hear how she rings?"

"Meraviglioso! Like a bell."

As the two men worked in the shop on Via Bertisi, hardly speaking, each concentrating on his work, the sun climbed higher in the Lombard sky, warming the air, bringing out the rich aroma of linseed oil and pine resin. Occasionally the sound of a violin could be heard from one of the other shops on the street. The old man would raise his chin a little, smiling. His eyes were useless, but his ears were keen; he could judge the quality of an instrument from just a few notes. Cremona, Italy, was the center of violinmaking in 1745, as it had been one hundred years before, and probably would remain for however long there were violins. Still, there was a tremendous range in quality among the instruments produced by its masters, journeymen, and apprentices.

At noon the men took off their aprons and went upstairs for a simple lunch of bread, slices of sausage, and wine, prepared by Grazia, the *padróne*'s only remaining servant, a woman nearly as old as he.

It was the habit of most violinmakers in Cremona to take a break in the early afternoon, especially during the summer, when the warmth made it difficult to stay awake leaning over a workbench, trying to concentrate on the finer work that required small, delicate, repetitive tasks. But time was precious to the *padróne,* and so the two returned to their labors after their meal.

In the middle of the afternoon, Silvio finished applying a coat of varnish to a green instrument. The *padróne,* who had no children of his own, had already passed the secret concoction on to Silvio, teaching him to mix it in a copper alembic that once belonged to an alchemist. He looked up from his work when he noticed the old man had stopped working and was looking up, his eyes focused, as they always were now, on something very far away.

"Is something the matter, *Padróne?*"

"Is the shop in order?"

"Of course, *Padróne,*" Silvio said, looking around to assure himself that this was indeed the case. "Except for the wood shavings on your apron. Why do you ask?"

"We are about to have visitors," the old man said, brushing the wood dust and tiny spruce curlicues from his leather apron. He turned toward the door of Serafino Violins with a look of happy anticipation in his sightless eyes.

As if conjured up by the old blind man's wizardry, four men appeared in the doorway. When Silvio saw who they were, his throat tightened the way it used to in the presence of the harsh master of the orphanage where he lived before he had the good fortune to be apprenticed to Archangelo Serafino to learn violin-making. Silvio had been anticipating the deputation's visit for a long time, and dreading it for the *padróne*'s sake.

First through the door was Fausto Scolari, the *presidente* of the luthier guild, wearing a rich velvet cloak and a hat decorated with a purple feather. Behind him was Carlo Tartini, a journeyman in Fausto's shop and an officer in the guild. If the presence of Giovanni Capelli, a master violinmaker who had once been one of the *padróne*'s apprentices, gave Silvio reason to hope, he did not know what to make of the other man, a thin young priest with a high forehead and dark, cold eyes.

"*Buon giorno, gentiluomini,*" the *padróne* said, smiling and opening his arms in a welcoming gesture.

"Good day to you, Archangelo Serafino," Fausto said without removing his hat.

"It is always a pleasure to have you visit my shop, Giovanni," the *padróne* said, looking in the direction of his former apprentice as if his sightless eyes could see him perfectly. "And you other three gentlemen are welcome as well."

Fausto and the priest exchanged a troubled glance, as if the feat were evidence of witchcraft, but Giovanni, like Silvio, did not seem in the least surprised. *Padróne* Serafino "saw" more with his ears than most men did with their eyes.

"Good afternoon, *Padróne,*" Giovanni said, removing his hat and bowing with grave solemnity.

Fausto cleared his voice to get the others to look at him, reminding them he was the one in authority among the visitors, a man who was, Silvio knew, well accustomed to putting himself forward.

"It seems you have not regained your eyesight, Archangelo."

"Your own eyes remain keen as ever," Archangelo said with a hint of humor.

"And yet," Fausto continued, ignoring Archangelo's comment, "it appears you are continuing to make violins even though you are blind. Can this be true?"

"God has taken my sight," the *padróne* replied, "but He has given me something much more precious in return."

"Has He indeed?" the priest asked.

Archangelo looked at the priest with a curious expression.

"Pardon me, sir, but I do not think I have had the pleasure of being introduced. I never forget a voice."

"I am Father Bartolommeo."

"You are not from Cremona, I think."

"No." The young priest drew himself up proudly. "I

am from the curia in Rome, from the office of the congregation."

Silvio felt his knees weaken. He had had a premonition something like this might happen when people started calling his master's recent instruments Angel violins.

"We are honored you would take the time to visit our little shop," *Padróne* Serafino said. "Is your visit personal, or are you here on behalf of the congregation of the Inquisition?"

Silvio began to say a hasty prayer, but it went unanswered before he could complete his silent request.

"I am here in an official capacity," Father Bartolommeo said.

"As are we all," Fausto added, as if there could be any doubt.

"A blind violinmaker is very rare indeed," Fausto said. "I do not know that I have ever heard of such a thing. You are fortunate you have Silvio to assist you."

"I thank God for Silvio's help every morning and every night in my prayers," *Padróne* Serafino said.

"And yet we are confronted with a serious problem."

"We are?" the blind man asked with what seemed like perfect innocence, even though Silvio could not imagine the master was unaware where the guild president was going with his line of questioning.

"You are blind, Archangelo," Fausto said, making the statement an accusation. "You cannot possibly continue to make violins. At least not here, in Cremona, as a member of the guild."

"But with all due respect, Fausto, that is absurd. I have never made better violins. Blindness has been nothing but a blessing to me as a violinmaker."

"That's absurd!" Carlo sneered.

"Why did we come here if not to hear *Padróne* Serafino's side of this?" Giovanni said. The anger in Giovanni's voice surprised—and heartened—Silvio. If he was willing to take his former master's side, there was a chance the old man would be allowed to continue making violins for what little time he had left. Giovanni was now considered the best violinmaker in Cremona. His opinion was not without consequence.

"Perhaps I might be allowed to say a few things on my behalf," *Padróne* Serafino said.

"That is precisely why we are here," Giovanni said, though it was clear from the expression on the faces of Fausto and Carlo that they were not interested in Archangelo Serafino's side of things.

"You know me. You know my shop. For fifty years I have done good work here. My violins are comparable to any that have been made in Cremona in my generation. And yet, if you will forgive me for saying it, my violins, like all the violins that have been made here in recent times, have been good but never extraordinary. Nobody makes violins that are the equal of instruments built by my mentor Stradivari or Guarneri del Gesu. Would any of you dispute that as a general statement?"

"We do make very good violins, violas, and violoncellos in Cremona," Fausto said, "the best in Europe."

"Yes, but something has gone out of our craft. We no longer achieve the highest level of the art. For a long time I thought it was as if some secret had been lost, though we still know the smallest details about the way Stradivari mixed his varnishes, the exact dimensions of his violins. Yet something seems to be lost. If you use your *ears,* gentlemen, you know it is true."

"*Padróne* Serafino is right," Giovanni said.

"Nobody questioned the quality of my work." The *padróne* smiled in his inquisitors' direction. "At least, not while I still had the use of my eyes. To be perfectly honest, I didn't question my work myself. I was among the best in Cremona. What if my instruments weren't as good as Stradivari's? Whose were? My instruments were in demand. I always had patrons waiting for deliveries. Who was I to worry that I could not reach the seemingly impossible standard set by the geniuses of an earlier age?"

Archangelo paused a moment as if to let Silvio and the others consider his words.

"But then a miracle happened. . . ."

The priest's attention pricked up at the word *miracle*. Silvio sensed danger there, but there was no way to warn *Padróne* Archangelo to tread lightly. He was too far away to jab with an elbow, and it wasn't any use shooting him a warning look.

"I went blind."

3

FAUSTO LOOKED AT Archangelo as if he were mad. "How can you call going blind a miracle? A violinmaker who loses his sight is no better off than a violinist who goes deaf. The one thing precludes the other. You might just as well have your hands cut off. You are finished."

"I confess I thought as much myself, when my eyes started to go. But when God took away my sight, He taught me how to hear, how to truly hear, for the first time in my life. And my sense of touch . . ." The blind man held his fingers up before his face and seemed to look at them with wonderment as he rubbed the tips of his fingers against his thumbs. "When I had my eyes, I relied on them to tell me if an angle was right, if a face of a violin had been shaved down to the proper depth. Now I 'see' with my fingers and my ears. Through the grace of God, the powers of my senses of hearing and touch expanded to make up for the loss of my eyes a hundredfold. I am actually a better violinmaker as a blind man than I was when I still had my sight."

"That is absurd!" Fausto said.

"Some respect for *Padróne* Serafino, if you please,"

17

Giovanni said in a warning voice. "He was a master luthier before any of us were born."

"I don't mind," Archangelo said with a laugh. "Were our positions reversed, I would be skeptical, too. When I think of how many violins I've built: I think I could carve the bouts and sound holes in my sleep! And I might as well have been asleep, judging from the instruments I built. Beautiful to behold, excellent tone, equal to any you could buy in Cremona, but still failing to achieve that highest distinction that only a few masters have ever been able to reach.

"It was only when I was going blind, a time of despair for me, when I was still learning that God was not finished with me as a violinmaker, that I began to realize that we have forgotten what the old masters must have known about our craft, the thing that had taken the soul out of the violins we make nowadays."

"Rubbish."

"Let him finish, Fausto," Giovanni snapped.

"A block of wood does not possess a soul," Father Bartolommeo said, looking at the *padróne* with his dangerous eyes. Silvio prayed that his master would be quiet, but he knew that he would not until he had had his say.

"He speaks blasphemy," Carlo said, pointing to Archangelo.

"If so. I apologize for my clumsy words," the *padróne* said. "All things, even a block of spruce, exist to do but one thing, and that is serve God. I used to think of spruce and maple as materials, lifeless, inert. But I was wrong. As I lost my sight, I was forced to rely upon my ears and fingers to guide me in my work. It was like awakening from a dream. I started to pay attention to what the wood was telling me, which in turn led me to make certain variations to the design of my instruments. These were small but important innovations, changes based not on whimsy or experiment but on a lifetime's experience as a master luthier. It made the difference in the way my violins sound and their response to the nuances of playing. That's why no two instruments I make are exactly the same, just as no two singers are exactly the same. I treat the wood with reverence, working with it carefully, gently, coaxing it to release the beauty God has given it. It is only through the grace of God that I have ever achieved anything. I build violins as expressions of my devotion to God, to release some measure of the beauty and divinity He put into Creation."

"And this is why you call them Angel?"

"To me, they are simply violins, Father."

"But you acknowledge they are called Angel violins?"

"Some people call them that," the *padróne* said.

For the first time, Silvio thought, looking at the old man, Archangelo Serafino seemed to realize the trouble he was in.

"Is this one of the miraculous creations?" Fausto took down one of the finished violins, regarding it with a skeptical eye.

"All of these are my instruments, sir," Silvio said.

"But surely you work together, you and the *padróne,* side by side, shoulder to shoulder in his shop, producing Serafino violins."

"Not since my sight grew dim," Archangelo said. "To be perfectly honest with you, gentlemen, once I was blind I did not know at first whether I would be

able to continue in the trade I learned as an apprentice
to the great Antonio Stradivari. I tried to get Silvio to
go into the service of another master, but he would not
leave me."

Silvio nodded at the other men, confirming it was
true.

"When my eyes were getting very bad, I told Silvio
the time had come for him to make his own violins,
start to finish. I did not think it would be fair to him. I
did not wish to injure his reputation as a competent
journeyman luthier."

"Aha!" Fausto exclaimed, pointing at *Padróne* Serafino. "You have just made my case for me. You yourself confess your violins are not up to the Cremonese
standard."

"It is true that I suspected they would not be, but
that did not turn out to be the case, through the grace
of God. While I can do the carving and fitting, it is true
that I am no longer able to perform the finish work or
apply the varnish and stain. I rely upon Silvio for that.
But I did with many of my violins before I lost my
sight. I'm sure it is much the same with you, Fausto.
No doubt you rely on Carlo and your other journeymen to handle certain mundane tasks."

This was as close as Silvio had ever seen the
padróne come to insulting anyone, but Giovanni, who
had once been Archangelo Serafino's apprentice,
seemed to realize the old man had just implied that
Carlo was Fausto's unthinking yes-man in this and
other guild business.

"If these violins are Silvio's, where are yours,
Archangelo?" Fausto made a show of looking around
the shop, like an actor in a pantomime. "Or are they

lifted into heaven by apotheosis the moment you complete them for use in the heavenly choir?"

"*Presidente,*" Giovanni said, resting his hand upon the handle of the dagger in his belt.

"My output is quite modest, as one might expect of a blind violinmaker," Archangelo said before Fausto had to make up his mind whether to apologize or risk being drawn into a duel. "I work slowly. Very slowly."

"Do you mean to tell us you have *no* violins we can examine?"

"I have one that was only just completed, *Presidente*. The patron who commissioned it takes delivery Monday."

"And what kind of patron would order a violin made by a blind man?" Carlo asked.

"The commission was for the Bishop of Florence," Silvio said when it seemed the *padróne's* modesty would keep him from answering. "Bishop Falcone is a violinist himself, you may know. He said he cannot wait for the instrument to be delivered to him. Ever since he heard one of the *padróne's* marvelous new instruments, the only thing he can think about, he said, is possessing one for himself."

Silvio was delighted to see how that news affected Fausto and Carlo, but then he saw the way Father Bartolommeo was looking at him and his blood ran cold. Silvio could see the circle of the Inquisitor's interest extending to encompass Bishop Falcone. Silvio told himself to close his mouth and keep it closed.

"Perhaps we could see this instrument," Father Bartolommeo said.

"Would you permit me to ask you a question, Father?"

The severe priest inclined his head.

"I understand why the guild masters are here. Like my young friend Silvio, I have been expecting their visit and am surprised that it took them so long to take notice of my recent efforts."

"It was only after hearing tell of the magnificent violins you were making, instruments that would put theirs to shame," Giovanni said.

"I resent what you're implying," Fausto said.

"If your honor has been compromised . . ." Giovanni said, straightening, not the least intimidated by the guild *presidente*.

"Gentlemen, if you please," Archangelo said, again interposing himself between the pair. "I was about to ask Father Bartolommeo what aspect of my business could possibly be a matter of official concern to the congregation of the Inquisition."

"We are the ones who have come to ask the questions," the priest said.

"Then do you have a question for me, Father Bartolommeo? There are no secrets between me and the Church. I am a loyal servant of God. I hope I have made that clear."

The priest looked at the *padróne* without replying. The silence unnerved Silvio, but it did not seem to affect Archangelo.

"Talk about 'miracles' and violins that sing with the voice of angels is . . ." Father Bartolommeo let the sentence hang a long moment before finishing. ". . . troubling."

"Why is that so, Father?"

Silvio cringed at the *padróne*'s naïveté, which almost—almost—made the priest smile.

"Because it smacks of blasphemy," the priest said sharply. "Ascribing miraculous gifts to God, gifts that give you the ability to make violins with the power to bewitch musicians and even bishops—these are very grave matters indeed, Signor Serafino."

"But if I cannot attribute these powers to the Lord," the *padróne* said, holding his upturned hands before him, "then to whom?"

"The devil."

"Oh, Father," Archangelo Serafino said, for once looking and sounding like what he was: a broken-down, blind old man very near the end of his life. "How could you think such a thing? You wound me to the very soul."

"Sometimes pain is necessary to obtain the truth," the priest said.

Even Giovanni was staring at Father Bartolommeo with horror. The fact that the Inquisition had not been much heard of in recent times did not mean the office was not continuing its work, but quietly. Of all the things Silvio had imagined might be in store for the *padróne*—exclusion from the guild, banishment from Cremona, imprisonment—he had not thought to include the possibility of torture and execution, perhaps even being burned at the stake. And, of course, whatever fate befell Archangelo Serafino would most likely include his sole journeyman!

"So you see, *signore,*" the priest continued, "it is not simply a matter of whether you will be allowed to remain a member of the Cremona luthier guild. The greater question is, Who do you truly serve: God or Satan? I need hardly tell you the implications."

"Then I have no choice but to let my work speak for

itself. I will let it alone argue for my livelihood and my life. But it falls to the Lord to judge my soul, as He will all of yours."

"Amen," Father Bartolommeo said.

"Silvio? Would you be so kind as to bring these gentlemen the violin I made for Bishop Falcone?"

Silvio went upstairs after the instrument. Overcoming a sudden impulse to jump out a window and run away, he returned with a rectangular case bound in leather. The visitors gathered around as Silvio unfastened the latch. Inside, nestled in a bed of green velvet, framed by the case lid and the two new bows it held, was a honey-colored violin.

Giovanni, quicker than Fausto, took the violin out of its case and held it up for closer inspection.

"Beautiful wood." Giovanni turned the instrument over. The maple was a fine medium-to-strong flame, perfectly matched. "You have always managed to get the best wood," he said, sounding a little envious of his old mentor.

Giovanni inspected the bouts, purfling, and scroll, which was, as Silvio knew, a little irregular. Before handing it to Fausto, he looked inside the F hole. The label, a rectangle of paper written in brown ink in his former master's familiar hand, read, *Archangelo Serafino, 1744 + VII*. The *padróne* had been putting crosses on his labels since going blind, in thanks to God for not forgetting Archangelo in his time of darkness. The "VII" was indicative of where the instrument came in the series of Angel violins Archangelo had made since losing his sight. In two years he had produced only seven violins, the output slowing to a trickle for an old man who had built more than six hundred instruments in his lifetime.

"I object to the finish," Fausto said.

"Yes, quite," Carlo chimed in. "It's far too light."

"Even before I lost my vision, I came to dislike the idea of staining my violins a dark hue."

"It is the way we make violins in Cremona," Fausto declared.

"If spruce and maple were dark woods, there would be no need to stain them. Why not bring out the natural beauty of the wood?"

"I think the violin has a lovely finish," Giovanni said. "The brilliant golden highlights flash in the sun."

"That's high praise for you, Silvio, coming from Master Giovanni."

Silvio bowed toward Giovanni.

"The instrument is narrow, too narrow, too feminine," Fausto said. "And look at the placement of the F holes. They are far too high on the instrument's shoulder. Perhaps you made it for a lady or a child."

"I have found that my violins sound better if I make certain modifications on the Stradivari model most violinmakers in Cremona follow today."

"Improve on Stradivari?" Fausto sputtered. "Now you do speak blasphemy, sir! Antonio Stradivari perfected the violin. The way to ensure that Cremona remains the capital of violinmaking in Europe is to adhere to his patterns."

"No one admires the great master more than I," the *padróne* said. "I apprenticed with him and worked hard to learn everything he had to teach."

"And failed."

To everyone's astonishment, the *padróne* agreed.

"You are quite right, Fausto," the old man said, and laughed. "I did not learn everything. I did not learn how to make violins that are the equal to the ones made by the great Stradivari. Close, but not equal. Not until I started paying attention to what the wood was telling my fingers and my ears. I realized I had to be willing to go beyond the forms that worked so well for the incomparable Antonio, but not so well for those of us who have come after him."

"What you say makes no sense," Fausto said.

"None whatsoever," Carlo said, echoing his captain.

"How can turning away from Stradivari result in anything but an inferior violin?"

"Because, my dear fellow, following the tried-and-true plan did nothing but produce inferior violins, inferior to Stradivari's. You follow Stradivari's patterns, Fausto."

"Without fail."

"Are the violins you make the equal of Stradivari's?"

"It would be preposterous to make such a claim. There was only one Stradivari."

"Giovanni? You are Cremona's preeminent violin-maker today, in my opinion." Archangelo Serafino touched a fingertip to his ear. "Judging with these, your violins stand above all others. Do the instruments you build, using Stradivari's patterns, best the old master?"

Giovanni thought before answering. "Some of my violins are good enough, I like to think, to be considered in the same general family as a Stradivarius. But no, *Padróne,* my violins do not have the same sound. Those instruments exist in a class of their own. There is nothing else like them. Perhaps there never will be."

"Then so much for following the old ways," the

padróne said. "Have you gentlemen ever considered whether Stradivari's methods worked best for him because they were *his* methods?"

"Do you have the arrogance to say your violins are the equal to Stradivari's?"

"I don't compare myself to other violinmakers, Fausto, and I don't compare my violins to other luthiers' instruments. That is for the others to decide."

"Then let us hear something played on this *fiddle* and settle the matter once and for all," Fausto said.

"Silvio, if you would do us the honor."

"But of course, *Padróne.*"

He accepted the violin from Fausto—the instrument fairly leaped into his hands—and put it between his shoulder and chin.

All violinmakers in Cremona played, of course, but as some were better craftsmen than others, some were better performers. Silvio could have easily made his living as a violinist, though his livelihood was better and far more assured as a member of the luthier guild. Still, he played in several local chamber orchestras to supplement his journeyman's income, and was much in demand as a player at balls and simple gatherings of his friends, where after several glasses of wine, Silvio would play and people would dance and sing. He had offered to work for Archangelo Serafino without pay in exchange for one of his magnificent instruments. The *padróne* had rejected his offer, but promised to build him a violin as a gift out of the next series.

Silvio played a few preliminary notes on the gut string, smiling to himself at the look of surprise on Giovanni's face at the shimmering clarity. The A string was a bit flat. Silvio adjusted the boxwood peg until

the instrument was perfectly in tune, then raised the
bow to play.

The horsehair danced across the strings as Silvio
closed his eyes. The world fell instantly away from him
and time stopped. His fears for his master, poor old
blind *Padróne* Archangelo, and for himself, were forgotten as Silvio went through the final brilliant allegro
"L'Inverno" movement to Vivaldi's *Four Seasons*. The
only thing that existed for him for those few minutes
was the violin and the music flowing from it like sunlight from the heavens.

The violin responded to the slightest change in expression as Silvio played. It was like a good lover, sensitive to his touch, but touching him in return, leading
as well as being led. Silvio had played the piece a
thousand times, but never like this. He heard and felt
beauty hiding within the music that, good as he was,
had escaped him before. The master's violins were like
magic looking glasses: they revealed things that had
remained hidden. It was like suddenly having the universe inside you—the sun, the moon, the planets and
stars, all turning in perfect harmonious order. For as
long as you played, you could see and understand it all
with perfect clarity, and it was all within you, and you
were within it, one with creation, with God.

The violin whispered. It sang, it cried, it roared. And
when the tempest was through, it left behind a scene of
absolute serenity.

Then, silence.

Silvio heard the ragmonger's cry from up the street.
The music was ended, the spell broken.

He slowly lowered the violin and opened his eyes.

The inquisitors were staring at him.

Silvio saw Fausto, the guild *presidente,* for what he was, absurd in his foppish hat. His garments were suited to someone above his station, a lord who spent his days occupied in hunts, not a man who made violins with his hands for a living. He stood there with his mouth partly open, like an uncomprehending idiot, struck dumb by the power of *Padróne* Archangelo's magic.

What pleased Silvio more than seeing Fausto and Carlo stupefied was the look of wonderment on Giovanni's face. The man acknowledged to be Cremona's leading violinmaker—a man in his prime, unlike Silvio's elderly blind master—had heard for himself the miracles inhabiting these familiar forms of spruce and maple.

It was not the guild masters who spoke first, but Father Bartolommeo, the priest from the curia.

"Blessed be the Lord in His infinite mercy," the priest said, and crossed himself. "It *is* an Angel violin."

4

THE SENSATION THE Paris concerts created made an invitation to Versailles inevitable. The royal command was not long in coming. It arrived during a production of Handel's opera about sorcery, *Alcina*. The only person in the box at the theater who seemed to mind the interruption was its recipient, the young Welsh violin prodigy whose name was on everyone's lips, Dylan Glyndwr.

Glyndwr's host, the Comte de Sévigné, and the *comte*'s other guests were well accustomed to being at the beck and call of Louis, the fifteenth French king to bear that name, and by all accounts the most dissolute and debauched of an exceedingly dissipated lot.

The honor of performing at Versailles brought several inconveniences, the greatest being that Dylan Glyndwr would be accompanied by the court chamber orchestra instead of the ensemble he had assembled from Paris's excellent supply of players. The king's men no doubt would be competent, but Glyndwr preferred performing with an orchestra of his own choosing. Even more than this, Dylan Glyndwr had a deep-seated aversion to bowing to the commands of any king who wasn't Welsh, but there were no more princes of Wales, unless one counted the heir to the English throne, the Prince of Wales—and Glyndwr most certainly did *not*.

As there was no graceful way of avoiding Louis's summons, the virtuoso would simply have to make the best of it.

Attired in full court dress—a ruffled lace shirt, waistcoat, heavy brocade jacket, silk stockings, and buckle shoes—Glyndwr arrived at the palace carrying only his violin. The scores had been sent on ahead for the orchestra to rehearse, though the press of other engagements had made it impossible for the virtuoso to work with the group before the actual performance. The program was to be a violin concerto in E major written by an obscure German composer named Bach. Glyndwr was much taken with Bach's music and hoped that by playing his music he might help ensure the composer's immortality. The violin was a Stradivarius he'd owned for some years. It was the best-sounding violin he had ever played.

Dylan Glyndwr's royal command performance at Versailles was late starting. Louis had spent the day hunting and lingered over supper in his private apartments while his courtiers were left to amuse themselves, the evening's entertainment awaiting the monarch's entrance. Louis was announced nearly two hours after the featured performance was to have started. He swept into the room surrounded *d'intimes,* his innermost circle of fawning lords, sycophantic ministers, and a retinue of women possessing beauty as dazzling as the jewels they wore. Madame Pompadour, whom Glyndwr had met in a Paris salon, came in on the king's arm. She whispered something into his ear as he seated himself on his throne, making him laugh.

The conductor, a tiny man in an enormous wig named Jean Graniont, bowed to Glyndwr. The virtuoso got up from where he had been sitting, holding the Stradivarius on his left knee, and tucked the violin under his chin.

The orchestra was far better than Dylan expected. Maestro Graniont had thoroughly drilled the musicians on Bach's complex counterpoint. Even better than their playing was the fact that they actually *listened* to the soloist. Midway through the first movement, the orchestra and the violinist were playing off of each other, advancing a musical conversation of sublime complexity under the careful eye of Jean Graniont, who wisely chose to shape rather than control the playing.

Dylan Glyndwr played with his eyes closed, thoroughly immersed in the swirling symphony of sound surrounding him. It was more than sound to the virtuoso. There was color and form, an evolving shape Dylan pictured as an enormous cloud building and billowing, blowing and boiling, the contrasting folds of darkness and light painted and textured by the rays of a brilliant sun. Like lovers in an embrace, Glyndwr and the orchestra moved and breathed as one, one body, one soul, forever joined outside of time and space.

It was when the violinist opened his eyes for the conductor's cue to start the next movement that he noticed Madame Pompadour had left the room. The king was still in his seat, although it was impossible to see more than the top of his wig because of the crowd of women encircling him, shielding him from view.

These selfsame women made a show of focusing their attention on the orchestra as it launched back into the Bach, while in their midst one of their members knelt on her knees before Louis, her face buried in his lap.

Glyndwr forced his attention back to the music, burning with rage to be subjected to such a royal lack of respect. Dylan played with a savage energy that took the orchestra by surprise. The nimble ensemble kept up with the music's new coloration, though only just, performing what was certainly the darkest interpretation of Bach's E major violin concerto anyone would ever hear.

"Très bien, monsieur. You well deserve the high praise people sing of your musicianship."

Dylan Glyndwr was carefully wiping the rosin off the fingerboard of the Stradivarius and did not look up. Rosin was an abrasive and would damage the Strad's varnish if left unattended. The woman's accent betrayed her, although her French was flawless. She was *English.* That alone gave him reason to hide his scowl. Given a choice, Dylan Glyndwr greatly preferred to prey upon the hated English.

They were alone in an antechamber off the grand salon, a room lighted by a crystal chandelier, with a marble floor and gilded furniture, where visiting dukes and bishops prepared for their audience with the monarch. He looked across at her, favoring her with a friendly look.

"You are very kind to say so, *mademoiselle,*" Glyndwr said in equally perfect French.

Such a beautiful woman, he thought, a lovely porcelain doll, small and delicate, with light brown hair, cornflower-blue eyes, and sensuous lips painted with a brilliant rouge. She wore a Parisian gown, like all the women at court, with a bodice cut scandalously low and compressed in a way to thrust the breasts upward. The French upper orders were depraved as well as unpractical in matters of dress. Even in the best society, it was common to glimpse a bit of areola peeking out from behind the fabric of a fashionable gown worn by a woman of high degree.

Together they made their way through the crowd, the genius of his playing evident even to the haughty French aristocrats. Pleading the need for air, he escorted Lady Caroline Hamilton to a balcony overlooking the gardens, where they stood sipping champagne. Glyndwr found Lady Hamilton to be amazingly transparent in the details of her colorful if not altogether proper life. She had been born in London, the unacknowledged daughter of a chambermaid and a duke. She had the good fortune to grow up beautiful and charming and had enjoyed several successful seasons on the stage. She had parlayed her acting career into a position as Lord Bolton's mistress. Bolton brought her to Paris, where he had the poor taste to succumb to gout and other complications of a lifetime of debauchery. But Miss Hamilton, like a cat, knew how to land on her feet. She was currently installed in the Versailles apartments of one of Louis's courtiers. Glyndwr took it as a matter of fact that the man the adventurous Miss Hamilton had her eye on was, ultimately, the king.

"You created quite a sensation tonight with your violin."

Dylan looked out at the garden, breathing in the

perfumed darkness, and frowned. "I do not think His Royal Highness was impressed."

"Louie lives only for pleasure, and music is not the diversion he loves best."

"Obviously not."

"He could not wait to get away to visit the Stag Park tonight. But I'm sure you have heard all about *that* place."

"I had not heard of it before now, my lady."

She leaned her head closer, near enough for him to feel the warmth of her skin, and spoke in a low voice. "The Stag Park is an old hunting lodge that has been converted into the royal brothel. According to rumor, there are ninety beautiful girls kept there, mostly young virgins kidnapped from their families to service the king's most wanton fancy. Does that shock you, *monsieur?*"

"Nothing shocks me, Mademoiselle Hamilton. I have seen much of the world."

"Alas, the truth is nowhere near as delicious," she said with a pout. "There are only a dozen girls invested there, most of them sixteen or seventeen. The scandalous talk of children is gossip circulated by enemies of the monarchy. I would venture to guess none of the Stag Park damsels were virgins when they spent their first night there."

"You seem to know a great deal."

"I have my sources, Monsieur Glyndwr. In the Court of Louis the Fifteenth, everyone does."

"What does Madame Pompadour think of the king's carousing?"

"Do not be naïve, *monsieur*. Precious little happens in court that Madame Pompadour is unaware of, and the truth is there is little she does not control. If only she were better at governing, poor Louis wouldn't be in such bad odor with the people." She stood on her toes to whisper in Dylan's ear, "Stag Park was Madame Pompadour's contrivance."

"I know the French are depraved, but that makes little sense to me. Why drive her lover into the arms of other women?"

"For two very good reasons. First, Pompadour is worldly enough to know it is in Louie's nature to have many lovers. The second is that the girls at Stag Park are *safe*. There is virtually no chance that any of Louie's liaisons with those hussies will take serious root and compromise more important lasting situations, like the one the king enjoys with Madame Pompadour. Better Louie find diversion in the arms of simple country girls than the cunning ladies of the court. Behind the pretty smiles and witty banter, the calculation and jockeying for position never stop. It would be far more dangerous to Madame Pompadour if the king were enjoying himself in the arms of schemers like Mademoiselles de Romans and de Forcalquier. Take it from me, *chéri*. If anyone would know, it is I!"

"I would think knowing too much about the king's intimate affairs could be dangerous."

"I am not afraid of danger, Monsieur Glyndwr. Would it surprise you to learn that my protector is there now, with the king and his intimates, sharing in their amorous capers?"

"And you don't object?"

"My dear Monsieur Glyndwr," Miss Hamilton said,

placing her tiny hand on his forearm, "it is only because he is gone that I am able to be here with you."

She wanted Glyndwr to kiss her, and he would have very much liked to oblige, but not in so public a place. Mademoiselle Hamilton, as sensitive to adjusting to the touch of a man as Dylan Glyndwr was to a violin, understood instantly.

"The night is becoming chilly. Would you be so kind as to escort me to my apartments in the palace? We can continue our conversation there, unless you are in a hurry to return to Paris."

A servant had come onto the balcony with more champagne, but Dylan waved him away.

"I have all the time in the world," he said, and held out his arm for Caroline Hamilton to take.

"A man of your talents could go far at Versailles, with the right friends," she said.

"Perhaps, but I am better suited for the life of a wandering virtuoso."

"Always a new city, a new orchestra, a new woman. . . ."

Dylan Glyndwr met her eyes.

"You are very good with your instrument," she said, her eyes filled with wicked light.

"I do what I can."

"I have seen what you can do . . ." She paused, arching one delicately drawn eyebrow.

". . . with your violin." She pointed at the case with a jeweled finger. "Do you take it with you everywhere?"

"It is my constant companion."

"There was a violinist here last winter, a Pole, who

played what he called the Angel violin. He was not half the musician you are, *monsieur*, but, ah, what tone! Even the king was mesmerized by his playing."

Glyndwr sat up from the divan where he had been reclining. "It is a new kind of violin?"

"No, I don't think so." She thought about it a moment, remembering. "He said the violin was a 'miracle.' That was the word he used: *miracle*. If that strikes you as sacrilegious, you wouldn't think so if you'd heard its rich, rare sound."

"How did it sound?"

"Like a violin, but different. It is difficult to explain in words how something sounds. I suppose it sounded like the voice of an angel."

"What was his name, the violinist?"

"I don't remember. It was . . . oh, I've had far too much champagne tonight! I think it was Janklincz. Yes, that was it. Janklincz. You know of him?"

Dylan Glyndwr shook his head.

"A tall, thin man, bony and angular, with long black hair."

Dylan stared across the room at the case holding his Stradivarius. The Strad was a magnificent instrument, the best he had ever heard. But the idea that a violin existed that would make his thoroughbred seem no more than a mule made him almost sick with despair and desire.

"Such a sour look, my love. One of these will make you sweet."

Dylan pushed aside the chocolates Caroline Hamilton was bending down to offer him and drew her down onto the divan beside him. "They cannot be as sweet as these," he said, burying his face in her breasts.

"Play me the way you play your violin," she whispered, her hand on the back of Dylan Glyndwr's head, her fingers in his hair, holding him against her. He kissed her warm skin, parting his lips, tasting her with the tip of his tongue. "Play me passionately, my love, until I sing you an aria of ecstasy. . . ."

Lady Hamilton's body stiffened when he bit into the silky flesh over her left breast, his blood teeth piercing the pericardium, pricking twin holes directly into the heart. Dylan was almost as surprised as she. The vampire had never experienced the sharp roar of blood so fresh from the heart, the wine of life rich with mysterious essences, infinitely more potent than the most powerful drug.

Centuries of satisfying the Hunger had not diminished the pleasure it brought Dylan Glyndwr by the slightest degree. Music could ease but not banish the despair from his soul, but there was always this to free him. Carried away on a flood of delight, he heard Caroline Hamilton gasp the final word of ecstasy in her short, passionate life.

"Deeper!"

Her heart beating slower and slower, they sank together into the blissful nothingness, until finally there was nothing left at all but the dimmest glimmer of a sound Dylan Glyndwr had never heard: the enchanted singing of the Angel violin.

5

IMPRESARIO RUDOLPH KRAUSE had excellent contacts throughout Europe. In his letter responding to Glyndwr, he reported he did, indeed, know of a violinist named Janklincz, but only just barely. The Polish violinist was a mediocrity, a second-rate pedagogue with delusions of a performing career. Janklincz had arranged his own debut in Paris the year before. Surprisingly, the modest affair had generated a certain level of notice, which Krause attributed to the masses being unable to discriminate between true virtuosos and poseurs. Janklincz moved on to Vienna but failed to appear at a theater where he was to perform. Krause had written an associate in Austria for additional information. He would write to Glyndwr again as soon as he was able to learn more about the violinist's whereabouts.

Too impatient to wait for another letter, Glyndwr left immediately for Vienna, traveling by private coach.

The stage manager at the theater remembered Janklincz from the previous winter and still bore him animus because of the refunds he had been forced to make when the performance was canceled at the last moment. He knew nothing of the musician's whereabouts, but when he saw the gold sovereign in Glyndwr's hand, he was more than willing to let him talk to orchestra members, who were just completing rehearsal.

The stage manager directed Dylan to a sallow viola player with a soiled scarf around his neck.

"Hans?"

The man looked up with a smile that displayed a mouth filled with bad teeth. Glyndwr explained that he was looking for a Polish violinist named Janklincz.

"Yes, I know poor old Jank."

Dylan Glyndwr pulled one of the chairs around and sat. "Why 'poor'?"

Hans tapped his chest with his hand. "Consumption."

"He is sick?"

The viola player nodded. "Sick enough that he had to cancel his performance with the orchestra. Karl was quite angry about it." Then he added, "Karl is the manager here."

"How is he doing?"

"Janklincz?" The man shrugged. "I cannot say. I just knew him from rehearsal. A nice enough fellow. And such a violin!"

Glyndwr concentrated on unfastening the top button of his waistcoat so as not to show too much interest. It was warm and airless in the closed theater. How the man opposite him could bear the muffler wound around his neck was beyond Glyndwr.

"He had a good instrument?" Glyndwr asked casually.

"I have never heard anything like it. It has the sweetest tone, especially on the upper strings, like musical honey. But real guts, too. Good projection. And it can really roar when he puts the bow to it. He calls it the Angel violin."

"A good name for it, apparently."

"It was Jank's angel in more ways than one. To be perfectly honest, there was nothing special about his playing. He could have sat with the first violins maybe, though more likely with the seconds, but that violin . . . extraordinary. The remarkable thing about Janklincz's playing wasn't the playing but the magnificent sound of the violin itself."

Glyndwr sighed and slapped his knees as he stood up, as if he were a busy man and had more important things to do than listen to someone talk about a violin.

"I don't suppose you'd know where to find him? There's a sovereign in it for you, if you do."

"What do you want with him? Does he owe you money?"

"Quite the reverse. His uncle has died and left him a piece of property. It's not much, but these details have to be taken care of. Solicitors, you understand."

"He was renting a room above a café shop when he was rehearsing with us. That's all I know."

"Can you give me directions to the place?"

"A sovereign, you said?"

"That's right," Dylan Glyndwr said, reaching into the pocket of his vest.

The passions of Vienna include music, coffee, chocolate. The café, a place specializing in pastries and rich German coffee, had not a single customer when Dylan arrived, but then it was the time when most people took their evening meal.

"A table, sir?"

There were two men working in the shop. The one speaking to the vampire was a fat older man, obviously the proprietor. At his side was a red-faced youth, skinny, with a perpetually startled appearance on his face. Both wore long white aprons around their waists that fell nearly to the floor.

"I am looking for a man, a violinist named Janklincz. I was told he rents a room from you. Can you help me find him?"

The two men looked at each other.

"He does not live here any longer, sir," the stout man said. "May I ask why you're looking for him?"

"I work for a solicitor," Dylan said, going on to tell the same story he had told the viola player, using exactly the same words.

"He no longer lives above the café, but Franz here can show you to his current residence. It's not far from here."

The fat man nudged Franz with his elbow. The younger man, blushing, stood frozen where he was, his hands held tight against his sides, as if he were afraid to move.

"Take this gentleman to see Mr. Janklincz straightaway." The big man's eyes narrowed. "Go on now, boy. Do as I say. He hasn't all evening."

The young man went by Glyndwr without looking at him and out into the street, still wearing his long white apron. He said nothing as they walked down the street and turned north, toward where a church steeple towered above the surrounding buildings.

Franz stopped and pointed.

"He's there."

Glyndwr looked. "Where? In the church?"

"Just beyond it. I don't know exactly where but you can look for yourself or ask at the church."

Dylan began to burn with rage.

Janklincz's new residence, the place to which the boy was directing him to find the Polish violinist, was a cemetery.

The lamplighter tipped his hat to the vampire, who brushed past him without acknowledging the polite gesture.

Dylan Glyndwr was in a poisonous mood, and anyone who so much as looked at him was risking his life. If the fat man had come along to observe the results of his practical joke, Glyndwr would have taken him by the ears and twisted his head around until the last thing he saw before the life went out of his eyes was the street he'd just waddled down. Dylan still might go back to the café, afterward, to settle the score. That depended upon the success of his present mission. It was only thanks to the helpful boy, the object of the café proprietor's bullying, that the fat man was still alive.

Franz's directions had taken Dylan to a rough part of Vienna. The dirty streets were narrow, and the houses leaned precariously overhead from either side, lines strung between the windows with laundry drying in the sooty air. This was the quarter one would visit to look for prostitutes, who lived cheek by jowl in Bohemian squalor with artists, pickpockets, students, petty thieves, and revolutionaries.

The pawnshop was on Moon Street, just past the square with the fountain and statue honoring some dead general, as Franz had said.

Glyndwr peered in through the window of the dimly lighted shop. On display inside was a chaotic array of tools, books, a navigator's sextant, china and flatware, and other of the more salable items from the shop's inventory of hawked secondhand goods. This was the dusty detritus of who knew how many indigent lives, their prized possessions converted to ready cash when there were no longer other alternatives available. The better merchandise—the jewels, the watches, perhaps a valuable painting or two—would be locked away someplace safe from the depredations of common smash-and-run thieves.

He went in, at first ignored by the bearded man wearing a nightcap bending over his ledger book, making entries by candlelight before retiring for the night. Given the chance that Dylan had come to sell rather than buy, it was a rather good strategy, he thought, for the pawnshop keeper to ignore him at first. Were he desperate to raise money by selling a ring or gold snuffbox, the pawnbroker's act of indifference might tend to make him more amenable to accept a lower price.

Dylan leaned an elbow on a glass case containing some bankrupt surgeon's operating devices. He was considering which of the cruel-looking tools he would use to torture the pawnbroker if he proved evasive when the man suddenly noticed his customer.

"It is late," the man said. "I was just getting ready to go to bed."

"I am interested in buying a violin. I suppose I could just as well go elsewhere."

The man's demeanor changed immediately. "I have

a selection of good instruments. How much are you thinking of spending?"

"Actually, I'm looking for a specific violin."

"A violin is a violin, sir."

"I understand that last month you liquidated the estate of a Polish violinist named Janklincz."

A genuine sadness came over the pawnbroker. "Precious little there was to dispose of. He didn't own enough to fully settle the bill with his landlord, or so the landlord claimed."

Dylan leaned over the counter toward the man. "There was a violin?"

"Of course. I have it right here."

The shelves were so narrow that the pawnbroker had to turn sideways to get through. He disappeared into the darkness, apparently able to locate items within his inventory by sense of touch alone. He came shuffling back, holding a violin case above his head.

"Here it is," he said, putting it on the counter. He started to open the case, but Dylan grabbed it away and opened it himself.

"A nice Italian violin," the pawnbroker said, lighting a lamp so that his customer could examine it. "It's a genuine Stradivarius. You can see that the label says so. They're very valuable."

Dylan turned the instrument over, studying it with a skeptical eye.

"If you sell many violins, you should know that every cheap copy bears a label that says 'Stradivarius.' "

"Do they really?" he replied. For a pawnbroker, he wasn't much of a liar, in Glyndwr's estimation.

Judging from outward appearances, the violin was completely ordinary. It wasn't a worthless piece of kindling, but there was nothing extraordinary about the wood or the craftsmanship. The back was made of two joined pieces of maple without noteworthy flame. The carving on the scrollwork was mediocre, and the F holes did not appear to be quite symmetrical.

"Are you sure this violin belonged to Janklincz?"

The old man nodded.

Dylan took out the bow—not a bad bow, amazingly enough—tightened it, then drew it simultaneously across the E and A strings to tune the instrument. From the first stroke, it was obvious to Dylan Glyndwr that the violin was entirely third-rate. He played a few measures from Bach's B-flat partita before putting the violin down.

"You play well," the pawnbroker said.

Glyndwr's only reply was to grab him by the lapels of his moth-eaten dressing gown and drag him bodily across the counter.

"That is *not* Janklincz's violin," Glyndwr hissed, feeling his blood teeth slip down from their cavity in his upper gum.

"But it was," the old man sputtered. "I can prove it. I have an inventory and receipts, all witnessed and signed. The authorities are demanding in Vienna."

"*Where* is it?" Glyndwr roared, hoisting the man high in the air with one hand. He lifted his face and leered up at the pawnbroker, giving him a good look at the twin scimitars of gleaming ivory that would pierce his jugular and drain him, fast, of his blood and his life, if he continued to trifle with Dylan Glyndwr. "Where is the Angel violin?"

The pawnbroker reminded Dylan of a fish pulled from water, his mouth opening and closing, gulping for air. "The landlord said . . ." He stopped to swallow more air. ". . . that he did have . . ." Gasp. ". . . a noteworthy violin. . . ."

Glyndwr realized he had done too good a job of throwing a scare into the old man. The pawnbroker's weak heart was giving out; Dylan could hear its sickly heartbeat—fast, with an ominous irregular flutter—when he focused his acute hearing on the man's chest.

"Calm yourself," he said, lowering the man to the floor but holding on to his dressing gown. "Look at me."

The old man's eyes were unfocused.

"Look at me!" Glyndwr repeated sharply. "Look into my eyes."

The pawnbroker did as he was told.

"You must calm yourself," the vampire said. "Slow your thoughts. Slow your breath, your heartbeat. You have nothing to fear from me. You are well and will be well. I require only information and I will turn you free and leave you in peace."

The old man stared back at him. He was terrified but at least he was listening, or his body was, to Dylan Glyndwr's commands. Still, the fact that Dylan continued to hold on to a handful of the man's dressing gown was the only thing keeping the pawnbroker on his feet.

"Now let us return to the previous subject. You were telling me the landlord said Janklincz had another violin, a noteworthy violin."

The pawnbroker nodded.

"Perhaps you have heard it referred to as the Angel violin."

No, the pawnbroker shook his head. He had not heard that.

"What became of the other violin—the Angel violin?"

"It . . . he," he began, stammering. The old man closed his eyes and swallowed before beginning anew. "Janklincz was in ill health. Consumption. It killed him."

"Yes. And the Angel violin?"

"He needed money for rent, for laudanum. He sold it. I think that is what the landlord said. To tell you the truth, sir, what interest would it have been to me? The property had already been disposed of."

"And that is all you know? You're not holding some small thing back from me?"

The pawnbroker shook his head.

"I am very wealthy and willing to spend whatever it takes to find the Angel violin," Glyndwr said, adopting the tone of the calmest, most reasonable man in the world. "If you have information about the instrument—a lead, an idea, anything—I would be delighted to pay you for it. And if you could give me the name of the person who bought it from Janklincz, you could set your own price. I am a generous man."

"All I can tell you is to go back to the landlord. Maybe he knows."

Dylan Glyndwr looked at him closely. He was telling the truth.

"I have told you what I know, sir. I can see you are a gentleman and a man of your word. Please do as you promised, and set me free."

"I shall," Glyndwr said.

And he did, but not in the way the pawnbroker wanted.

The vampire returned to the café after midnight.

The matter of the transaction transferring the Angel violin to its present owner had been strictly between Janklincz and the buyer, the landlord swore. The only thing the landlord knew was that the man who had visited Janklincz in his sickroom was from France and acting as an agent for the real buyer, evidently also French. That was as much as the fat man knew, and Dylan was well convinced of it, having tortured the man without mercy just to be certain. He killed him and he killed Franz, the young waiter, so as to leave no loose ends in Vienna.

He roused his sleeping driver, insisting they begin the return journey to Paris immediately.

Dylan Glyndwr lolled on the rich black leather cushions in his carriage as they set off through the deserted streets of Vienna just before dawn, still intoxicated from the elixir he'd drained from the three men, gorged like a Roman glutton after an imperial banquet. He was blood-drunk enough to momentarily overcome the rage of knowing that he was no closer to the Angel violin than that night at Versailles, and that the chances were good that he would *never* find it.

6

DYLAN GLYNDWR WANDERED among the ruins of Pompeii. He had come by moonlight to view the mosaics most recently uncovered by archaeologists. Vesuvius loomed in the darkness, still smoldering more than a millennia and a half after wiping out the Roman city with such quick fury that the ash-encased bodies of the victims were discovered lying together in the villas, entire families embracing in death.

He sat on a toppled column to study a mural showing young women being initiated in the mysteries. A satyr led the procession, playing a lyre. On the steps of the temple the priestess awaited, wearing a laurel and holding a wicker basket from which peered the head of a viper. The precise meanings of these symbols were lost in time, but it was easy enough to guess the ritual for the comely maidens—a beautiful symbolic death; the descent to the underworld; the return to the land of the living, innocence exchanged for knowledge, shadows and darkness giving texture and depth to the soul.

Somewhere in the distance, a nightingale began to sing.

Glyndwr looked up, his brooding eyes roaming over the remains of the city, lovely even in its blasted desolation. He had come here many nights to be alone. He thought it strange there were no ghosts in Pompeii, a city where ten thousand met an unexpected and violent end. He had seen no signs that the ruins were haunted, except by himself. He was, he thought, a kind of ghost.

The vampire listened to the song echoing among the ruined fills and baths. He had lately started to write his own music, and the achingly beautiful sound of the melodious bird would find its way into the sonata he was presently creating.

If the soul is the seat of the emotions, the organ that feels, dreams, and imagines, Dylan Glyndwr possessed a very great soul, one capable of profound depths of sensitivity. Such was often the case with vampires. The ones not driven mad by the *passione* of blood followed their souls toward pure artistic pursuits. Glyndwr's path was music, the only anchor preventing him from drifting completely into darkness. Evil exerts a powerful pull on anyone with power, and no more powerful creatures walk the planet than the *vampiri,* blessed with eternal life and unfathomable powers of intellect.

The marvelous bird—it hardly seemed possible that it was an earthly thing that would one day be reduced to a pile of dry bones. The perfection in the creature's soul was manifest in its song, a reflection of the higher beauty too ethereal for worldly beings to possess but for fleeting instants.

The nightingale set the vampire to thinking, to brooding, about another miraculous songbird, the Angel violin. The sweet vision of the miraculous violin served as his Holy Grail, and the search for it had given him purpose and meaning. For the first time since his exile from Wales, after the bloody English killed his family and stole his castle and estates, there was hope in the vampire's heart, an object to believe in, to venerate, to serve.

After returning to France from Vienna, Dylan hired agents to gather the names of every violinist with the skill and means to have collected so singular an instrument. His search started in Paris and spread outward into the countryside. Within the first year, his quest reached the outermost provinces. Dylan visited every city in the country, listened to every orchestra, no matter how humble, his preternaturally keen ear alert for the sound of something miraculous and extraordinary. The vampire broadened the cast of his net to take in wealthy dilettantes, amateurs of independent financial means, dealers, and collectors, but all without result. Dylan knew the owner and location of every Stradivarius and Guarneri in France and the Low Countries, but he had not found the Angel violin.

In the course of his journeys Dylan acquired many violins, as a diversion, and to keep excellent instruments from languishing in the possession of the unworthy. He made a good profit from his dealings, though he was not beyond selling at a loss, or even occasionally giving violins to struggling young virtuosos. He became equally familiar with French violinists, and used his influence with impresarios like Rudolph Krause to promote—or end, if so deserved—careers.

In the course of quietly becoming the foremost private authority on violins and violinists in France,

Dylan Glyndwr found not so much as a single lead on Janklincz's violin. Like its late owner, the violin seemed to have emerged but briefly from the gray mists of anonymity before plunging back into oblivion.

Time made Dylan despair of ever finding Janklincz's violin. It also made it impossible to continue his quest beyond a certain point. Even in a cosmopolitan city like Paris—crowded, busy, people coming and going with the seasons, as changeable as the latest fashion—people began to notice that Glyndwr did not appear to age the way normal people did.

With the quest for his grail not so much ended as postponed for lack of information, Dylan decided it was time for him to become someone else for a while. He booked an extensive tour of Germany and then crossed into Hungary. Using a new name for his performance in Budapest, he wandered southeast, through Macedonia and Greece, traveling in a black coach with the Glyndwr family crest—a red dragon—on the door. He performed sporadically and only when the fancy took him. With a great accumulation of wealth stored away in the banks of Geneva and Venice, there was no need to work. Sometimes he would play with a chamber orchestra, but just as often he performed solo, exploring the infinite variety of his beloved Bach partitas.

An affair with an Italian princess with a strange fondness for pain brought Glyndwr to Naples. Their passion led Dylan to drink of her too often, and in her weakened state the change began to take her, leaving Dylan to choose between seeing her become immortal or killing her while he still could. He stayed on at her palazzo after her quick, unexpected death. They had been wed shortly before she died, so he might use her estate for as long as it suited him.

Was the Angel violin real, like the nightingale singing to him, or was it only a myth, like the Pans and satyrs whose dance was frozen for eternity on the walls of Pompeii through the work of a forgotten artisan?

Perhaps he would never find out.

Dylan rode back to the palazzo and gave the reins for his stallion to the waiting groom. He went inside, his riding boots tapping on the terrazzo, calling for wine to be brought to the study. He drank off the goblet, his eyes on the serving girl who brought it to him. The lusty young wench made the Hunger stir in him, but he would not touch her as long as he wished to use the estate. When he wanted to lose himself in the intoxicating wine of life, he would repair to one of the many brothels in the city, rough places along the waterfront, where it attracted very little notice when a dead prostitute or two were found in their rooms.

Dylan dismissed the girl and went to his desk. A pile of correspondence awaited him, neglected for weeks. There were letters and parcels, some sealed in wax, others tied with ribbon, according to the habit of the time and place of origin. Requests for him to perform, social invitations, letters from his banks, correspondence pertaining to the operation of the estates he had acquired during his haunts.

A letter from his shop in Paris peeked from the middle of the stack. He drew it out, slitting the seal with a silver knife.

Dylan Glyndwr had established a little violin shop near the university to look after the instruments he'd collected on his search for the Angel violin. The shop had taken on a life of its own, and continued to thrive after all these years due to its reputation, entirely deserved, as the place for discriminating musicians to buy—or sell—a quality violin or viola.

The letter brought news of the Angel violin.

Dylan spread the note flat on the desk and pulled the candle closer, startled by this unexpected and exciting bit of intelligence. The man running the shop for Dylan had a visit from an Italian violinist who, in the course of chatting about having an instrument appraised, reported that the Angel violin was not a single violin but rather a series of violins made by a luthier in Cremona who had gone blind. Apparently in return for his lost sight, the maker had been blessed by an uncanny ability to build excellent instruments.

It was one of God's jokes, Dylan muttered to himself.

There had been only a few Angel violins made, perhaps no more than a dozen, before the blind luthier died. In some respects they were reported to be awkward in appearance—as one would expect of violins built by a blind man, the letter said. However, the instruments all had extraordinarily fine tone. Indeed, the violins were said to be "miracles," according to the few people who had ever heard them.

The vampire had not been able to find Janklincz's violin, but it didn't matter if he could find one of the other Angel violins built by the blind Cremonese luthier Archangelo Serafino.

Dylan pulled the bell cord and was smiling when the

girl came in to see if her master cared for more wine. Such a momentous occasion called for celebrating with more than mere wine, he thought, looking at the girl in a way that made her blush.

Dylan Glyndwr was going to Cremona.

7

WHEN THE FIRST cry of a carriage came up from below, Consolata Capellini was naked in bed on her hands and knees, the fat tavernkeeper going at her from behind.

"*Avanti!* Carriage!"

Consolata looked out the open window and saw it, a fine coach-and-four of the sort only a nobleman or rich merchant could afford. She tried to pull away, but Santorini's big hands grabbed her by the hips. He was too close to let her go, even at the prospect of an easy profit. Santorini picked up his pace, his enormous paunch slapping her naked rear. It was the way Consolata preferred him to take her, when he gave her a choice. He practically crushed her when she was on the bottom and he on top.

She lowered her head and moved herself against him, which he liked. She had been told that she would tire of men soon enough, but she was new enough at whoring for it to give her pleasure. She had always been given to wantonness, which was how a girl from a small village in the Italian *campagna* had come to be the new whore at the country tavern on the road to Cremona. The bed creaked and rocked. The sweat trickled down Consolata's face, some of it mopped up with her hair when she tossed her head as Santorini rode her down into the mattress at the apogee of his passion.

The door banged open and a withered middle-aged woman with a sharp face flew in.

"Carriage!" Tiberia shrilled, kicking at her husband.

Santorini avoided her eyes as he pulled up his pantaloons from around his ankles.

"We finally get a chance to make back some of our investment in this *puttana,* and you are up here filling her with your stinking seed!"

Santorini was out the door, moving away from Tiberia with speed he seemed capable of achieving only in her presence.

Tiberia soaked a rag with some of the wine from the bottle of *vino di casa* Santorini had brought with him when he'd pulled Consolata up the stairs by the wrist to take his daily pleasure of her.

"Here, wash yourself with this." Tiberia threw Consolata the rag, pointing to her own privates with her other hand, as if Consolata were too ignorant to know what she meant. Tiberia helped Consolata into her good dress and brushed her hair with furious brutality.

Gavino was handing a flagon of wine to the driver when Consolata came out into the courtyard. The coach was even finer than she had thought when she'd seen it from the upstairs window. It was finished in rich black lacquer, with delicate gold-leaf accents around the curtained windows. A coat of arms, a red dragon, was painted on the door, which had a silver handle.

"I invite your master to sample our hospitality," Santorini said. He nodded in Consolata's direction.

Consolata smiled at the driver and drew in a full breath, glancing down to see the way her full breasts were threatening to burst free of the low, tight bodice.

Santorini shielded his mouth with his hand and whispered to the driver in a voice loud enough for Consolata to hear words that should have made her burn with shame but only made her feel a wicked desire: "*Fóttere . . . prostituta . . . còito . . . scopare . . .*"

The words went fast to work on Gavino, who seemed suddenly uncomfortable in his bulging trousers. Santorini would not let the footman pleasure himself with Consolata unless he paid, and, of course, the poor man did not have money for such diversions. Perhaps she would go to the barn, take his manhood in her mouth, and stand him to a free *pompino*.

The coach's curtain, wine-colored velvet of such a deep hue that it seemed black except when the light caught the folds, moved a little as the passenger pushed them back far enough to look out. Consolata could not see the gentleman inside, his face lost in shadow against the brilliant Tuscan afternoon light.

Consolata smiled and took a few dainty steps toward the carriage, turning her face in profile so the man could see how young she was, and healthy. Santorini looked from Consolata back to the coach, his busy eyes revealing that he was already tallying the money to be made.

Three sharp raps rang out against the roof of the coach, the passenger rapping with his cane.

"I beg your lordship to reconsider," Santorini said, but he had misunderstood.

"We will take the girl with us."

"Oh, no, sir. Tell your master the girl is not for sale."

"Everything is for sale for the right price, *signore.*"

"But she is my niece," Santorini said. "Her mother entrusted her to me. I invite you to enjoy her many charms, but I could not let you take her from me."

The driver said nothing but looked displeased. When no further communication came from within the carriage, Santorini began to sweat even more than he did just standing in the sun.

"I will not charge you for the room. Stay as long as you like. Be my guest for the night. The day will soon begin to die."

After an uncomfortable moment, a hand came through the curtain. It was not an old hand, as Consolata expected, but young and well-turned, with long, strong fingers and the neatly trimmed, polished fingernails of a lord. The ring worn on the middle finger caught the sun, the large square-cut emerald flashing in the light. The hand opened and a leather pouch fell to the dust with a bright clatter of coins. Santorini grunted as he bent over to snatch up the pouch, opening it with clumsy fingers, spilling gold coins into his waiting palm. His bad teeth showed as his lips parted in an ecstatic smile.

"I have never been one to stand in the way of someone bettering themselves in the world," the tavernkeeper said. "Should she gather her things, or will your master be sending her back when he's had his fill of her?"

"My master will take care of everything," the driver said, turning to take up the reins.

Santorini looked at Consolata, then jerked his head toward the carriage.

When she ran gaily past Santorini, he said in a low voice, "You can come back here, you know."

Of course she could, Consolata thought, but not if she could help it.

The carriage door swung open, shutting as quickly as Consolata disappeared through it, frustrating Santorini's attempt to get a glimpse of Consolata's wealthy new benefactor. The driver cracked the whip over the heads of the team, and the carriage was on its way, leaving Santorini and Gavino staring after it.

The moon was coming up when the carriage pulled to a stop along a deserted stretch of road, responding to the order rapped against the roof. The driver did not drop the reins or turn his head.

The carriage door swung open. Consolata's body tumbled out, rolling to a stop on its back on grass cropped short by the sheep that had grazed there the day before.

8

SILVIO WAS PUTTING a clamp on a violin when he looked up to the sound of footsteps in the doorway. He had grown old in the years since the master's death. He was bald but for a crown of snowy hair. His eyesight was failing, yet he had not produced any of the miracles Archangelo made after going blind.

The visitor was a tall man, thin but radiating a sense of great strength, with the smoldering eyes of a traveling virtuoso. He was not from Cremona. That was obvious by the pallor of his skin and the cut of his clothing—fine gentleman's clothing but foreign in design. He wore his hair long and untied, the locks tucked behind his ears.

"Good afternoon, sir," Silvio said with a stiff bow. "Welcome to Serafino Violins."

"Good day." The man inclined his head slightly. His voice sounded English but there was something else to it. Scotch or Irish perhaps. Silvio had done trade with the British but had no great knowledge of the race.

"I have a violin in need of repair," the visitor said, speaking in excellent Italian. "You do that sort of thing here?"

"Repairing fine instruments is a specialty," Silvio said. "I handle all repairs myself."

He said repairs were the only work he entrusted to himself. Violinmaking was a younger man's vocation, requiring a fine eye for detail and exactitude of spirit. He left that part of the work to his grandson and the two other journeymen he employed, all gone to Florence for the festival.

"This is a rather fine instrument, I think you will agree," the visitor said, the case on the bench.

"A beautiful old Stradivarius." He looked up at the man. "May I?"

"Please," the man said with a flourish of the hand, giving him leave to examine the valuable instrument.

Silvio brought the violin near his face, studying the crack in the front, running parallel to where the bass bar was mounted inside.

"The breach has affected the tone only slightly, but I am anxious to have it repaired before it gets worse."

"Very wise of you, sir," Silvio replied. "A violin is like a woman: the attention you pay them is returned a dozen times over, but you neglect them at your risk. You have had the Stradivarius a long time?"

"Seven years," the visitor said. "I call it Jupiter, because of its regal tone." The stranger looked around. "You are the master of this shop?"

Silvio dipped his head. "Silvio Pietro, at your service."

"You knew the Serafino whose name is over your door?"

"But of course," Silvio said. "I had the honor to be *Padróne* Serafino's last apprentice. Having no children, he left the shop to me when he died. He was a kind man."

"How long has he been with the Lord?"

"It has been fifty years since the master's death." He gently put the Strad back in its case. "You are English?"

A dark scowl crossed the visitor's face. "England be damned and all the English with her. I am Welsh. My home is Cadair Idris. Do you know Wales?"

"No, but I have heard it is a beautiful land."

The visitor sighed. "I have not been home in a long time. Cadair Idris is a mountain in Snowdonia, the northwest part of the country. Some might find it gloomy, for it often rains, but it is some of the loveliest country you will ever find. If you see it, you will never get it out of your bones."

"You will return there soon, I hope, sir?"

"Unfortunately, no. I next sail for Madrid, where I am to perform some quartets by that phenomenal German, Beethoven."

"I once repaired a violin for Herr Beethoven."

"You have met the man?"

Silvio nodded.

"How did you find him?"

"He knew exactly what he wanted," Silvio said. "He was a discerning client."

"You mean demanding."

"You know the Germans," Silvio said, and smiled. "I tried to tell him you cannot make a German violin sound like one built in Italy, but he believed otherwise. Eventually I convinced him he would be satisfied with a different instrument."

"One of yours?"

"It was not such an exceptional instrument. Much inferior to your Stradivarius, but better than the German box he was playing. The 'Jupiter' will be in good hands with me. You plan to remain in Cremona a few days?"

"However long it takes," the visitor said, presenting Silvio with his card.

"It is a pleasure to meet you, Signor Glyndwr. There aren't many of Stradivari's instruments left in Cremona."

"Help settle an argument for me," Glyndwr said. "You are from Cremona and know these instruments. Which is better. A Stradivarius or a Guarneri del Gesu?"

"It is all a matter of preferences. For workmanship, the Stradivarius. For power of tone, the del Gesu. I have heard some roar like cannons. However, for delicacy of tone and responsiveness, most players prefer the Stradivarius. For a virtuoso given to pyrotechnic playing, perhaps the del Gesu would be preferable."

"You are saying neither violin is better than the other."

"The ultimate telling is in what the instrument does in the hands of the person who plays it," Silvio said diplomatically.

"Yet surely you would agree that a superior violin will coax something extra out of the player, leading him on toward new levels of expression and passion?"

"It is my experience that that is true, Signor Glyndwr."

"So tell me," the visitor said in the manner of a man with time to ponder philosophical matters, "who, in your learned opinion, is *the* violinmaker par excellence?"

"The best ever?"

Glyndwr nodded.

"My answer would be neither Stradivari nor del Gesu. The best violins ever made in Cremona—with all due respect to your excellent violin . . ."

"I promise not to take offense," the visitor said.

"The master luthier of them all was my old master, Archangelo Serafino."

"The maker of the exquisite Angel violins."

"You've heard of them?" Silvio asked, surprised.

"But of course," Glyndwr said. "And I have been led to understand that *you* are one of a small handful of people in the world who own one. I wonder if you would do me the very great favor of playing it for me?"

Silvio's expression changed to pleasure. When he was still a young man, when his bow arm was still nimble and the name Archangelo Serafino was remembered and honored, people would sometimes visit the shop and ask to see the Angel violin and hear him play. These requests diminished over the years, as people forgot and time obscured the *padróne*'s work. It was only natural that the instruments of Stradivari and del Gesu got the most attention and came to be thought of as the most desirable; there were so many of them, relatively speaking, even if they had gradually gone away to owners in other parts of Europe, like the Israelites' exodus from the Promised Land.

The extreme scarcity of these rare Serafino instruments—the *padróne* had made only thirteen—contributed to their obscurity, but, strangely enough, so did the existence of Archangelo Serafino's earlier violins. There were many Serafino violins in circulation, all of them excellent instruments, the life's work of a master artisan. After the master's death, when people still spoke of the Angel violins, unscrupulous dealers would pass off earlier Serafino violins as Angel violins. Silvio had even seen some of *Padróne* Serafino's earlier violins with forged labels, for it was only after going blind that he started marking his label with a tiny cross in black, to symbolize his devotion to God.

"I thought the world had forgotten," Silvio said softly.

"Not quite," the visitor said.

"You will not be disappointed, Signor Glyndwr," Silvio said, turning to unlock the cabinet where he kept his most prized possession. He lovingly carried the case to the workbench. "I must tell you straightaway it isn't for sale at any price."

"I would not expect you to willingly part with so precious a treasure," the visitor said. "I will gladly pay for the privilege of seeing it."

"No, no, I wouldn't hear of it. You are clearly a connoisseur. It is a great pleasure to meet someone who can appreciate such an exquisite creation."

Silvio opened the case. It was there, his jewel, the spruce a wonderful shade of gold, lightly stained to suit *Padróne* Serafino's tastes toward the end. He hadn't wanted to do anything to change or mask the natural beauty of the wood.

Silvio carefully lifted the instrument out of the velvet-lined case. Inside, the label, written in the master's own hand, said, *Archangelo Serafino, 1744 + XIII.* The number Thirteen, an unlucky violin, at least in the sense that it was the last Archangelo made before his heart gave out. Silvio cradled it in his arms like an infant, though he knew well enough that the instrument was a lot sturdier than it looked, a masterful feat of engineering, force against force, joint against joint, capable of singing in the most robust—or subtle—voice. How long had it been since he'd played it? A year? Two years? He opened and closed the fingers of his left hand around the neck. They were stiff, the movement awkward. They looked like the fingers of a very old man, and, strange as it was to realize with such clarity at that moment, Silvio was an old man.

"I no longer play more than a few notes after making a repair," Silvio said. He looked up at the visitor and saw the eagerness in his eyes. Silvio was no longer capable of doing the Angel violin justice. The realization that at some indefinite point in the past he had played the violin—*really* played it—for the last time, made him want to cry.

"Would you care to play it for yourself?" he said, so struck by the grief in his voice that he did not really hear what the visitor said as he took the violin from his hands.

Glyndwr put the violin to his chin and began to play. Silvio did not recognize the music. It was a moody Hungarian piece, a rhapsody filled with rapid chromatic scales and minor chord arpeggios. The Welshman was a fiery player, and yet Silvio could see the Angel gather him up in its wings and carry him off to that familiar timeless realm of pure beauty, where creation unfolded endlessly, like a mirrored hall with an infinite number of looking glasses, each reflecting even the smallest flourish an infinite number of times.

By the time Glyndwr lowered the violin, tears were running down his cheeks.

"So now you understand—and believe in the power of the Angels."

Silvio turned away out of deference as the visitor touched a silk handkerchief to his eyes. People often reacted emotionally to being touched by the light, the bliss, the incomparable, ineffable, indescribable perfection of the Angel's voice.

"And the other violins—where are they?"

"Only God knows that, Signor Glyndwr. They have dispersed, the other twelve disciples of the *padróne*'s blessed hands."

"No one has ever brought one to the shop to have it repaired or authenticated?"

"Only once. A man came to the shop and asked about one of the violins *Padróne* Serafino made for Bishop Falcone. The bishop had died, and the man was thinking of buying the violin. It was the number Seven. They each have a number, you see, one through thirteen."

"What was his name?"

"He did not tell me. I remember that he was very secretive. He was Swedish. Or perhaps Russian. I gather he was acting on behalf of a wealthy patron. That must have been all of thirty or forty years ago. Where does the time go?"

"And you have no idea where I might find one of these magical instruments?"

"I am afraid not, Signor Glyndwr. I like to think the Angel violins are highly valued and appreciated by their owners, though I suppose some of them may be sitting in a music room, forgotten."

The visitor reached out and grabbed Silvio by the neck so quickly that he did not see the man move. Glyndwr's cold green eyes seemed devoid of the least sign of human feeling. Silvio knew, even before the vampire opened his mouth, that he was about to die for the Angel violin.

9

CAPT. JEAN MASSENET stood at the elbow of the pilot as the *Juliette* came around the southwest corner of Sardinia. The *Juliette* rode deep on the starboard side, a good wind filling the sloop's sails so that she fairly flew over the waves where the Tyrrhenian Sea becomes the Mediterranean.

Captain Massenet squinted into the light, searching the sky. He stood with his arms behind him, turning his lucky jackknife over and over again in his right hand. The most direct route from Naples to Valencia would have been around the north end of Sardinia, but the route between the islands of Sardinia and Corsica was too treacherous. The strait was narrow, without much room to maneuver or run. It would have been better to skirt farther south, but then there were pirates from Tunisia and Algeria. There was no such thing as a safe course to chart in these troubled times, not for a merchantman flying the tricolor flag and most of the European powers at war with France.

The island mountains came down to the sea, rocky crags dotted with olive trees bent and twisted by the constant wind and rocky soil. The only thing that gave Captain Massenet the least comfort was the fact that

Bonaparte was from Corsica. But Cagliari, the only city of substance on the southern end of the island, was long behind them. Trouble, if it came to them, would be on the high seas, where not even Bonaparte himself would be able to assist them.

The last bit of land, an island jutting up from the water as if hurled down from Olympus by an angry Zeus, was a mile off their starboard, a black outline with the sun falling into the sea beyond it in the west.

"Well, Georges," Captain Massenet told the pilot, "it appears the famous Massenet luck has not deserted—"

"*Bateau!*" one of the mates called down from his perch in the mainmast rigging. "Ship!"

Captain Massenet raised his glass, but it was useless to him against the blinding glare dancing on the water. He lowered the instrument and rubbed his eyes. Then he saw it. About a mile away, a sizable ship sat behind the island, turned into the wind, barely moving. Waiting, Captain Massenet thought.

The pilot was looking back at him. The man had asked him a question, but he hadn't heard it.

"*Ferme,*" he said. He indicated that the pilot should hold a steady course, pointing with his jackknife in the direction they had been sailing, toward Valencia, in Spain, many, many, many miles away, across the water. "*Solide,* Georges."

"A complication, it appears."

Captain Massenet did not answer or turn to look at the Marquis de Saint-Veran.

"A British man-of-war, I'd hazard."

Captain Massenet nodded absently, busy watching the sailors on the still-distant ship scrambling through the rigging, dropping the canvas that instantly filled with wind and began to strain against the still-loose sheets. Within a matter of minutes, every inch of canvas from the royal to the fore mainsail would be set, pulling the ship through the water at a quickening pace.

"It looks like the *Diligence.* May I have the use of your glass, Captain?" He studied the ship. "Indeed it is. She's a third rate ship-of-the-line, with a complement of eighty guns and a five-hundred-man crew. Commander's name is Holland, Captain Samuel Holland. Well loved by his men. There are said to be fewer floggings on the *Diligence* than on any other ship in the Royal Navy."

Captain Massenet was looking at the Marquis de Saint-Veran with nearly the same suspicious disregard he had in his eyes watching the *Diligence* get under way.

"For a French citizen, Marquis, you seem to know a great deal about British warships."

"The *Diligence* was docked in Genoa until recently, as was I. I had gone there to meet with shipbuilders about commissioning a vessel. The comings and goings of ships in the harbor were the wine of everyday conversation during my visit."

"And yet you sailed for Spain, and from Naples, not Genoa. Would that not have been a more direct route?"

The marquis smiled thinly but said nothing.

"I noticed you boarded the *Juliette* in haste. Was it going to Valencia that interested you, Marquis, or merely getting out of Italy in a hurry?"

"You are a perceptive man, Captain. Several Austrian agents anxious to interview me were somewhere behind me. I was convinced they would be too vigorous in their questioning of me for my continued good health."

Captain Massenet looked back at the *Diligence*. The man-of-war seemed to have charted a tack to intercept the *Juliette*.

"And why would Austrian agents wish to question you, Marquis?"

"They were under the absurd impression that I was a spy," the Marquis de Saint-Veran said. "It was really all quite beyond me. They concocted some mad delusion about me scouting out the Austrian enforcements under General Michael von Melas, in advance of a surprise attack by Bonaparte across the Alps." The marquis laughed merrily. "I have no idea how they dreamed up such a preposterous story."

"They're here because of you?"

"I do not honestly know, Captain. It is possible. But Britain is at war with France. The English might just as easily be prize hunting. They are in the right place at the right time. Indeed, here we are."

A puff of smoke appeared from the end of one of the *Diligence*'s cannons. It was a moment longer before Captain Massenet heard a distant boom, but almost immediately there was a shriek through the air above their heads. The gunner had overestimated his range and overshot the ship.

"They're trying to get your attention, Captain," the marquis said. "They didn't miss."

The noise brought his other passenger up on deck, *Monsieur* Glyndwr, the violinist.

"Did that ship fire at us?" Glyndwr demanded. Angry rather than afraid, Captain Massenet noted with satisfaction.

"*Oui, monsieur.* They intend to board us, if they can."

"Can you outrun them?"

"You would want to outrun the Royal Navy, *monsieur?* Why would a British subject risk his neck trying to escape a man-of-war?"

"I am Welsh, not British," Glyndwr snapped. "I hate the bloody British even more than you do. The enemy of my enemy is my friend. That makes us allies. What are our options?"

"We could heave to and be boarded," the marquis said.

"Meaning they would take my ship and my cargo." Captain Massenet's eyes narrowed. "And maybe they would take you, Marquis, and hang you for a spy."

"Or you could help me get to Valencia. I promise Bonaparte will pay you a handsome reward for certain documents in my possession. On the other hand, if the British take your ship, they may hang us all for spies."

"Begging the captain's pardon, there is a third choice," the pilot said. "We could hug in close to the coast, trying to lose her in shallow water, where we can go and she can't."

"But that's dangerous. We could end up on the rocks ourselves," Captain Massenet said.

"You did not answer my original question, Captain," Glyndwr said. "Can we outrun the man-of-war?"

"Easily, I think. Especially if we get around in front of her, where her guns can't get to us. It'll be dark soon. With just a little luck we can be miles away by dawn."

"Then run hard and run fast, Captain," Glyndwr urged.

"Bring her around ten degrees," Massenet told the pilot. "Get in front of her, where she can do us no harm."

The *Diligence* fired off another half dozen rounds, the last shots falling dangerously close to the ship. The sun was down, the sky quickly turning to purple, with a darker band of black spreading from the eastern horizon behind them, promising to shroud the *Juliette* in a protective mantle of darkness.

Captain Massenet stood at the stern of the sloop with Dylan Glyndwr and the Marquis de Saint-Veran, watching the man-of-war growing smaller in the dusk. He was smiling a little. He was lucky, very lucky. He always had been.

"They're giving up," Glyndwr said.

"What do you mean, *monsieur?*" the marquis said.

"They're turning."

"You must have very good eyes, *monsieur,* to see that in this light."

"Quiet!" Captain Massenet ordered, lifting the glass to his eye. The British warship was slowly turning, swinging into the wind until she was showing the *Juliette* her starboard side. He could just make out the officers, gathered on the quarterdeck between the mizzen and mainmast.

"A broadside from a ship like the *Diligence* can put one thousand pounds of iron in the air," the marquis said with his usual ironic tone, but there was a tightness in his voice.

There was a sudden flash of light from the direction of the ship, as if forty or more fireworks had suddenly burst. For a moment the man-of-war was perfectly illuminated in the bright white light, the glow lasting long enough to pick up the billowing puffs of gunpowder smoke swirling up from the cannons.

"Did you know, Monsieur Glyndwr," the marquis

continued in a mock didactic tone, "that an eighteen-pound gun can throw a five-pound shot with enough velocity to penetrate a one-foot-thick oak hull at a range of one thousand yards?"

They heard the deafening roll of thunder, followed by a high-pitched shriek of projectiles hurtling toward them.

A little short or a little long, Captain Massenet thought. It would be too dark to make their range in a matter of minutes. If only his luck held a few more minutes. They wouldn't try to blow a valuable prize out of the water just for the sport of it. It had to be the marquis, Captain Massenet had time to think, just as the cannonballs fell out of the sky on the little sloop.

It was dark when Capt. Jean Massenet awoke. He was lying on his back, looking up past furled sails at a starry sky. Someone was shrieking in the distance. It was an inhuman wail, like the cry of a banshee. Except it was human. Every minute or so the cry would form itself in the twisted semblance of two words: *My* and *violin.*

Captain Massenet drifted back into unconsciousness. The next thing he knew he awoke, still on his back under the night sky, being tended to by an English doctor. The doctor was bandaging his arm. No, not his arm, for there was nothing there, just a stump of bloody flesh with a bit of bone protruding. He thought he was going to faint from the sight but he didn't. His mind was strangely clear. He knew he was in shock, and that it would wear off, but it didn't matter. For now there was no pain, and the realization that he'd lost an arm and maybe more—he could not lift his head to examine himself—was only a dull awareness.

"You have to let us help you or you're going to drown," he heard an English voice say.

Then a second voice, this one more authoritarian, an officer, Massenet guessed: "You should be damned glad just to be alive. To hell with the bloody violin you keep wailing about, sir. Act like an Englishman."

Captain Massenet managed to turn his head slightly to the left. Two tars were helping Dylan Glyndwr onto the deck. He was wet and looked completely deranged. Massenet knew the violinist placed an inordinate value on his instrument. He'd taken care of it as if it were an infant and even called it "Angel." By the look of anguish on his face, you'd have thought he'd lost his entire family in the sinking of the *Juliette,* and not just a violin.

Glyndwr seemed to notice the officer who'd been berating him. He grabbed the man by his jacket with sudden fury.

"He doesn't like to be called an Englishman," Captain Massenet said, but he said it in French and nobody was paying any attention to him anyway. They were all watching Glyndwr, who instead of striking the officer appeared to be biting him on the neck. There was a spurt of arterial blood in the light of the ship's lanterns as Glyndwr threw the officer's dead body aside and disappeared into the rigging above.

Captain Massenet felt himself slipping backward into the darkness, wondering if what he'd seen had really happened, and, if he woke again, if there would be anybody left alive on the man-of-war besides him and the vampire mourning for his lost violin.

ADAGIO

The Present

10

JANE CRITTENDEN DISMISSED the Friday-afternoon faculty meeting early and went back to her office, Katarina Eck following close behind, like a German shepherd nipping at her heels, wanting to discuss a problem student. The discussion would have to wait until Monday, Jane said, adding only that she was disinclined to allow another postponement to Maggie O'Hara's juried recital for admission to the music school's performance-study program. The girl's muscle problems with her shoulder and arm were unfortunate, but the recital had already been put off twice, and enough was enough. Jane was beginning to share Eck's belief that the problems were psychologically induced. Not every violinist, no matter how talented, was cut out for life as a performer.

The chairperson of the university's music department lived in a new development of quarter-million-dollar homes in a wooded valley on the edge of town. The house was a contemporary two-story brick with a three-car garage and a spacious deck in back with an in-ground hot tub. It was situated between property belonging to a lawyer and his wife, who did public-relations work for the university, and a Mormon dentist with five children.

The Volvo bounced coming over the curb. The far-left bay in the garage was filled with storage boxes, the lawn mower, and assorted junk. Jane parked on the right, her spot. Her partner, Camille, parked in the center. It was Camille's yoga night. She wouldn't be home until after eight.

The house was conspicuously neat, floors freshly vacuumed or scrubbed, the furniture dusted. Their cleaning lady, Yolanda, usually came on Monday, but Jane had asked her to make a special trip back on Friday because she was having a guest. There was a big bouquet of flowers in a crystal bowl on the dining room table. Camille had a passion for flowers.

Jane put the bottles of California wine on the breakfast bar between the kitchen and great room and ran upstairs. She washed her face and ran a brush through her short hair, black shot through with steely gray. She was in the closet in the master bedroom, reaching for a fresh blouse, when she heard a car in the drive. It was a black BMW, she saw, looking down from the window that covered the top half of the open stairway leading down to the foyer. It wasn't one of the baby Beamers that were popular with the faculty, but a big, sleek sedan. Curious: Jane didn't know you could rent a car like that, at least not outside of a city like New York or Los Angeles. Maybe it belonged to a wealthy patron, she thought. Surely the conductor hadn't bought it for the few short weeks of residency in the United States. Perhaps she'd had it shipped from Germany.

The driver's door swung open and a woman's leg

emerged—a sandaled foot, then a few inches of tanned leg disappearing into a long silk skirt.

Jane opened the door before the bell rang.

"Jane Crittenden?"

"Hello. It is an honor to meet you, Maestro."

Jane held out her hand but the woman came past it and embraced her.

"I would be pleased to have you call me Maria, Professor Crittenden."

Jane had seen photographs of Maria Rainer, yet she expected an older woman when they met in person. Publicity photos tended to be chosen for propaganda value. But in this case the subject looked as good as her pictures in the press—better, in fact. Maria Rainer could have passed for being Camille's age—which was twenty-four—although she was prettier than Camille. The German conductor was not much more than five feet tall, yet she exuded the air of command, a natural aristocrat. Jane wondered how someone so young could have gone so far so fast, becoming conductor of the Berlin Philharmonic at such an early age. Jane felt a surge of pride. It had been a tremendous coup for her to get Maria Rainer to agree to be featured guest conductor at the university's Mozart festival.

Maria insisted on accompanying Jane into the kitchen while she opened the wine. Jane felt an instant bond of friendship, charmed by the conductor's potent combination of warmth and charisma. They took their wine onto the deck, which overlooked a meadow falling away from the back of the homes on the cul-de-sac. Though the cottonwoods overlooking the creek in the distance had lost most of their leaves, there was still color in the maples and oaks on the opposite hillside.

They talked casually, discussing Maria's flight and
the university, and the music school's emerging reputation for placing string players with some of the nation's leading orchestras. The talk would be more
formal the next night, during the dinner the university
president was hosting to honor their distinguished
guest; everybody would be too busy being important
or obsequious, as their role demanded, for any real rap-
port to develop. That was why Jane had invited Maria
to drop by for a glass of wine. They could get to know
each other, and Maria would have a chance to learn a
little about the people she would be leading, who was
good and who was not so good. They could go over the
rehearsal schedule and make sure everything was
agreeable. And Jane would have an opportunity to
learn whether the conductor had any special needs or
wishes, as well as discreetly identify potential problems to avoid. Conductors could be temperamental,
and nothing would turn Jane's triumph into a career-
damaging disaster faster than having a distinguished
maestro storm off the podium and quit over some
minor problem that could have been easily rectified.
Jane's antennae, which were quite finely tuned by
years of bloody internecine academic warfare, battling
herself to the top of the university music department,
picked up not the slightest whiff of trouble from the
German conductor. Maria had definite ideas, but it was
equally clear that she knew how to get things done
without resorting to cold appeals to authority, humiliation, or any other dark tricks.

Jane opened the second bottle of wine and brought
it out with a plate of cheese and crackers, which
neither woman touched. The discussion turned to

Mendelssohn. Maria's most recent program with the Berlin orchestra had included his Symphony No. 4, the Italian Symphony.

"The thing about Mendelssohn is you keep expecting him to let up, but he never does," Maria said. "He keeps coming and coming at you until you think, 'When is this man going to take a break?' I think of it as 'the Mendelssohn engine.' It's always there, pounding, pounding, the pulse, the heartbeat."

Jane took it all in, smiling, thinking how clever and fortunate she was to have gotten the young phenomenon to agree to conduct the Mozart festival. In her short career, Maria Rainer had become one of the world's preeminent conductors. And best of all, she was a woman. It was important—and still all too rare—for women to hold the orchestral baton. The German conductor was the perfect embodiment of the New Woman, in Jane's estimation. She was masterfully self-possessed yet feminine at the same time, strong and decisive without surrendering the part of her that was most distinctly *not* masculine. Women who tried to covertly emulate men missed the point of feminism, Jane thought. Gender was something the head of the university's music department thought about a lot. She wanted to found a department of women's music studies, but the idea was too avant-garde for her Midwestern university.

"Of course, we won't be concerning ourselves with Herr Mendelssohn at your Mozart festival," Maria was saying. "What have you selected for the program?"

"Something light and charming to get things rolling."

"Light and charming—ah, yes, the very essence of Mozart."

"I quite agree," Jane said, and smiled. "I was thinking the Violin Concerto in G Major."

"Perfect. Who will be the soloist?"

"I have arranged an audition to give our best students an opportunity to play for you. We have several outstanding violinists in our graduate performance program. This isn't Juilliard—not yet, at any rate—but I think you'll be pleased by the caliber of playing."

"I am certain of it."

Dusk fell as they talked. Jane lighted candles on the deck and put a CD of Beethoven piano music on, the languorous music just loud enough on the deck speakers to fill the pauses in the conversation with delicious sound. Jane was in the kitchen, refilling their glasses, when she heard Maria come in behind her. She sensed the other woman's presence near her a moment before Maria laid a hand on her shoulder. Europeans, Jane thought: so physical in their demonstrations for friendship.

Maria pressed her body close against Jane's from behind.

The sudden act of intimacy set a flock of butterflies to flight inside Jane. She felt a powerful physical attraction for the woman, but she had not considered acting on it. By appearances, Maria was twenty years Jane's junior, and beautiful, famous, and wealthy enough to have as many lovers as she wished. It had not occurred to Jane that Maria was as drawn to her as she was to Maria.

"Maria . . ."

"Hush, my love," Maria purred in her ear. "Let me take care of everything."

Jane's eyes found the clock. Camille wouldn't be home for another hour. And if she came home early . . . what did it matter? Jane realized that she had fallen completely under the beautiful German's spell. It was dangerous to give herself over to such abandon, but what was love without recklessness? That was how it had been with Camille, but Jane sensed that she was about to experience something far sweeter still.

Jane melted backward into the other woman's embrace. The light, warm, wet touch of the tip of Maria Rainer's tongue on her neck sent an electric thrill of excitement through Jane Crittenden that ceased abruptly when the vampire sank her teeth into her neck.

11

MAGGIE O'HARA STOOD in the Upham Hall practice studio with her back to the closed door. She tucked the violin under her chin and regarded the music propped in front of her on the stand with fierce concentration: Sibelius's Violin Concerto in D Minor, op. 47.

Beautiful music, if you could play it.

She raised her right arm. The bow felt well-balanced as she lowered it to the strings, a fulcrum counterpoised between the thumb and little finger of her small right hand. The bow, a carbon-fiber Coda bow her grandfather had given her for Christmas, was, like her Chinese violin, good enough for a serious student at the university, though not quite professional quality.

The strategy was to lay siege to the Sibelius, conquering it one movement at a time. If Maggie attacked the concerto straight on, from start to finish, it would eat her alive.

In an earlier, more puritanical age, the violin had been known as "the devil's instrument," suspect because it was thought to lure the innocent into committing the sin of dance. The better reason for associating the violin with Lucifer is that it is fiendishly difficult to play.

Unlike the piano, which has eighty-eight keys to guide the hands, or the guitar, which has frets, there are no guideposts on the violin fingerboard to assist the player. Only years of diligent scale and étude practice had won Maggie's fingers the muscle memory required to fall exactly where they needed to be to play in pitch.

The challenges to the right hand and arm are more demanding still. The violin comes closer to the human voice than any other instrument, and the almost infinite variability of the bow is why. But to make the violin sweetly sing, Maggie had devoted years to practicing the delicate manipulations of speed, pressure, control, and motion required to play spiccatos, arpeggios, ricochets, and octave-leaping scales.

She drew in a sharp breath, feeling the rhythm with her entire body, and began to play. She got most of the way through the movement before she lost the bowing.

She started over.

When she got to the passage where she had the trouble, Maggie lost her bowing a second time.

Her mouth was set in a taut line as she attacked the music for the third time. She was determined to play the passage correctly, even if she had to repeat it again and again, until security threw her out when they locked the building at midnight.

The door opened, but Maggie didn't look over her shoulder. Possession was the only thing that mattered in the practice studios. First come, first served. There were no time limits. The room was hers until the building closed. Ignoring the intruder, she started to play again, murdering the dynamics, distracted despite her dogged effort to concentrate.

"I thought we were going to get something to eat."

Maggie began the passage again.

"Maggie!"

The bow screeched over the strings, startling the visitor as she spun to face Peter Hill, a young man, handsome and intelligent-looking, with wire-frame glasses and a ponytail.

"I thought I told you never to interrupt a rehearsal."

The sharpness of her voice surprised Peter. It surprised her.

"You said you'd meet me at six. It's nearly seven-thirty."

She felt her defiance waver. She had promised. She had to look away from him.

"I lost track of the time."

"Again."

Maggie felt an unpleasant warmth flush through her face.

"You don't have any idea how difficult this is."

"I didn't say it wasn't," he said evenly.

Peter was always so controlled, so perfectly self-possessed, which only served to increase Maggie's irritation. She was exactly the opposite—passionate, emotional, vulnerable.

"Sibelius is a bear."

"He must be. All you do is practice that piece."

"And all you do is study, now that you're in med school. Do I make an issue of it?"

"I still have time for you, Maggie."

"Don't play that card with me. You know everything is riding on this recital."

"I understand," he said, and nodded.

"No, you don't."

He tried to put his hand on her arm, but she pulled away.

"I understand, Maggie. I really do."

Maggie couldn't hold his eyes. She was upset with him for interrupting, with herself for overreacting, and with her inability to master the Sibelius violin concerto. Mainly she was mad at herself, although she was working hard to direct her anger outward at Peter.

"You need to let up on yourself a little, Maggie. You've become obsessed."

"Obsessed," she echoed, reaching for sarcasm but managing only to make it sound like an admission of guilt. She *was* obsessed. Her entire future balanced on her ability to master the piece well enough to pass the juried recital and gain admission to the music school's performance program. It was bad enough that the muscles in her arm, shoulder, and back kept going into spasm. The recital had been postponed twice. Her violin teacher, Dr. Eck, had already warned Maggie she would be granted no further extensions.

"I think your playing would improve if you would step back a little, relax, and enjoy what you're doing," Peter said. "If you try too hard at anything, you tense up and your performance declines. It's a physiological fact, but it's also just plain common sense."

"This is my one shot at this," Maggie said, her voice rising with each word. "It's not as if I can take another science class, the way you did, and raise my grade point enough to impress the admissions office at the medical school. This recital is it. It's the only thing I care about at this point."

"Does that include me?"

"Yes," Maggie said with brutal coldness. "It does."

Peter started to speak but stopped himself, as if unwilling to trust what he might say.

"Why don't you just leave, Peter?" Maggie said dismissively, as if bored with the conversation and impatient for it to end. "I have work to do. Go have something to eat, see a movie, study organic chemistry—do whatever you want, just leave me alone. I have my violin. That's the only thing I need."

"Maggie, you're twenty years old."

"Yes, Peter." She started to tap her foot.

"The university is a good school, but this is hardly Juilliard."

"If you have a point to make, hurry up and get to it, because I have practicing to do."

"I've heard you play plenty of times, Maggie. I think you're good. In fact, I think you're very good. But if you had what it took to be a concert violinist, you wouldn't still be trying to prove it to people."

Maggie's mouth fell open at hearing Peter utter the unspeakable.

"I don't know what happened to shake your confidence, but since the fall semester started you've been inching closer and closer to a breakdown," he went on. "I thought you'd harness the frustration and pressure and make it work for you, but I don't see that happening. The problems with your arm and back . . . if you ask me, they're psychosomatic. Your body is sabotaging itself."

It was all true, of course. Maggie knew what Peter was saying was true, but she wasn't about to quit now.

"Whether you get into the performance program at

the music school is not a matter of life and death, no matter how much you think it is. Life will go on whether or not you get it. Maybe what you want, or think you want, isn't meant to be. If not, you need to figure out where you fit into the world of music and make your peace with it."

Maggie clenched the violin so tightly by its neck that it began to shake. Her voice was low and strange when she spoke, as if channeling the spirit of someone who choked to death on the bitterness of unrealized dreams.

"I hate you," she hissed.

Peter didn't say anything. He looked at her closely with what, after a moment, Maggie recognized as pity.

"Get out!" she screamed.

Peter turned without another word and left, shutting the door gently behind himself, as if in deference to Maggie and all the other musicians who had come to pray to the black Manhasset music stands pressed into service as altars to art.

Maggie O'Hara stared at the empty space where Peter Hill had stood, knowing he would never again occupy that space in her life. She had given everything else for her music. Peter was but the latest sacrifice. As the stakes became dramatically greater, it seemed fitting that the price should correspondingly increase.

She turned back to Sibelius, concentrating too hard to be bothered by either the tears or the pinching pain in her shoulder muscle that flared up whenever she practiced too long. And even though she attacked the blizzard of notes with her determination redoubled and her attention sharply focused, the truth was that she played it very poorly.

12

OLD CAPITOL WAS the heart of the university. Built in the 1840s, the limestone building was a prairie interpretation of a Greek temple, even if it was topped with a Roman dome of copper painted gold. When the legislature moved the state capital west to the center of the state, Old Cap became home to a fledgling landgrant university. Four more buildings were added to the grassy park surrounding Old Cap during the early years of the twentieth century. Old Cap sat in the middle of the complex, known as the Pentacrest, with the five buildings overlooking the meandering river below.

The town and university spread in all directions from Old Cap, growing in tandem, partners in the same prosperous enterprise. University buildings multiplied, from the Pentacrest west toward the river, and to the north and south. The town's business district was east of the Pentacrest, a bulwark against expansion in that direction. To the northeast of the Pentacrest was the original residential neighborhood, with rambling frame or brick houses that the first professors and administrators built for their families.

The university continued to gradually consume the blocks nearest the Pentacrest. Beyond the dormitories, the Merissac School of Business, the Chemistry Building, and other university properties, were transitional areas of small businesses and single-family houses divided into apartments. The slow commercial creep would continue until the university decided to swallow up another gulp of property in one of its periodic expansions. There was no telling when the university would stop growing. Perhaps never.

East of the Botany Building and north of the State Historical Society headquarters was the 600 block of Cedar Street. It was a street of single-family homes and houses converted to apartments, with only two businesses on the block. At the corner was a camera shop in what had been a neighborhood grocery. Next to it, in the lot to the north, was a violin shop.

Ivaskin Violins occupied Graham Cottage, named for Oliver Graham, an Episcopal priest who served with the Union Army as an infantry captain during the Civil War, losing his eye and his faith at the Battle of Gettysburg. Graham became a philosophy professor at the university after the war. The smallish house he built of dark brown brick had a modest front porch and steeply peaked gables over the two front windows placed symmetrically on either side of the door. The outermost gables incorporated windows to the garret bedrooms on the second story.

A great deal of attention had been given to small details in building Graham Cottage. It was not known who designed the house. Most agreed it had been Graham, though it was a simmering matter of dispute among local preservationists, whose love of old buildings was sometimes superceded by a fondness for bitter, take-no-prisoners battles over issues of provenance and preservation. Be that as it may, the person who planned the cottage seemed to have set out to prove that imagination, not wealth, was the vital ingredient in transforming the ordinary into the noteworthy. The steeply canted roof was finished in alternating shades of slate, the shingles scalloped at the bottom to resemble a series of small waves tumbling toward a beach. The bricks were set at angles at the corners and either recessed or protruding here and there to produce cornices and overhangs and other fanciful masonry effects.

A bronze plaque mounted in the bricks beside the doorway proclaimed that Oliver Graham's house was on the National Registry. Thanks to the designation, it was unlikely that the block would ever be occupied by a parking ramp, which university officials were always proposing with great zeal as a solution to the town's chronic shortage of parking, and because of the revenue such facilities generated.

Today, converting Graham Cottage into a commercial establishment would result in a pitched battle, replete with demonstrations and even acts of civil disobedience. There had been no such controversy in the 1960s when Ivan Ivaskin, a music professor at the university's school of music, retired and opened up a violin shop in the Graham home on Cedar Street.

The only outward sign of Graham Cottage's commercialization was a small wooden sign in the shape of a violin hanging horizontally above the door at a right angle to the wall, like a sign outside an English tavern. Lettering on the glass in the front door said *Ivaskin Violins.* The enterprise's scope was further defined in smaller letters: *New & Collectible Instruments & Bows*.

From inside Graham Cottage came the sound of a violin playing Beethoven's Violin Sonata in A Major. The music stopped. The A string was plucked, the tuning peg adjusted, the string plucked again. The adjustment proven satisfactory, the playing resumed.

Unlikely circumstance had played such an important role in Carter Dunne's life that he had almost come to expect the strange, occasionally bizarre quirks of fate that characterized his existence.

Carter had gone to college in South Dakota, thinking he might one day become an art teacher. He had always liked art, and had been fortunate enough to be born with a good sense of line, proportion, and color. He was also very good with his hands, and his affinity for the tactile and mechanical as much as anything led him toward a master's degree in pottery. But it was not in the cards for Carter to spend his life teaching high school students to throw bowls and glaze pots. During the semester he was finishing his master's thesis, an uncle who owned a Ford dealership in Milwaukee invited Carter to design a ceramic stove for the sailboat he was building on Lake Michigan. Carter ended up working on the boat that summer. One of the chandlers in the boatyard was a man Carter's age who was interested in computers and a new thing called the World Wide Web. He had an idea about selling Carter's ceramic stoves on the Internet.

The two young would-be entrepreneurs found there were advantages to working in a boatyard that built custom sailing yachts. The clients had money and business experience, and many of them had an eye for the next big thing. The fact that their Internet business wound up selling airline and travel reservations, not Carter's ceramic stoves, was just another element of the unexpected in Carter's life.

By his thirtieth birthday, Carter Dunne had amassed more wealth than he ever would have imagined possible. The business became more complicated after they took their stock public, so the partners brought in a bright young woman with an MBA from Wharton to run things. It was boredom and luck, not business sense, that led Carter to sell his share of the venture not long before the dot-com bubble burst and the company ended up in Chapter 11.

Carter spent a year traveling the world. He went on a safari in Africa, spent a week in Antarctica, fished for salmon in Russia, and nearly died attempting to climb Mount Everest with a crew of rich Americans. He got engaged to a Japanese student whose father was a vice president of Toyota, but it didn't work out because of the differences in race: her family thought all Americans were barbarians. Carter spent the winter in a house in the Keys after that, licking his wounds, drinking rum, and waiting for circumstance to push him out the door and in the direction of his future.

Thinking he might like to get back into business, he came to the Midwest on a tip from a business broker to check out a small factory that made Shaker-style furniture. He wasn't able to come to an agreement on a price with the owner, a Mennonite who apparently didn't want to retire as much as he said he did. Carter stayed in town after the deal fell apart to continue seeing a woman he'd met. Karla was a beautiful but moody graduate student in art. It wasn't likely to develop into anything serious, but the sex was good, and Carter kept extending his stay at the Sheraton a day or two at a time.

He found himself walking down Cedar Street one morning, cooling off after his daily five-mile run. He was supposed to have lunch with Karla, but they'd quarreled the night before and he didn't know if she was going to show up.

Ivaskin Violins was the sort of place that had the power to capture Carter's attention and ignite his imagination from the first glance. There was something bewitching about the little cottage with its intricate brickwork, gingerbread roof, and artfully kept ivy. It was almost like something out of a fairy tale. Perhaps the sensation that Carter had seen the house before, as if in his dreams, was due to the fact that it looked so much like it belonged in a storybook.

The attraction had nothing to do with violins. Carter did not play the violin, although he wasn't too bad on the guitar and had a rather decent Martin back in his hotel room.

He stood on the sidewalk and looked at the violin shop for a long moment. It felt as if the cottage was inviting him to come in. He started up the brick sidewalk out of curiosity. A business card was wedged between the molding and glass in the lower right-hand corner of the door, its back to Carter. Written on it in a neat hand was the message, *Shop for sale, inquire within.*

A tiny bell attached to the inside of the door jingled when he went in, but no one answered the summons. The place appeared deserted. Sunlight poured in through the windows, the golden light reflecting off the surfaces of the violins and violas hanging from the ceiling and the walls. Some violins—apparently the more rare and valuable—were displayed on sumptuous beds of red velvet in glass cases.

These were not factory-made violins, but handmade instruments. A few looked new or almost new, but it was obvious that most were quite old, though not old as in decrepit and used up, but in the way an old master painting is old. It had never before occurred to Carter, but violins were actually works of art and therefore immortal; they had conferred upon their makers and previous owners a shared immortality, paid in recompense for the gently carved scrolls, for the exquisite attention to detail, for the years of loving care.

The smell of the place . . . it was almost intoxicating—beeswax, spruce, varnish, rosin powder. It was a warm, complex aroma, like the alchemy of good brandy cellared a century or more in the cool, dark, cobweb-crossed depths of a subterranean vault.

Carter drew in a slow, deep breath and closed his eyes, feeling the magic in the little violin shop. What stories these violins could tell of their previous owners, whose hands, long turned to bone, to dust, had danced along the ebony fingerboards. And what would the violins tell of how they came into the world, the children of brilliant Italians, earnest Germans, mercurial Frenchmen. The best materials. Incomparable workmanship. Perfect finishing work. Still good after so many years, time only enhancing the violins' tone, making their song deeper, richer.

Carter Dunne had thought of his 1940 Martin as old, but how much older and exquisite some of these violins must be. He wished he played, for it would be interesting to try out some of the violins, testing their tone and projection.

"Buon giorno."

A thin, elderly man with a neatly trimmed white mustache was coming downstairs carrying a partly disassembled violin under his arm. He wore a white shirt and carefully knotted tie beneath a faded blue denim apron. The man walked with the solemn dignity of a courtier, back straight, head erect, eyes bright, alert, intelligent.

Carter wasn't often at a loss for words, but standing there in his wet T-shirt, surrounded by an array of instruments he knew nothing about, he felt as embarrassed as if he'd gotten up in front of a boardroom only to realize he'd forgotten to put on his pants before leaving home in the morning.

"How may I be of assistance, *signore?* You have come to inquire about a violin? We have many fine instruments, as you can see."

"Are you the owner?"

"Oh, no, *signore.* The owner is Mr. Maxwell. I am only the luthier." He extended his hand. "I am Gianni Felici. May I be of assistance?"

"Maybe," Carter said. "I think I might be interested in buying this shop."

13

THERE WERE PLENTY of open spaces in the hospital parking ramp on Friday night. Maggie threw a blanket over her suitcase and book bag in the backseat. She took the violin, her most valuable possession, with her. Nobody in their right mind would break into the battered Escort looking for something worth stealing, but it would have been foolish to leave the instrument in the deserted parking garage.

Corrine Gooding smiled at Maggie as she came off the elevator and headed past the nursing station.

"I think he's asleep."

"How's he been?"

"As well as can be expected," the nurse said. "We can talk later, if you have time."

The door was propped open. The lights inside the room were turned off, leaving the monitor screens to throw a sinister greenish glow over the scene. What caught the eye was the rococo profusion of wires, tubes, IV bottles, and medical equipment encircling a bed with high chrome side rails. A close look was required to see that the subject in the center of this elaborate lab experiment was a human being. The formidable array of science and technology had been brought to bear to sustain the flickering flame of life that soon would go out, though not even the doctor-professors, with their godlike status at the teaching hospital, could say for certain when that time would come.

Maggie stood in the doorway, looking down on her grandfather's visibly diminishing form. There wasn't much left of him. The big Irishman who had once liked to sing bits of corny Dean Martin songs in an exaggerated, mocking voice had been reduced to a few wisps of white hair and a skeleton wrapped in nearly translucent skin.

"Hello, darling."

He smiled, his eyes still closed, smelling the Jean Naté perfume he'd given her for her birthday every year since she was thirteen.

"Hi, Grandpa."

She went to kiss him, feeling a jolt of recognition, then pain, when he opened his blue-gray eyes to look at her. His eyes were the only thing about his appearance that had not changed. The kindness, the intelligence, the humor were all still there even at the end. As good as it was to see how much remained so close to the end, it was also a bittersweet reminder of what Maggie would miss when he was finally out of his misery.

"Why aren't you in school?"

"It's Friday evening. I drove back for the weekend."

"It's hard to keep track of the days here," he said. "I hardly know one from the next."

She put her hand over his and squeezed it. He squeezed back, but barely. Maggie looked up at the television suspended on the far wall, studying it intently, as if it were turned on. This was hard for her, very hard, and yet there was no place she would rather be than with her grandfather during his final days. But he had insisted she stay in school and visit only on weekends. He was stubborn about things like that. He liked to say that he was "from the old school," though Maggie was never sure exactly what that meant except that you worked hard, did what you were supposed to, and stayed out of trouble.

"How do you think the Bears are going to do Sunday?"

He didn't answer. He'd fallen asleep.

Over cups of coffee from the pot in the family lounge at the end of the hall, the oncology night nurse gave Maggie a quick rundown on her grandfather's condition. It didn't take long. Treatment options were limited to trying to moderate his suffering during whatever little time he had left.

"How is college going for you, girl?" Corrine asked. She knew almost everything there was to know about Maggie from talking to Sam.

"I'm having a lot of trouble with my shoulder and arm. It's interfering with my playing a little."

"Nerve trouble?"

"It might be a disk, but they're not sure. The doctors have not been a lot of help."

"Nerve trouble can be tricky."

"I've been trying some alternative therapies. I've been seeing an acupuncturist."

The nurse frowned.

"I know what you're thinking. I would have thought the same thing, except that it's helped. She's a woman who works with a lot of people in the college of music and the orchestras in the area. There's an amazing amount of repetitive stress injuries with musicians."

Corrine Gooding's expression didn't change.

"My neurologist is the one who suggested I try acupuncture," Maggie explained, "so how crazy can it be?"

"Honey, that's all I needed to hear," the nurse said, and laughed. "Most neurologists I know are half-crazy."

It took Maggie a moment to be sure the nurse was joking. "My acupuncturist says my energy is blocked," Maggie said. They both giggled.

"My doctor—I'm talking about the neurologist now—thinks I may to have to give up playing the violin for a while. It might be for the best. I'd have time to concentrate on getting my master's in music education."

"I thought your dream was to be a performer and travel all over the world, leading a life of glamour."

"It was."

"You're ready to give that up?"

"I don't know," Maggie said, and looked out the window. It was night but there were so many lights in the city. She hadn't liked living in a small town when she first went to the university, but there were parts of it that had grown on her. You could see the stars at night, for one thing.

Maggie sighed.

"Maybe it's time for me to put away my dreams and be more realistic."

"That's one way to look at it, and maybe that's right," the older woman said, looking at Maggie with an unblinking stare. "But if you're ready to give up on your dreams, girl, you have more than you want in common with some of the people in this ward. And I'm not talking about your granddaddy, you understand. He is a fighter."

That much, at least, they both knew for certain.

"The medicine makes me sleepy."

"That's okay, Grandpa. I was talking with Corrine."

"Did you play your recital yet, the one to get into the performance program?"

"It's coming up."

"Are you practicing?"

She nodded.

"There's a price for everything," he said. "The only place that success comes before work . . ."

". . . is in the dictionary," Maggie said when the old man's voice trailed off. He was full of quotations and aphorisms. "I've heard that somewhere before," she added, leaning forward to look at him in the shadows. His eyes were closed again. She thought he was asleep until he started to speak.

"When I was in Germany during World War Two, I bought a violin off a German officer," he said, talking with his eyes still shut. "I always wanted to learn to play the Irish fiddle, just like you did, before you got into the orchestra and started to study music seriously."

"I still like to play fiddle tunes. Whenever I play a reel or jig, I always think of you, Grandpa."

The old man opened his eyes and smiled, though both seemed to exhaust his meager reserve of strength.

"I think he was a German officer. He had a suit on that he'd gotten somewhere that didn't fit him too well.

But he was wearing officer's boots. And he looked and acted like an officer, if that makes sense."

Maggie nodded.

"He was a Nazi, of course. He let on that he'd been attached in some way to Hermann Göring's staff. Göring was Reich marshal, one of Hitler's top dogs."

Maggie had heard her grandfather's stories about the war, how he'd lied about his age to enlist, about being wounded at the Battle of the Bulge and being awarded a Purple Heart; but she'd never heard this story before.

"Everything was finished for the Germans after the war. The cities were bombed out, the people hungry. This guy said the violin was worth a lot of money. He wanted a thousand dollars U.S. I just laughed, Maggie. I didn't have that kind of money. I was a sergeant, for crying out loud. But it was an old fiddle in good condition, and it seemed like a good deal at the time, if I could buy it right. So I sold a couple of Lugers I'd gotten off of Germans and managed to scrape up one hundred dollars, which turned out to be enough to buy the thing. The German told me the violin had been in his family, but who could really know? The Nazis were gangsters. I didn't believe him, but I didn't have any reason to disbelieve him. If I didn't buy the violin, somebody else would. I figured, Why not?"

Sam O'Hara's head settled against the pillow and he shut his eyes. A minute passed. His breath became a little less labored as he recovered from saying so much.

Maggie was ready to fall asleep herself. She had attended her classes before making the four-and-a-half-hour drive to Chicago. Bed was going to feel good. She was leaning forward to get up when her grandfather spoke again.

"I want you to have it."

"The violin? Do you still have it?" Maggie said, trying to disguise the surprise in her voice. Her first thought was that he was becoming delusional. The only violins she had ever seen around the house were the instruments he had rented or bought for her over the years.

"I always intended for you to have the fiddle, Maggie. I was saving it as a present for when you graduated from college."

"That's sweet, Grandpa." She didn't want to ask where it was. This was more painful than she thought it would be. Maybe she would return to the hospital one day and he wouldn't know her, his mind eaten away by cancer and painkillers.

"I've kept it put away, a surprise."

She nodded.

"It's in the attic, in a steamer trunk with some army gear—my old uniform, a helmet, junk really, mementos. Before you go back to school, go upstairs and find it. The trunk key is on the ring inside the basement door, the one with the spare keys to the house and the garage. Dig out that old fiddle and let me know what you think of it. Promise?"

"Yes, but only if you promise to be quiet now and rest. You're wearing yourself out with too much talk."

The old man nodded, too weak to say more. He closed his eyes and fell fast asleep.

The light in the back hall flared and made a dull pop before going dark. Maggie felt her way up the steps to the kitchen. The overhead fluorescent balked but flickered on after the initial hesitation. There was a huge stack of mail on the table. Jan Dunham, their next-door neighbor in Elmhurst, collected the O'Hara mail weekdays and left it in the kitchen. Maggie would go through it on the weekends, paying the bills, throwing out the junk mail, taking magazines to the hospital, where they sat untouched on a table next to her grandfather's bed. When Maggie put her book bag on the table, the pyramid of mail trembled and began to slide onto the floor.

Maggie, who wasn't in the habit of cursing, swore.

She put her bag and her violin in her room and went around the house, opening windows. It was a little chilly, but the house had a closed, musty smell and needed airing. Water was running somewhere. She went into the bathroom and jiggled the toilet handle and it stopped. Everything was falling apart, as chaos began to pick apart the edges of her world.

There was a half-empty bottle of chardonnay in the refrigerator from the previous weekend. Maggie poured a glass and sank into her chair in the living room, next to Sam's, facing the television where they had watched Cubs and Bears games when she was growing up. The TV was off now, the living room dark except for light from the kitchen.

She took a sip of wine and sat back, weariness bearing down on her like a vast, formless weight. Inevitably she began to dwell on the Sibelius concerto, her nemesis. It almost made her neck and arm ache to think about it. She'd first experienced the ill-defined physical problem while preparing to play the recital for admission to Juilliard. She botched that audition, ruining her chance to attend the conservatoire. Then the pain and cramping vanished as mysteriously as they'd come. She'd been healthy for her first years at the university, moving through her studies at an accelerated pace. But the nerve and muscle problem returned as her senior concert approached. Her teacher, Katarina Eck, a concert violinist who did not believe in coddling students, had gone so far as to imply she thought the problem was not in Maggie's neck and arm, but in her head.

And maybe Dr. Eck was right, Maggie thought.

She took another sip of wine.

Maggie was putting off going into the attic to find her grandfather's violin. Assuming the whole thing wasn't a delusion, there was almost no chance the instrument was worth anything. Buying a violin was a tricky business even for people who knew what they were doing. Most cheap violins had *Stradivarius* written inside them—meaning only that they were Strad copies. The likelihood that her grandfather had been cheated was almost a foregone conclusion.

Maggie took another sip of wine, and her mind began to play what-if.

At the end of World War Two, Europe in chaos, anything would have been possible.

The German officer had asked for a thousand dollars. How much would that be in today's money? Ten thousand? If, while desperate, he'd been willing to sell it for such a price, what might it have really been worth?

"Don't be stupid," Maggie said aloud to herself.

She put her feet up on the hassock, but when she shut her eyes she saw an imaginary picture of the violin in the attic, hidden away for more than half a century. It called her, like a ghost demanding not to be recognized. She knew she wouldn't be able to sleep unless she had a look, even though she was certain she would only be disappointed with what she found.

A cloud of dust floated down on Maggie as the stairs unfolded out of the hall ceiling. It had been years since anybody had been up in the attic. There was a socket with a single bulb mounted on one of the ceiling joists. She pulled the string, which broke off in her hand without turning on the light. Fortunately there was enough chain hanging from the socket for her to pull on the dim yellowish light.

The attic was filled with everything from old folding lawn chairs to wardrobe boxes containing her grandmother's clothing, which Sam hadn't been able to bring himself to give away or throw out. There were boxes of her parents' things in the attic, too. Someday she'd have to go through all of it—someday soon, maybe.

There was no sign of the trunk Sam O'Hara had described, but that was hardly surprising. She began to work her way through the clutter, sliding boxes to the side, restacking things, constantly having to move one way or the other to keep from blocking the light at the top of the collapsible stairs. There was an old dresser near the far eave, but it was pulled out a few feet from the wall. It was too heavy for Maggie to move. She climbed up on it to look behind. Stacks of old issues of *Reader's Digest*s were tied in neat bundles sitting on an oblong box. There were brass fittings around the corners of the box. It was her grandfather's army trunk.

She made a second try at moving the dresser again, but it wouldn't budge. She opened a drawer. It was filled with clothing for a little girl—her clothing. One

by one, she pulled out the drawers and set them to
the side.

It was difficult to imagine her grandfather's reluc-
tance to part with things. Maybe it was his way of
hanging on to the people he'd lost, his only son, his
daughter-in-law, and his wife, and, of course, his
granddaughter.

Once the drawers were out, Maggie could rock the
dresser toward her and pull it to the side, making a big
enough space to squeeze through. She tossed the
stacks of magazines aside and knelt to open the trunk,
only to find it was locked. She remembered what Sam
had said about the keys and had no choice but to thread
her way through the clutter to fetch them.

When she returned to the attic, Maggie realized she
felt equally conflicted between hoping the violin was
something special and knowing that it almost certainly
was not. She put in the key and opened the center
latch, then the latches on the side, and, holding her
breath against the dust, threw open the lid.

On top was an old army blanket. She set it aside
with careful reverence. There was something sacred
about her grandfather's personal property. Touching it
made her think that soon these material things would
be all that was left of him in the world. She lifted a
steel army helmet painted pea green, then the woolen
army shirts, scratchy to touch. Underneath was a box
containing medals she'd never seen; her grandfather
was a modest man and, it would seem, also a brave
one. There were more shirts and trousers; then, at the
bottom of the locker, packed between black army
boots still shiny with polish, was an old-fashioned fitted violin case.

Maggie took the case from the locker and carried it downstairs to open it where the light was good.

The slider button on the center latch would not budge. The case was locked. She pulled on it, thinking it might pop open, but the case was a lot sturdier than it looked. There had to be a key somewhere.

Back up the stairs she went, hurrying now, banging her head painfully against one of the low slanting rafters in the dim light. She took the key ring from where it hung in the trunk latch. There was a small key on the ring, tarnished silver and antique-looking. That had to be it, she thought, the anticipation suddenly unbearable.

The key fit in the lock, and when she turned it the latch popped and the case came open with an audible sigh, as if the genie within groaned with exhausted relief to be freed after more than a half century of captivity. A familiar aroma filled the air—the faint perfume hinting of wood, varnish, and rosin, the smell more focused and concentrated after being held within the confines of the velvet-lined case. There are similarities between a violin case and a coffin, but in the case of the former, the precious object is lovingly protected not in death but life, awaiting only the warm touch of the musician's hands to awaken and sing songs that can soothe, arouse, or move a listener to tears.

Maggie hooked her thumbs into the gap between the body of the case and the lid, opening it to reveal the legacy bequeathed to her by her dying grandfather.

And there it was: a honey-colored violin in pieces. The neck had detached from the body; two of the old-fashioned gut strings were broken, the others slack; the bridge had collapsed flat against the face of the instrument. It was, it appeared, ruined, destroyed by years of neglect in an attic where the temperature was scorching in summer, freezing in winter.

Maggie blinked rapidly, holding back the tears, and lifted the violin out of its case with the same extreme care she'd use to pick up an injured bird.

The finish was lighter than the older European instruments she'd seen, which gave it an interesting, even distinctive look. The wood in the spruce top was tightly grained, the quality of the material far better than the wood in her Chinese violin, which had cost as much as the new car she should own instead of the rattletrap Escort. The back was a single piece of maple with magnificent flaming in the grain. And the pegs were carved from boxwood instead of ebony or a cheaper wood dyed to look like ebony. That was curious. Boxwood pegs had become popular in newer copies of famous violins, but typically with older violins, the pegs were ebony, except on instruments made by master Italian violinmakers.

Maybe the violin could be repaired, although it would take somebody knowledgeable to tell her whether it would be worth fixing.

Maggie held the violin up to the light and turned it so she could look into the F hole to see if it had been signed by its maker or if it was the product of some anonymous craftsman. There was a strip of paper affixed to the inside of the instrument, inscribed in brown ink in an antique style of writing.

It said, *Archangelo Serafino 1744 + VII.*

14

THE AUDIENCE APPLAUDED politely as the musicians filed between the marble colonnades and into the room, carrying their instruments.

The Focke Paleis in Amsterdam was an excellent setting for Vivaldi, whose music always sounded a bit sterile in a concert hall. The marble floor in the palace's great hall, and the high vaulted ceiling—a clever trompe l'oeil of angels peaking down through an "unfinished" ceiling—meant lively acoustics that would help the music breathe.

The musicians in the St. Edmund's Baroque Orchestra played period instruments strung with gut strings and old-style bows. The ensemble's dedication to "authenticity" extended to every facet of the performance, from their free use of grace notes to the absence of vibrato, a nineteenth-century development.

Vivaldi's *Four Seasons* was a bit overfamiliar with most audiences, almost, yet not quite, a cliché. As a staple of the repertoire, it got performed enough that on an uninspired night its distinctive features lost their sharpness, like a coin that has been in circulation long enough to become worn by passing from hand to hand. Still, the St. Edmund's ensemble was noted for its ability to infuse new blood into timeworn pieces, primarily thanks to their leader and principal violinist, whose deep affinity to the period was exceeded only by his fiery playing.

The musicians were seated and ready to perform, moving chairs, tightening bows, adjusting music stands to catch the light for the candlelit performance. An A was played and everyone checked their tuning. All eyes turned to the principal violinist, who also served as the group's conductor. He used the tip of his bow to indicate the rhythm and then, with a nod of the head, they fell together into the piece.

He had anticipated an unusually good performance from his agitation beforehand. While an unsettled temperament can lead to a disastrous concert, inflamed passions can fuel extraordinary playing.

The first movement, "Le primavera," went very well, the individual players blending together to shape a voluptuous sound. It was in the second movement, "L'estate," "Summer," that the concertmaster began to feel the other musicians listening to him, watching him at times. This was the elixir that transformed what would otherwise have been yet another performance of *The Four Seasons* into something magical—a passionate and transcendent performance by the lead violinist.

For those in the hall, whether they were in the audience or orchestra, the palace dissolved and along with it the rest of the world and all its sad cares. In their stead there was only the music, music that seemed to come from a place beyond time and space, a place where beauty, creativity, and emotion were the only realities.

By the *allegro non moto* movement of "L'inverno," "Winter," the principal violinist was slashing at the strings with his bow, drawing every nuance of expressiveness from the music. His playing during the slower, emotional *largo* movement contained such tender sadness that several of the more sensitive people in the audience had to resort to their handkerchiefs.

The crowd burst into applause and cries of "Bravo!" at the end, awakening from the exquisite dream.

The violinist sat with his eyes closed, feeling as drained as if he had poured out his blood during the performance.

The other musicians were standing, acknowledging the cheers, glancing with uncertainty and some concern at their leader, who continued to sit there, lost in his thoughts. At last he got to his feet and bowed, cradling his violin the way a falconer would hold a favorite bird that returned from the hunt only to have its heart burst.

The crowd exploded with more cheers and applause. Several men whistled through their teeth. The orchestra took their seats again, but the violinist remained standing for the *Partitas,* which he performed solo as an interlude before Corelli's Concerto No. 8 in G Minor.

The Bach would quickly revive him, Dylan Glyndwr thought. Playing Bach fed his soul the way blood fed his body and the Hunger.

Glyndwr put in a perfunctory appearance at the reception after the concert, then disappeared alone into the room that had been set aside for his use. He turned on the tap in the sink in the lavatory and filled his cradled hands with cold water, burying his face in them, wanting to brace himself, to wake up from the desire threatening to overtake him.

He loosened the hair on the bow and put it into the case. He used a cotton cloth to carefully wipe the white film of rosin powder from the fingerboard and face of his violin. It helped to focus on simple tasks. Such acts had a certain meditative power. It was like prayer, although it had been a very long time since he had been able to pray.

Someone tapped on the door.

Glyndwr ignored the intrusion. He secured the suspension strap across the violin's neck, covered the instrument with its protective velvet blanket, then closed the case, shut the double latch, and drew shut the two zippers.

There were four more raps on the door, this time a little louder, a little more insistent.

The vampire pulled on a long black overcoat, its tails falling nearly to the floor. He threw the white silk scarf around his neck and picked up the instrument.

He opened the door, and there she was, as he had sensed she would be. She was young, beautiful, American, and very rich. She wore her long blond hair up on her head, to better display the perfect line of her perfect neck and the necklace of diamonds she wore around it. Real diamonds, the vampire saw, and of the best quality.

"I'm sorry to interrupt, but . . ."

He sensed she was not in the least bit sorry to intrude upon his solitude. In her hands she held her program and a gold pen.

"I have never been so moved by music," she said, extending the program to him to autograph.

He did not take the paper but reached past it and took her gently, but firmly, by the wrist.

She began to smile after the slightest hesitation. He saw the image of her husband reflected in her sparkling emerald eyes—he was about seventy, more than a bit overweight, with a white mustache and thin wisps of hair on his nearly bald head.

She came forward as he drew her to him, pulling the door shut behind her, parting her lips just enough for him to see the cherry tip of her tongue.

Dylan slipped the strap of the violin case over his shoulder with the same smooth motion he used to turn her and slip his arms around her, lowering his face toward the hollow, toward the perfumed declivity between her neck and shoulder and the pleasure he would find there.

15

CARTER DUNNE LOOKED up as the door opened and a woman came in with a violin case.

She was a student, he guessed, but that would have been a safe bet with any woman her age in the university town. She had a fair, clean-scrubbed complexion, and was dressed simply in running shoes, blue jeans, and a cotton blouse. The woman had a pretty, though not beautiful face, with bright green eyes, high cheekbones, full, well-formed lips, and long auburn hair pulled back in a bun. She was probably a Flaherty or an O'Conner, Carter guessed: Irish.

"Good morning. What can I do for you?"

The girl set the violin case on the glass display counter and put her hands on top of it protectively.

"I have a violin in need of repair."

"Then you've come to the right place," Carter said, and grinned.

But she gave Carter a skeptical look. "The violin is old. It might be valuable."

He looked at the battered case and nodded, not wanting to be the one to have to explain that just because it might say *Stradivarius* inside the instrument, it didn't mean it was valuable.

Carter turned and called up the stairs, "Gianni? Do you have a minute?" Then, back to the girl: "We have a real expert on the staff."

"Really?" she asked.

"Really," he said, still smiling. "Ask anybody at the music school if they know Gianni Felici."

"I will," she said, as if it were a weighty business matter requiring verification. "I'm in the program there."

Felici came down the stairs, walking lightly, a thin, elderly man with a well-trimmed mustache and silver hair combed straight back from a high forehead. Beneath his shop apron he wore a white dress shirt and tie. When Carter bought the business, he told the luthier he didn't need to wear a tie to work, but the old Italian replied that he would feel undressed without it. Anybody who chose to continue working when they were eighty years old could dress however they wanted, Carter thought.

"Good morning, miss," Felici said, bowing his head. The girl nodded.

"She has a violin needing repair. She thinks it might be valuable."

"Aha," Gianni said, as if pleasantly surprised. He exchanged a brief look with Carter, but nothing the girl would have noticed. "Shall we have a look then?"

The girl's hands tightened visibly on the violin case. Carter thought she might snatch it up and run out of the shop.

"Gianni is the best in the business," Carter said. "He trained in Cremona before the war. World War Two, I mean."

That bit of information seemed to jar something loose inside the peculiar customer.

"My grandfather was in World War Two," she said. "He brought this violin home with him. He left it to me when he died."

"The instrument will be in good hands with Gianni. He's worked on his share of Strads. Being centrally located in the middle of the country, he gets work from some of the premier touring and orchestra players. We have a Guarneri upstairs he's appraising for an auction house in Boston."

Felici's eyes flickered at the mention of the Guarneri, but it didn't matter if the girl knew it. The luthier was tight-lipped about clients, as if the Sicilian law of *omerta*, silence and secrecy, governed the violin business.

The girl took her hands off the case.

"Thank you," Felici said. He turned the case toward him, unfastened the latches, and opened it to reveal what looked to Carter like a hopeless wreck.

"A lovely bird with a broken wing," Felici said, giving the instrument a good look before touching it. "May I ask how long you have had the violin, miss?"

"Not long. It was in storage in an attic for a long time. Can you fix it?"

"But of course."

For the first time, she smiled.

"Reattaching the neck is relatively simple. If there is nothing else structurally wrong, I can put strings on it, set it up, and have it for you in a week."

Felici leaned over the violin, running his eyes over the instrument, yet not touching it. "It appears to be a fine old Italian violin. It is a valuable instrument."

"Really?" the girl said in a funny way, as if she were surprised and not surprised at the same time.

"Really," Felici said, a solemn pronouncement. The luthier did not joke around when it came to work.

"My grandfather brought it back from Germany after World War Two. He bought it from a German officer, someone who was down on his luck. My grandfather intended to learn to play some reels. My family is Irish. But he never got around to playing. I guess he left that up to me."

"You play the violin?" Carter asked.

The girl nodded. "I hope to be admitted to the performance program at the school of music."

"Then you *are* a violinist," Felici said, looking up from the violin.

The girl didn't seem to be as sure of it as the luthier.

"I'm afraid this violin was packed away in an unheated attic for years."

"That can be hard on a violin, but central heating is a relatively modern convenience," Felici said. "A violin as old as this one would have seen its share of temperature extremes."

"So you think it's old?"

"It appears to be."

Carter saw the excitement in the girl's face. He felt it himself. But he was not just glad for the girl. It was exciting to discover that the instrument was more than a sad old fiddle.

"The man who sold it to my grandfather said it was valuable."

"It certainly is," Gianni Felici said. "The question is how valuable. It's definitely not a Stradivarius, though there are similarities in both the workmanship and wood. The finish on the scroll at the top of the neck is a little like a del Gesu. Guarneri tended to get in a hurry on the finishing work."

"You think it is a Guarneri?" Carter asked, hearing the excitement in his own voice. The girl was staring at Felici in disbelief. It was one thing to think the violin might be valuable, but a Guarneri!

Felici turned the violin over in the light, looking at the back and sides.

"No," he said. "But there are similarities. I have a sense that I have seen this violin somewhere, but I can't place it."

Gianni Felici put the violin back in its case and took a penlight from his pocket to help him see inside the instrument through the F hole. He snapped off the light after the briefest inspection and drew himself upright. He looked at the girl as closely as he had been looking at the violin a moment before.

"What is your name, miss?"

"Maggie O'Hara."

"I knew there was something familiar about this violin, Miss O'Hara. I have worked on it before. It was a long time ago, during the war, in Germany."

"The label inside . . . it says 'Archangelo Serafino.' "

"Indeed it does. He is little known today, but one of Cremona's preeminent luthiers."

"Do you mind?" Carter said, tilting the case slightly and causing the light to shine through the F hole so that he could read the label, too. It said, *Archangelo Serafino, 1744 + VII.*

"Do you think this is really one of Serafino's violins?" Maggie asked Felici. "You don't think it's just a copy, like one of the thousands or millions of violins that are labeled Stradivaris?"

"I know it is a genuine Serafino. I worked on this instrument. I can personally authenticate it."

"And it is valuable?"

"It is priceless," Felici said. "Archangelo Serafino was a student of Stradivari's who went blind late in life. His final violins are without parallel. Their sound possesses an otherworldly beauty. That is why they are known as 'Angel' violins. They are miracles. One by one they have become lost to time. Indeed, it was thought that the Seven was gone forever. But it seems that what was lost has now been found."

But then the delight went out of Felici's eyes.

"What's wrong?" Maggie said.

The luthier looked at the violin.

"Perhaps nothing," he said, and sighed.

16

THE VAMPIRE SAT in church, eyes closed as if in prayer. Oude Kerk was the oldest building in Amsterdam. Dutch for Old Church, the building was originally a simple wooden structure surrounded by a cemetery. It grew along with the port city, and by the 1300s was a sprawling Gothic church. It was consecrated as St. Nicholas of Myra, the patron saint of sailors and traders. The Oude Kerk was blessed in more ways than one: the structure had an amazing, even miraculous power to escape destruction. Huge fires ravaged Amsterdam in 1421 and again in 1452. The Oude Kerk emerged unscathed from both infernos.

In 1566, a fury over the use of religious images raged through Christendom. The Oude Kerk's magnificent medieval altars were savagely damaged during the iconoclastic frenzy, as zealots sought to purge the church of the rare and priceless images newly judged to smack of idolatry. A second wave of religious upheaval occurred in 1578, when Amsterdam became a protestant city during the Alteratie. Any decoration associated with Catholicism was torn from the church at the same time religious rituals that had developed over one and a half millennia were branded anathema.

Later alterations to the church were less destructive. In 1724, a wonderful pipe organ was installed. The organ was the reason Dylan Glyndwr had come to the church. He listened carefully, eyes closed, as the organist played the recessional, Bach's brilliant Prelude and Fugue in D Minor. The organ sang like a choir of seraphim, ringing to the rafters and roaring in the Oude Kerk's foundation, like a mighty celestial spirit.

Glyndwr continued to sit with his eyes closed as the last strains reverberated through the cavernous Oude Kerk. The vampire was a tremendous fan of pipe organs. Next to the violin's incomparable virtuosity, the pipe organ was the musical instrument that came closest to imitating the voice of God. If the violin was best at illuminating the beauty and ethereal light of the Almighty, the majestic pipe organ, the leviathan of musical instruments, was the voice of the Lawgiver come to issue governance to the people and to smite the wicked.

Dylan Glyndwr did not attend church. He did not think much about God. But whenever he played the violin or listened to good music, he felt as if God were speaking directly to his ancient, shadow-filled heart.

Glyndwr had been raised Catholic, though the Wales of his youth was a wild place, more pagan than Christian. The son of a high lord, he had learned Latin and taken catechism from a bishop. Yet Dylan had also danced around Midsummer's Eve bonfires at the stone monoliths the Druids left scattered across the countryside. He knew his share of witches as a young man, and was taught to maintain a healthy respect for the faeries that haunted the lonely valleys and windswept crags of Cymru, before the hated English drove them all from the lands.

It goes without saying that becoming a vampire complicated Dylan Glyndwr's relationship with God. The usual assumption is that vampires are infernal creatures, monsters preying upon helpless mortal beings, lusting to possess their bodies, their blood, and their souls. The woman who turned Dylan into a vampire did not share in this notion. To her, vampires occupied an exalted place in creation as God's immortal servants on Earth.

By the time Dylan Glyndwr had become a changeling, he had already known enough tragedy to break his heart. His had seen too much savagery and perversion inflicted by the wicked to maintain any real faith in the divine order. But neither could he imagine himself eternally cursed or his soul lost. He was, like the mortal he had been, almost equally capable of good and evil. He found it easy to succumb to the orgiastic delights of the blood, yet he learned early on to control himself. Excesses always led to trouble.

Unlike his benefactress of the blood, Dylan Glyndwr did not think it mattered one way or the other if he killed. He was, more than he chose to admit, a product of his time. He had been born into an era of warfare, when lives tended to be brutish and short. The lives of individuals did not count for much. Men and women were cut down for looking the wrong way at a lord, hanged for stealing bread, hunted down like animals and skinned alive for poaching on manorial grounds.

As the years went by, Dylan's perpetual wanderings hardened his heart. The main consideration in choosing whether to take a life became essentially a matter of practicality. Killing tended to be inconvenient. One had to dispose of the body. Suspicions were raised. Questions were asked. Under certain circumstances, the local population could become panicked.

By the time Europe experienced the Enlightenment, with the disturbing erosion of morality that was the inevitable counterpart to men and women thinking for themselves, Dylan Glyndwr had already become ambivalent about morality. He had ceased believing in heaven and hell just as he had ceased believing in goblins and banshees. Because he did not have to worry about dying, he no longer pondered into what state his soul would pass after death.

Dylan Glyndwr became an existentialist centuries before anybody knew what existentialism was. He was alone in himself, a universe of one, free to make of himself—and to do—whatever he chose. He lived for the moment, with little thought for the past or future, instead investing himself wholly in the present. The feel of the violin strings under his fingers, the smell of a woman's expensive perfume, the sweet intoxication of the first swallow of blood—the vampire lived a life of the senses, a sensual creature. Eternity was not a period of time but an experience, in Glyndwr's way of thinking. To live, to die, the joy of creation, the ecstasy of playing the violin, of making love, of drinking blood—were these not all but different manifestations of the same unbounded essence?

Dylan Glyndwr opened his eyes.

The Oude Kerk was deserted and quiet as only a church can be, where even the silence itself seems to be consecrated. He looked at the patterns of light and shadow falling from the windows set high in the ceiling's wooden barrel vaults and smiled. He might have been an artist, had he not become bewitched by the sorcery of music.

A soft buzzing in his jacket pocket interrupted the vampire's waking dream.

"Dylan Glyndwr," he said, pressing the cell phone to his ear. He spoke softly, but his voice echoed in the empty church.

"Mr. Glyndwr, this is William Tritt speaking. I have some good news for you. Some very good news indeed."

Glyndwr came forward in his seat, his eyes narrowing in response to the triumph in the Englishman's voice.

"Tell me more, Mr. Tritt."

"I found what you are looking for, sir, after all these years."

"Do not say it," Dylan Glyndwr said, but Tritt mistook the vampire's lack of trust in the security of cell-phone conversations for disbelief and surprise.

"I have found an Angel," Tritt crowed.

The Welsh vampire began to smile.

17

MAGGIE CAME UP the stairs, the case containing the Chinese violin slung over her shoulder, and turned down the corridor toward Dr. Eck's office. On weekday mornings the hallway was crowded, especially between classes, when a mass of students made the space come alive with conversation and movement. But now, late in the afternoon, with time devoted mostly to private lessons, the passage was deserted.

The door to Katarina Eck's office was closed. Maggie was early. She was always early for her sessions with Dr. Eck, who had been educated in Europe and maintained a strict, formal, even authoritarian relationship with her students.

Maggie turned away, waiting. When it was her time the door would open, at precisely 3:30, and she would be admitted to the violin professor's inner sanctum.

The sound of a piano could be faintly heard from one of the rooms, a haunting melody from another place, another time—Debussy. A door shut behind her. Maggie turned but saw no sign of anyone coming or going. A piece of paper began to flutter on one of the bulletin boards. The building's ventilation system must have come on. She wandered toward it, as if unconsciously

133

drawn by the stiff, beckoning motion. It was an audition notice to try out as soloist with the guest conductor who was coming from Berlin to lead the school's annual Mozart festival. It made Maggie's palms sweat to even imagine exposing herself to pressure that intense—to have her playing judged by the distinguished visitor, Dr. Eck, and the other professors. She turned away, swallowing against the sudden queasiness in her stomach.

Maggie returned to her station outside the violin instructor's office. She heard faint voices inside—two women, then laughter. Maggie had never laughed in Dr. Eck's presence. Whoever's turn it was in the lion's den was braver than she, Maggie thought.

The door opened. Nicole Hoffman came out carrying her violin case. She owned a gorgeous violin that her father had paid $20,000 to have custom-made for her by one of the best violinmakers in America. Maggie knew all this because Nicole was the sort of person who liked to talk about her possessions. She also had a one-carat engagement ring from her boyfriend, who was in his last year in law school, and a new Miata sports car. She planned to spend the Christmas break skiing in Aspen.

"Hi, Nicole," Maggie said. "I heard that you were admitted into the performance program. Congratulations."

Nicole pushed her long blond hair away from her face with her right hand, the one where she wore the gold ring embossed with three triangles, the insignia of her sorority, Tri Delta. Without speaking or even acknowledging that she had heard, she stepped around

Maggie and went down the hall, wearing high-heeled shoes that matched her skirt and sweater.

Maggie's face burned with embarrassment at the cut. Was there something wrong with what she'd said to the other young woman? She meant it as a compliment. Nicole Hoffman had never been very friendly. She was from a rich neighborhood in Naperville and acted as if her money and looks made her superior to others in the orchestra, like Maggie, who came from more ordinary circumstances.

But maybe Nicole was better, Maggie thought. Nicole had passed her audition and gotten into the performance program.

"Do you intend to stand out there all day or are you going to take your lesson?"

"Sorry." Maggie went into the room, which was long and narrow, with bookcases rising on either side toward the high ceiling and a black baby grand piano at the far end, near the window. For once Maggie was happy to have Dr. Eck's imperious attitude command her attention.

First came the Flesche scales and arpeggios. Eck was a stickler for the basics and always began with scales. Maggie had been playing them since junior high and thought she played them well, but Dr. Eck always managed to find things to criticize.

After the warm-up, it was time to show Dr. Eck the progress she had made on the dreaded Sibelius, the audition piece she was working on for the committee that would decide whether she would be admitted with the select few, including Nicole Hoffman, to the performance program. Maggie didn't get far before she was stopped.

"Wait! Let me see your bow hand."

Maggie held it up, looking at it, her expression as dubious as Dr. Eck's was severe.

"Look at the angle of your little finger."

Maggie did as she was told. It looked perfectly fine to her, but she knew something was wrong or Dr. Eck wouldn't be glaring at her.

"Honestly, Miss O'Hara, I don't know how you can have any control over the bow at all if you are going to hold it in such an ineffective manner."

Maggie was glad to escape alive at the end of her hour, during which Dr. Eck had gone out of her way to make it clear that she did not think Maggie had what it took to escape the music-education track at the school, and an eventual future teaching music in a high school somewhere or giving private lessons in a music store. She carried her violin by the handle because of the pain in her shoulder. Coming toward her in the hall was the head of the department, Dr. Jane Crittenden. It was Dr. Crittenden who had granted her two previous extensions on her recital because of her muscle problems. There would be no more extensions, Dr. Eck had reminded Maggie during their lesson.

The older woman strode toward Maggie, walking quickly, swinging her arms. She always seemed to know where she was going and what she wanted to accomplish.

Maggie smiled uncertainly as Crittenden passed her, going the other way. The music school dean gave her a crisp, prim nod without slowing. Everything about Dr. Crittenden's manner seemed to say that she knew all about Maggie and her so-called health problems and was willing to give her only one more chance before dropping the ax on her grandiose plans for a career as a performing violinist.

Maggie kept going, too, but she felt herself starting to shake. She ducked into the first room she came to, a darkened classroom with music staffs painted on the chalkboard for theory classes. The sharp white lines blurred against the green background as the tears filled Maggie's eyes.

18

"SO WHAT DID you think?"

"Of Alan Webber?" Maria Rainer turned onto the highway leading away from the enclave of big houses overlooking the lake outside of town. She pressed on the accelerator and the BMW shot forward, quick and powerful, the road in the car's headlights a winding ribbon of silver threading between the oak trees.

"He isn't what you expected, is he?"

"His German is good."

"That's not what I mean."

"I know, Jane. I expected someone more modern, in the bad sense of the word. I thought he was extremely humble for someone who has won the Pulitzer prize for music."

"He was a god on campus after that."

"I was surprised that someone famous for following in Schoenberg's atonal footsteps would be so interested in Bach."

"Alan has a thing about fugues," the music school dean said.

"I do not know how you get from twelve-tone serious compositions to fugues, but I found him utterly charming."

"Watch out for deer. This winding stretch of road is treacherous. The trees come right down to the road."

Maria nodded. "It is a shame it is so difficult for him to leave the house."

"He's been in a wheelchair since his stroke. It took him a year to learn to speak again so that you could understand him. It's hell to get old."

Maria nodded again.

"He left big shoes for me to fill."

"I think you're doing a wonderful job," Maria was saying when they came around a curve and she hit the brakes. Ahead of them was an SUV that evidently had rolled over several times before coming to a stop upside down with the passenger side smashed up against a tree. One of the rear wheels was missing, the remaining tires spinning aimlessly in the air.

"What are you doing?" Jane asked as Maria unfastened her seat belt and opened the door.

"Seeing if I can help," Maria said, and jumped out, leaving the other woman staring after her.

Maria ran to the car, calling out but getting no answer. She smelled blood before she saw it, a powerful aroma as rich and potent as fine cognac. A woman's hand and part of an arm extended out of the driver's-side window, palm up. Blood trickled down the fair skin from a wound beyond what Maria could see inside the car, already enough of it to form a small red pool in the BMW's lights.

Maria got down on one knee and looked in through the window. There was only one person in the car, a young woman, possibly a student at the university. Though she was suspended by her seat belt, the balance of her weight rested on her arm and shoulder against the Explorer's crushed roof. Maria tried the handle but the door wouldn't open, damaged when the vehicle rolled.

"Are they alive?"

Maria glanced up at Jane, who had finally gotten out of the car and was now standing a few feet behind her. Her face was white as milk. Maria thought she looked as if she might faint.

"There's just a girl, and she's alive, but she will not live long at the rate she is bleeding. Use your cell phone to call for an ambulance. And please hurry."

It took a few seconds for the message to register in Jane's stunned mind, but when it did, she turned awkwardly and ran back to their car.

Maria was feeling dizzy herself, not from the shock of witnessing carnage—she had seen more than her share of that—but because of the fresh blood pushing her to the verge of an ecstatic swoon. The crash victim's blood steamed lightly in the cool autumn night air. Maria touched the tip of her finger lightly to the pool and brought it to her lips, but that did nothing but send a spike of mad desire rushing through her. She could taste the unmetabolized Jack Daniel's in the blood. No wonder the woman had flipped the SUV. She had poisoned herself to a degree that it was difficult to imagine she had been able to stay conscious long enough to get on the road.

Jane was in the front seat of the BMW, one hand covering her eyes as she spoke to the police. Maria grabbed the door and pulled hard. The metal complained as she bent the steel far enough to get to the woman but, she hoped, not so far as to make the rescue workers wonder how she'd gotten it open.

She had a tourniquet on the girl's arm by the time the EMTs arrived, just ahead of a sheriff's car, both vehicles racing up with lights flashing and sirens wailing.

"I'm amazed and impressed—but mainly impressed—that you had the nerve to stop and save that girl's life," Jane said as they continued their interrupted journey back into town.

Maria let out a long sigh and tried to calm herself. She could smell the blood in Jane's veins, not nearly as sweet as the girl's but sweet enough, and feel the pulse from each beat of Jane's heart as plainly as if Jane were beating a drum in the seat next to her. It was all Maria could do to keep from pulling the BMW over to the side of the road to drink her fill of the other woman. But such a thing would never do. It would come too soon after the last time she had availed herself of Jane Crittenden to feed both the Hunger and her passion. Too much of that would plant the seed in the other woman and bring on the Change. Maria had enough to occupy her without adding a fledgling vampire to her responsibilities.

"We have an obligation to help people in need," Maria said, speaking carefully to keep the tension out of her voice. "People in trouble, people who can't protect themselves—coming to their aid is the essence of morality."

"Of course you're right, but the blood . . ."

Jane's voice trailed off. Glancing at her out of the corner of her eye, Maria could see that Jane was trying hard to remember something that seemed just beyond the grasp of memory. Jane touched her fingers to her neck, as if feeling the pulse beating there, strong and regular just beneath the skin, could bring it all back.

"I come from a different culture than you," Maria said. "In Germany we have seen only too well what happens when people refuse to help. There is a saying that the only thing it takes for evil to triumph is for good people to do nothing."

Jane was looking at her, looking at her closely, but she kept her eyes ahead. It was dark and the road, scenic by day, was treacherous and filled with hidden danger at night.

19

THE KITCHEN IN the little violin shop was mostly as it had been when the cottage was still a residence. The gas-fired stove was from the 1950s, so ancient-looking that Maggie first took it for a retro reproduction. There was nothing antique about the refrigerator, a state-of-the-art model with a water-and-ice dispenser mounted in one of its stainless-steel doors. She could see where the oak cabinets had been modified to fit the oversize refrigerator.

Carter Dunne seemed to be the kind of man who liked to spend money on fancy gadgets. He kept the store's inventory on a Palm Pilot, a handy way to keep track of inventory, though it didn't hide the fact that the shop's new owner was still learning the business. The espresso machine on the counter was another perfect example. It wasn't a small home unit, but a large black Italian machine of the sort you saw in restaurants and coffee bars. He was standing with his back to her, making skim-milk lattes.

"How long have you owned this shop?"

"A couple of months," he answered without turning around, concentrating on the task at hand.

Maggie would have bet the espresso machine was a

recent acquisition, his newest toy. The lanky, sun-burned man was an unlikely match with the shop, Maggie thought, though that was only her intuition. She had the impression Carter was wealthy and well traveled. He was older than she, somewhere in his thirties. Maggie knew, in the way she always could tell, that he was thinking about her as potentially more than just a customer. Of course, maybe what he was really interested in wasn't Maggie but her rare Serafino violin.

Despite their difference in age, Maggie was interested in him, too. Or she would have been, had she been of a mind to be interested in a man. Her affair with the violin, unhappy as it had been as of late, left no room for other lovers. The abrupt breakup with Peter Hill had demonstrated, yet again, that music demanded her complete dedication.

"What made you buy a violin shop? You're not a musician, are you?"

"I play the guitar," Carter said, a little defensively, Maggie thought. The espresso machine hissed as he steamed the milk.

"So why didn't you buy a guitar shop?"

He gave her a funny look as he served her and sat down across the table with his own cup. The fact that she was confronting him in a half-teasing way meant something, but he wasn't sure what, and neither was she. It could mean Maggie was attracted to him and was trying out how it felt, but it could just as easily mean she disliked him.

"If I had found a guitar shop that was as charming as Ivaskin Violins, I would have bought it. Do you believe in love at first sight?"

Maggie frowned at him across the top of her over-size cup.

"I didn't either, until I stumbled onto this place entirely by accident while running one day. I was immediately bewitched." He looked around and smiled. "There's something magical about this place. I'm not sure whether it's the cottage or the violins, but it has a certain . . . if I said 'vibration' would you laugh?"

Maggie politely shook her head.

"It defies logic, I suppose. I can't put it into words. It's like a quaint little house in a fairy tale, the cottage where the kindly old wizard lives. I wouldn't go so far as to say there's magic in the violins we sell here, but there is the closest thing to magic there is in the real world. Which is to say beauty, craftsmanship, art, culture, and tradition. And when our violins are picked up by someone with talent, truly extraordinary things happen. If it isn't magic, I don't know what is."

A tinge of a blush came into his sunburned face. He'd said too much, Maggie could see him thinking. Except he hadn't. Not as far as she was concerned.

"What did you do before owning a violin shop?"

"I had an Internet business. I was one of the few who were fortunate enough to get in and out early, while there was still money to be made. It was dumb luck, really."

"So you're, what—a programmer?"

"I have an MFA in pottery. Plan A was to become an art teacher." He laughed and shook his head. "I've never been able to guess where life is going to take me, but at least I'm smart enough to know what I like when I see it. As long as you do something you love, things have a way of working out."

He took a sip of coffee and looked at Maggie, and it seemed to occur to them both at the same time that he might be talking about her.

"Gianni should be back anytime," he said, trying to push the conversation back toward safer ground. "He's pleased with what he was able to do. He put your violin back in perfect condition."

"How does it sound?"

"Gianni strung it up and tuned it, but he says he hasn't played it. He said the honor belongs to you. A violin like yours raises some questions."

"Oh?" Maggie asked, feeling suddenly wary.

"An old violin is a kind of mystery. Where it came from, who owned it, how it passed from hand to hand over the years."

Maggie stared at Carter across her coffee, saying nothing, hoping to avoid the subject she knew was impossible to escape.

"You're lucky in one respect," Carter said. "Gianni was able to authenticate the violin from the first. That's important. Sometimes we think a violin is *probably* this or that, but what we know falls just short of what's needed to authenticate it. It makes a big difference in value if you can prove or at least make a very good case that a violin is made by somebody, as opposed to only being able to say it probably is a certain maker's work or the product of his shop or school."

"I'm not all that concerned about the violin's value," Maggie said.

"You should be. It's priceless. A treasure, Gianni says, and he knows the subject dead cold."

The front door opened and closed. Carter started to rise, then sat back down. Gianni Felici came into the kitchen. He was wearing a white shirt and tie but not his apron. Judging from the stack of mail in his hands, he'd been at the post office.

"Miss O'Hara," he said, bowing his head. "It is a pleasure to see you. I apologize for making you wait."

"It's okay. I got a free latte out of the deal. Is my violin ready?"

"Yes, it is." But instead of going to get it, he pulled out one of the chairs and sat down a little stiffly, the way old people do. Maggie saw the way he glanced at Carter, who nodded. *Uh-oh,* Maggie thought, clenching her jaw as the muscles in her left shoulder pinched into a knot. This had been her fear from hearing the first confirmation that the violin was rare and valuable: that they—whoever *they* were—would try to take away the most precious thing her grandfather had left her when he died. She could feel the fear hardening within the muscles of her shoulder, in the pit of her stomach, in her heart, cold and hard, like a rock.

"I would like to speak to you about the violin, if you do not mind."

Maggie gave what she hoped looked like a casual smile of agreement. Had the violin been sitting on the kitchen table, she would have snatched it up and run from the shop and never returned.

"When a violin like this is found, there are always questions of provenance."

"I beg your pardon?"

"Provenance, Miss O'Hara, as in the instrument's origin or source."

"I know what *provenance* means," she said a little shortly. "Why should that be an issue?"

"Violins this valuable do not usually turn up in

somebody's attic," Felici said. The expression in his eyes softened, and he added, "Although it does happen."

"I didn't steal it," Maggie said, instantly wishing she could call back the words. Gianni Felici looked as if she'd just stabbed a dagger into his heart.

"I must most humbly ask your pardon if I made it seem as if I thought that even remotely possible," he said in a stricken voice.

"You didn't," Maggie said, slumping in the chair. "I am the one who should be sorry. If I were in your position I would want to know more myself."

"I asked Gianni to make discreet inquiries," Carter said. "There are places that serve as clearinghouses for certain kinds of information. There are even a few Web sites," he said, and smiled nervously, apparently concerned he wasn't handling the situation with the delicacy it required.

"To check if the violin is listed as stolen, you mean," she said.

Carter nodded.

"And?" she asked, looking at Gianni. She knew even before the old man answered that the news was good. The knot in her shoulder instantly loosened.

"There is no mention of it posted on any of the watch lists. I would have known anyway, but I checked to be certain."

"Would a missing violin be listed after all this time?" Carter said. "The war was more than fifty years ago."

"But of course," Gianni replied without hesitation. "A Strad taken from a dressing room in the nineteen-fifties was recovered only last year. An instrument like the Seven, as this particular Angel violin is called in the historical literature, is an art treasure. There is no statute of limitations when such a thing is stolen. Valuables stolen by the Nazis are still being recovered today, though not with the frequency that they once were."

"But you said there is no evidence that the violin was stolen."

"No, Miss O'Hara," Gianni said, "but there is no evidence that the man your grandfather bought the violin from owned it. And if he did, it is almost inconceivable he would have let the Seven go for so little. He would have had to have been a complete fool."

"Or hungry," Maggie countered. "Or desperate to get his hands on enough hard currency to get out of Germany. If he was a Nazi, maybe he had done things that made him want to disappear after the war, before the hangman could catch up with him."

The old Italian nodded, his eyes filled with sadness that must have come from remembering the war, Maggie thought. Her grandfather had not liked to talk about the war. War was glamorous and heroic only for people who hadn't ever been in one, he told her once after she had been playing soldier with the neighborhood children.

"The problem is, there is an important gap in the violin's history. We know who had it during the war, but we do not know whether he bought it or stole it. That, in turn, has a bearing on who the violin's rightful owner is today."

"I own it," Maggie said.

"As much as I dislike having to disagree with you, Miss O'Hara, you only possess it," Gianni Felici said in a gentle voice. "If there is one thing I learned during the war, it is that there is a difference between ownership and possession."

"Maybe if you told her about your experience with
the Seven during the war, Gianni, she'd begin to understand," Carter said.

"You said you'd worked on my violin during the
war," Maggie said, saying *my violin* on purpose. "In
Germany, I think you said when I brought it in for repair."

Gianni nodded.

"Tell me about it. I want to know."

"You have a right to know," Gianni said. "Indeed,
you should know."

20

"I HAVE THE unhappy distinction to be the last living expert to have seen the Seven before it disappeared at the end of the war," Gianni Felici began. "One of the stranger coincidences is that I am the first expert to see it now that it has resurfaced, a half a century later, a half a world away from where I last saw it.

"The violins Archangelo Serafino made are very good instruments; all of the surviving examples are collectible and valuable, and yet they are just short of the extraordinary quality of a Stradivari. That is, all except for the final series he made at the end of his life, after losing his sight. Those violins, the so-called Angel violins, have the reputation for being the best-sounding violins ever built. The fact that he made them after he lost his sight, with only his sense of touch and hearing to guide him, makes the Angels all the more miraculous. Who can say? Perhaps Serafino really did have an angel guiding his hands as he worked.

"Serafino numbered each of the Angel violins. The one you brought to me to repair is called the Seven, for it was seventh in the series of only thirteen Angel violins built before Serafino died. The Seven belonged to Paganini for a time, so I suppose it might as well be called the Paganini Angel. Some say the violin itself is what turned him into such a monstrous prodigy. According to legend, Paganini sold his soul to the devil in order to become the world's greatest violinist. At least, that is what people say. Another version of the story, much less commonly known, is that the devil upheld his part of the bargain not by simply giving Paganini extraordinary talent, but rather by arranging for a wealthy patron to present the young violinist with the magnificent Seven. For so long as Paganini played the Seven, every concert was sold out and the wealthiest and most beautiful noblewomen of Europe literally threw themselves at his feet. Of course, that is all just legend. Or so we think today, but who knows for certain?

"The rest of story—and this much is true and part of the historical record—is that Paganini lost the Seven gambling. But another patron gave him the famous Guarneri del Gesu Cannon he played the rest of his life, so it didn't turn out so badly for Paganini, though his later career never equaled its early heights. Paganini did seem to have led a life that was charmed and cursed at the same time. Which is exactly what one would suspect of someone who made a bargain with the devil.

"After Paganini lost the Seven, it changed hands, from one dealer to the next. For a time it belonged to a German violinist, a beautiful woman who inspired Johannes Brahms to write several of his lovelier sonatas and trios for piano, violin, and cello. The Seven disappeared from the records after that. Perhaps it was sold to a wealthy amateur or a professional player whose heirs were unaware of its value. It is difficult to imagine, but important instruments do become lost. Perhaps the person who knows its value dies unexpectedly and no one else realizes what they have. To the average person, one fiddle looks the same as another.

"From the eighteen-nineties until the war, the Seven's whereabouts were unknown, a mystery. And then, as inexplicably as it disappeared, it returned, in the possession of a man who is without question one of the most notorious collectors of all time."

Gianni broke off his story and looked at his hands, which seemed strong and nimble despite his great age, though the backs were lined with bluish veins. When the silence became uncomfortable, Carter asked Gianni if he would like an espresso. Gianni said yes, please, and so the interruption continued while Carter again busied himself with the elaborate coffeemaking apparatus. He opened the refrigerator for a lemon. Maggie noticed the refrigerator was filled with imported beer and white wine. Carter cut off a bit of lemon peel and put it on the saucer beside the demitasse.

"Do you ever suspect there are unseen connections between some people and even between people and things?" Gianni said, picking up the cup, its handle between his thumb and forefinger.

"What do you mean?" Carter asked.

Gianni dabbed his mouth with a napkin, smoothing down the edges of his neat gray mustache.

"I was just thinking how peculiar it was that Miss O'Hara should walk in here and present the Seven to me for repair. It is almost as if there is a bond between me and that violin."

"Maybe there is," Carter said, "or maybe fate is just playing with you."

"There are some extraordinary coincidences," Maggie said.

"It has been a long time since I have gone to Mass," Gianni said, suddenly looking very old. "Maybe it is a sign."

"You're going to live forever," Carter said with a wave of the hand. "Tell us about your first encounter with the Seven."

"I was in the Italian army. I had been a young luthier in Cremona. I did not enlist. I was conscripted after the war had begun. I was a reluctant soldier. I was not a fan of Mussolini's, even if he did make the trains run on time. When he threw in with the Germans, I knew it would end badly for Italy. And in the end it did. But wars can't be fought without young men, and so I found myself in the army, like all my friends.

"I went for training but was taken aside after a few weeks and given special treatment. No more marching and shooting. Nobody seemed to know why. I wasn't a big shot. I didn't come from an important family. I wasn't much good at soldiering, but others were worse. 'Orders,' the officers told me. They didn't know either. I cannot say that I objected. Why would I?

"I was sent to stay in a hotel in town. There was a pretty girl who worked in a café. She would bring me coffee, and we would talk about things. It was very pleasant. We became friends. Later we wrote each other letters. After the war she came to America. That is why I eventually came to America, to marry her."

"Ahhh," Maggie said, smiling. She liked this part of the story.

"One day a captain arrived with my orders. I was to pack my bags and accompany him to the station. He put me on the night train for Berlin. That was a complete surprise—Berlin. What need could they have for an Italian private in Berlin? I was more than a little nervous about it. The Germans are the same as anybody else: some are good, some not so good. But I was afraid of the Nazis. The fascists in Italy could be dangerous, but they were mostly playacting, like characters in a bad opera. But the Nazis meant business in a way that is difficult to understand today. Imagine a country ruled by thugs who had the power to do whatever they wanted to anybody anytime for whatever reason. It was not a situation that inspired comfort in anybody except other Nazis.

"A German lieutenant named Ritter, who spoke good Italian, collected me at the station in Berlin. He was friendly enough, although he wouldn't tell me where we were going, saying only that I would find out when I got there. We climbed into a Mercedes touring car and set off into the country, leaving Berlin behind us. We drove for a long time before we entered the gates of a vast estate. The driver took us around to the back, where the servants entered. Lieutenant Ritter told me we had reached our destination, Karinhall, Reichmarshal Göring's castle. I broke out in a cold sweat. Göring was Hitler's second-in-command. What did he want with me? What had I done?

"The soldiers patted me down for weapons and searched my bag to make sure I wasn't hiding a bomb. They led us down a corridor that seemed to be a kilometer long, down a winding staircase wide enough for six men to walk shoulder-to-shoulder, then back up

another corridor. I will not try to describe the place
except to say it was opulent beyond all imagining—
the best furniture, the finest Persian carpets, rare tapestries, and old master paintings hanging on the walls.
Most of it was stolen, for Göring was the most accomplished of all the Nazi freebooters.

"At last we came to a door like the door to a vault.
Two troopers were stationed outside, machine pistols
slung over their shoulders. One of Göring's factotums,
the man we had been trailing after during the long trek
through the castle's bowels, unlocked the gate and then
worked the combination to the bomb-proof door. My
knees were weak by the time he pushed it open. I was
expecting a torture chamber, but what I beheld instead
was a room that appeared to have been replicated from
Versailles—golden furniture, chandeliers, mirrors,
more paintings and tapestries. Some of the glass-
topped tables were in fact display cases that held
Göring's collection of musical instruments. The room,
one of many like it, was where the Reichmarshal kept
his collection of rare violins and violas.

"Göring's servant led me to one of the cases and
opened it with a golden key. Inside was a violin, the
Seven. I was told to carefully inspect it. There were
guards watching me all the time, their machine pistols
in their hands, ready to shoot me if I tried to steal the
Angel, or dropped it.

"As I looked at the Seven, I noticed that the pegs
were in need of attention. Ritter told me my new job
was to maintain the violins and violas in peak condition. I was to effect any repairs I deemed necessary,
periodically change the strings, and generally serve as
conservator to that part of Göring's collection.

"It would have been a wonderful job, had it not involved working on violins I assumed were mostly stolen. And I cannot say it was a pleasure to work for Reichmarshal Göring, who would have had me dragged out by my heels and shot if he suspected I was not performing the job perfectly.

"In the year I was at Karinhall, I never did see Göring. To tell you the truth, I do not know whether he ever visited the collection. Judging from what I heard, his activities at the estate were confined mainly to injecting himself with morphine and playing with a huge model train set.

"I eventually secured leave to visit my home. Things were beginning to collapse for Germany and Italy by then. Before I could return to Karinhall, I was handed a rifle and ordered to the front. I was in combat for a month as the Yanks drove us back. Eventually I had the good fortune to have my company surrounded by the Americans. We were only too happy to surrender.

"Who knows what would have happened had I made it back to Karinhall? I probably would have been killed fighting in Germany. I can't imagine anything worse than dying for Hitler."

Gianni's eyes met Maggie's.

"I might have even ended up being the man who asked your grandfather if he wanted to buy the Seven. Except that if I possessed the Angel, I would not have let her go for any price. Perhaps it was Ritter or one of the others who sold the Angel. It was chaos at the end. It is a miracle so many of Göring's stolen treasures survived destruction."

Gianni drank off the rest of the espresso and sat looking at his folded hands.

"So we don't know whether Göring had legal title to the violin," Carter asked.

"We do not," Gianni replied.

"And we do not know whether the nameless officer who sold it to Maggie's grandfather had any right to sell it."

"Again, we do not," Gianni said, shifting his gaze to Maggie. "It is impossible to establish a chain of possession. There are no bills of sale extant, letters, or supporting documents."

"What are you getting at?" Maggie said, feeling the emotion building up in her again.

"I am not hinting at anything, but merely trying to sift through the facts. Frankly, it is doubtful Göring obtained the violin by legal means. The same is true for the man who sold the Seven for a pittance to your grandfather."

"I don't like where this is going," Maggie said, pushing her chair away from the table.

"Please sit down, Miss O'Hara. You are jumping to conclusions."

"That's funny. It seems to me that's exactly what you are doing."

"Even so," Gianni said, motioning her back into the chair with his hands. "The fact that the violin has been in your family's possession for more than fifty years, along with the fact that there appear to be no competing claims, seems to argue fairly convincingly to me that you can claim legal ownership of the Seven, at least if nothing definitive comes to light to the contrary."

"I'm sorry if I lost my temper," Maggie said, smiling.

"There is no need to apologize," Gianni said. "There is a great deal at stake."

"Well then," Carter said and clapped his hands. "I think it's time we gave Maggie her violin."

Maggie turned her smile toward Carter. She could have kissed him.

21

THE JAGUAR ROLLED down the darkened mews with its driving lights on and slipped into the one open space on the street in the fashionable London neighborhood. The door opened. A woman got out. She looked behind her before crossing the street, though there was no traffic on the quiet lane near where it ended in a cul-de-sac. She was a brunette with her long hair piled up on her head and fixed with Chinese combs. From Dylan Glyndwr's vantage point in the drawing room window, he could see the pulse beating against the pale skin in her neck. He closed his eyes and smiled, experiencing the same tingle of anticipation he found vibrating within the woman's mind.

She was going to meet her lover.

Glyndwr had always liked London, despite his hatred of the bloody English. A great city like London belonged to the world. Besides, there were fewer English in London each time he visited. There were more Asians there than ever. He had heard an American in Victoria Station refer to the city as "Londonistan." Americans. Dylan did not know many, but he was not impressed with them. They had no culture, so far as the vampire could judge.

"Would you care for a spot of sherry, old boy?"

Dylan turned away from the window to face his host. William Tritt was an American, though he had done his best to disguise his origins, and wisely so. Like most Anglophile Yanks transplanted to the United Kingdom, he had labored long and hard to make himself more British than the British. The vampire liked Tritt. In spite of the fact that Tritt had grown prosperous as a dealer in rare and collectable violins, Dylan found him to be one of the more scrupulous traders he had dealt with over the years. The violin dealer lived alone in a house furnished with enough antiques to make Dylan feel at home in time. Still, Tritt was a bit of a fop, in his purple smoking jacket, with a shock of white hair and a girth that had expanded throughout the course of their association.

"What is your secret?"

"Which one?" Dylan said, accepting the drink. "I have so many."

"No doubt you do," Tritt replied with a suggestive chuckle. "I mean your rakish good looks, old boy. How do you manage to stay so young?"

"Clean living and prayer."

Tritt snorted. "We've been doing business for . . . Goodness gracious, how long has it been, Mr. Glyndwr?"

"I bought my Vuillaume bow from you ten years ago."

"Ten years! The years fly, don't they? They fly."

The vampire smiled sadly.

"Look at the two of us. I was a rather good-looking young chap when first we met, if I dare say so myself. A decade has turned me gray and ruined my figure. I should color my hair. It's a wonder I don't, considering how particular I am about my appearance. Alas, these days my vanity must be confined mostly to clothing and jewelry."

Tritt lifted his sherry in salute.

"To you, Mr. Glyndwr, the living portrait of Dorian Gray."

Dylan clinked glasses with Tritt.

"And I remember the Vuillaume, of course. An excellent bow and a bargain at the price you paid for it during what was a sadly depressed market. I am more than happy to take it off your hands, should you ever care to part with it."

"I make it a point never to part with anything, if I can help it."

"An excellent philosophy, for they aren't making antiques the way they used to," Tritt said, and winked a porcine eye. "I bought that bow from the estate of a Portuguese doctor who lived in South Africa. They had no idea what it was worth. I gave them a fair price for it nonetheless. Not too fair, but fair."

"You have always been more than reasonable," Dylan said. "Honesty hasn't prevented you from doing very well for yourself at Taylor and Morris."

"Ah, yes, the venerable old firm." He shot Dylan a look over the rim of his glass. "Shall we get down to business?"

Glyndwr tipped his head.

"You've come about the violin, of course."

"Of course."

"I could have given you the information over the telephone and saved you the trip from Amsterdam."

"I do not trust the telephone. And the mails are even more suspect. You have followed my directives?"

The smallest hint of indulgence crept into Tritt's face. He was used to dealing with eccentric customers. Their peculiarities were a source of private amusement.

"I have obeyed you to the letter, sir. Nothing has been written down, except for this, which is meaningless in and of itself."

Dylan frowned as he took the calling card from Tritt. He had expressly told the man that *nothing* was to be written down, though the joy it gave him to be approaching the end of a two-century quest made it difficult to feel more than a little put-out. On the back of the card, written in Tritt's neat hand, was an address, telephone number, and name: *Maggie O'Hara.*

"And you spoke to no one about this?"

"Excepting the person who provided the information, not a syllable. Considering the size of the retainer you gave me to keep an eye out for one of the Angels, I am surprised I even told myself," Tritt said, and chuckled at his own joke.

"Is your source reliable?"

"Oh, quite. He's one of the most in-the-know dealers in Cremona." Tritt raised an eyebrow. "He is exactly the person I would call to inquire about potential legal problems with a rare instrument."

"Meaning whether it was stolen."

"Quite," Tritt agreed.

"I do not care whether or not it is stolen. The only thing I am interested in is finding it."

"That is entirely your affair," Tritt said equably. He leaned forward as much as his girth would permit and whispered: "It's the Seven."

The Seven! That violin was reputed to be the most remarkable of the very remarkable series of Angel violins. Glyndwr had come close to the instrument and would have had it, if Paganini, the impulsive idiot, hadn't gambled it away while Dylan was stuck in Turkey, marooned by an outbreak of the plague.

"Did you learn where it has been since 1945?"

"I never believed the instrument was destroyed after disappearing from the Göring collection," Tritt said. "The details about its postwar history are a bit vague, but no matter. According to the story my man in Cremona was told, a German officer sold the Seven to an American soldier. It's more likely the soldier 'liberated' the violin from a cache of spoils without realizing what he had. We still don't know how Göring acquired the violin, but there don't appear to be any complications in that area."

Tritt told Glyndwr how the violin had spent the past fifty years in an attic before passing to the daughter of the former soldier, who had recently died.

"Absent any unforeseen complications, the man's granddaughter is the violin's legal owner."

"I had always suspected it would turn up in a Japanese collection. They had all the money in the world for a few decades and are mad about collecting."

"It somehow doesn't seem right," Tritt said, "all those van Goghs and Monets hanging in Tokyo."

"How much is the O'Hara woman asking for the Seven?"

"I'm not sure she wishes to sell, Mr. Glyndwr."

"She will sell, Mr. Tritt. Trust me."

"You're a sly one, Mr. Glyndwr. I have no doubt you're right."

"Can we rely on the discretion of your contact in

Cremona, Mr. Tritt? I do not want him sharing this information with others."

"He was well paid for his discretion, but to be perfectly honest I wouldn't count on it, Mr. Glyndwr. The news is bound to get out. The Seven is a legend. I myself am dying to hear an Angel and see if they sing as sweetly as the old stories say."

"They do."

Tritt gave Glyndwr a curious look.

"You will have to take it on faith. I have seen many things and know many secrets." The vampire raised his glass. "I salute you and your agents in Cremona and around the globe. It has been a long search."

"To the successful conclusion of your quest, Mr. Glyndwr."

"And what about you?" The vampire put the empty glass on the table beside his chair. "Can I rely on your discretion? I prefer not to have other suitors competing for the violin."

"For what you've paid me, Mr. Glyndwr, I will happily take the information about the Seven to my grave."

"Yes," the vampire said, "you will."

After arranging things to create the impression that the violin dealer had hanged himself, Dylan rifled through Tritt's address book and files, searching for the address of any dealers in Cremona. He suspected the information was locked in the computer on the desk in Tritt's study, but he had no idea how to work the newfangled contraption. Just as well. It would be foolish to travel to Italy just to tie up a loose end when he could fly to America.

Dylan Glyndwr had business, urgent business, with Maggie O'Hara.

22

"YOU WILL NEED to insure the instrument."

"I know, Carter." Maggie looked at the violin, remembering how she had found it, in pieces, in her grandfather's house. "I wonder how much it will cost."

"For an instrument this valuable, it will not be cheap, Miss O'Hara," Gianni Felici said.

"I'm a student. My grandfather had a little money, but he ran through most of it being sick."

"I'll tell you what," Carter said, smiling. "I will take care of the insurance."

"I couldn't let you do that."

"Then consider it a loan, if you like, but it would be more than fair for you to let me pay for the insurance for the time being. This will be news, when it gets out. You're going to tell people Gianni realized what the violin was, and that you allowed him to work on it?"

"Of course."

"The publicity alone will be worth what it costs to insure the violin," Carter said. "You've heard of guilt by association? Think of this as profit by association. We'll benefit no matter what, so you might as well get something in return."

"I wasn't brought up to take charity."

"Not charity, Maggie, business," Carter said. It was the first time he'd called her by her first name. She liked the way it sounded. But her doubts were never far behind. He probably was just being nice to her because of the violin.

"Of course, there will be other considerations for the insurance company."

"Considerations?" she asked.

"The insurance company will insist the violin be kept in a secure place. They will need assurances not only that it is reasonably safe from theft but also from fire and environmentally adverse conditions. Temperature and humidity control are critical."

"After what the Seven went through sitting in an attic for fifty years?"

"Even more so because of its recent history," Felici said to Carter. "The Angel violin is a treasure but a delicate one." His expression was grave as he looked at Maggie. "Upon the Seven's owner fall the considerable responsibilities of conservatorship. In a sense one does not own a Stradivari or Serafino so much as one cares for them for the present and future generations. You have not been given a violin but a trust, my dear girl."

"Oh, my." She felt a little guilty looking down at the instrument, which she still had not played. Indeed, the extent of her thoughts about the violin had been what it would sound like—and whether she would be disappointed. "I hadn't thought of any of that."

"I suppose that's natural, considering," the elderly luthier said.

"This violin is going to change your life, Maggie."

"Do you really think so, Carter?" she said, trying out

the shop owner's name for the first time herself to see how it sounded to her ear.

"Just wait, Miss O'Hara," Gianni Felici said. "Think of what it would be like to find a lost painting by Rembrandt. But rare as they may be, there are probably hundreds of original Rembrandts in collections around the world. The Seven is one of only two known Angel violins remaining in the world. The other is in the Hermitage collection in Russia. It has been locked in a display case and hasn't been played since 1917."

"What do you plan to do with the violin? Will you sell it?"

She looked up from the instrument.

"It would bring you tens of millions," Carter said.

"Easily," Felici said.

"It's not for sale," Maggie said. "It was a present from my grandfather. I could never part with it. Besides, I'm a violinist. I'm going to play the Angel."

Maggie saw what she thought was worry in Felici's eyes, as if she were a little girl proposing to ride a dangerous horse. But if the violin really had the powers people said it had, maybe it would elevate her to something more than one of the thousands of talented music majors who graduated each year and sank immediately into a tepid sea of anonymity.

"There it is, ready to play," Carter said. "Let's hear something. I've been dying to hear how this legend sounds."

Maggie felt herself blushing. The thought of playing the violin for Carter made her feel exposed and vulnerable. The old Italian nodded encouragement.

"Just a few notes, Miss O'Hara, to see if there is

anything I need to attend to. The honor of awakening the Angel belongs to you."

Maggie picked up the violin, holding it carefully, as if it were a delicate glass object and would shatter if she breathed on it. But the violin felt balanced in her hands. She attached the Kun shoulder rest Carter or Gianni had put in the new case that now held the Seven. Gianni Felici tightened up the bow that had come with the violin—a nineteenth-century French bow that was rather nice once he replaced the horsehair. He ran the rosin back and forth a few times and handed it to her.

"The sound may be a little tight at first," Felici said. "An instrument needs to be played to open it up. This bird has been caged a long time. She will need to limber up her wings and learn to breathe again."

Maggie tested the tuning, then adjusted the E string. She played a three-octave G scale to get the feel of the instrument. The first sounds from the violin were promising—a warm, shimmering tone balanced across the strings, which seemed to brighten the sunlight flowing into the room as Maggie's fingers climbed higher on the fingerboard. Her playing initially was tentative and a little uncertain. She was nervous.

Maggie had intended to play a few scales and arpeggios to see how the instrument sounded, but found herself launching into a solo violin piece. Paganini's Caprice No. 24 begins with deceptive simplicity but quickly plunges into nearly four minutes of demonically difficult playing, requiring the fingers to leap up and down the neck, gobbling great handfuls of fingerboard and reaching for two-finger double-stop passages that sound horrible unless the violinist's intonation is dead-on perfect.

If her playing was suddenly confident, it belied the fact that her soul was lost in a long primal scream of horror to have attempted something so difficult. It was like when she was a little girl and got onto a roller coaster, only to realize, as the car crested the top of the incline to the first stomach-dropping dive, that she would not be able to get off until the ride was through, and then only if she survived the experience.

Fortunately, her fear dissolved in the celestial sound pouring from the violin. By the time she was in the second variation, she was playing with her eyes closed and her lips slightly parted, like an ecstatic in the grip of a religious trance. On and on they raced together—the caprice, the violin, the violinist made one. It was as if she were possessed by the ghost of Paganini, who had once owned the Seven and no doubt played the same piece onstage before the kings and queens of old Europe. Or maybe she was simply possessed by the spirit of the Angel known by its number, Seven.

When the music was ended, Maggie stood with her eyes closed, her lips parted, a few locks of hair stuck to the perspiration wetting her temples after the physical and emotional exertion required to play the Caprice No. 24, perhaps as well as only Paganini himself had ever played it.

Gianni Felici spoke first, his accented English barely more than a whisper.

"You are exactly right, Miss O'Hara. You must keep the Angel, and you must play her."

23

THEY WALKED SLOWLY and without deliberation, like people without a destination to reach, even though they did have one. The conversation had lapsed, but it was the sort of thoughtful quiet neither of them felt compelled to break to make a point, or to say something just for the sake of ending the silence.

Carter tended to talk more freely with people he didn't know well. When you speak idly to a near stranger, everything you have to say about yourself—or hear from your opposite—is new and interesting. There are no positions to hold, no accommodations to maintain, no subjects mutually recognized as out-of-bounds. It was because Carter and Maggie were only slightly acquainted that their conversations over the past few days had tended to occur on a deep level. With people who are good friends or business acquaintances, the focus on small, practical, day-to-day matters tends to push to the periphery discussion of the bigger issues comprising the foundation of what people think about life. It had occurred to Carter—in the midst of trying to explain to Maggie without sounding pretentious why he thought it was important to actively pursue a strategy of living in the present, rather than in

the future or the past—that he realized the irony in
how it was easier to have an intimate conversation with
someone you didn't really know than with a lover,
good friend, or family member.

It was late in the day and pleasantly warm, though
the sun had already moved noticeably lower in the
southern sky with winter's approach. As soon as the
sun dropped beyond the pin oaks on the Pentacrest, it
would become chilly.

Maggie's footsteps slowed until she was not walking
at all.

"What time do we need to be there?"

"We ought to have enough time if we're there by
four-thirty."

Maggie looked at her wristwatch. "I'll buy you a
cup of coffee. It's only fair after all the lattes and cap-
puccinos you've made for me, not to mention everything else you and Gianni have done to help me."

"Sure," Carter said.

It was a delaying tactic on Maggie's behalf, and
Carter knew it. She had become so attached to the
Angel violin that it was amazing she could part with it.
She had taken it everywhere and slept with it next to
her bed, she told Carter. He had become equally attached to hearing her play. Maggie had eaten supper
with him and Gianni three out of the past four nights,
performing informal concerts for them afterward.
Carter didn't know which was more extraordinary:
Maggie's playing or the violin's amazing sound. Together, the woman and the Seven worked an intoxicating alchemy on Carter. He was in love. And Maggie
was in love, too, but with the violin. Carter hoped she

was also falling in love with him, but she was a difficult read.

Carter and Maggie had the Novel Café to themselves at that hour. The usual habitués, students from the university writer's workshop and English department, had deserted the place so close to the supper hour. Students still downtown were drinking beer at Joe's or the Airliner. The Novel Café wouldn't get busy again until later in the evening, when students would filter back in for caffeine-powered journal-writing sessions and study breaks.

Maggie was looking at Carter with a sort of amusement when she returned to the table with their coffee. This continued until he finally said, "What?"

"I've been reading about you."

"Oh?" He tried to sound nonplussed.

"You were one of the golden boys."

He gave her a crooked smile. "Were?"

"Before you sold your stock in the company you founded and got out of the Internet business."

"I have always had good timing."

She leaned toward him across the table, her eyes locked on his, looking at him as if he were a piece of complicated music she wanted to understand.

"What are you doing hiding out here?"

Carter blinked with surprise.

"Who said I'm hiding out?"

"What are you doing working in a violin shop if not hiding out?"

Carter laughed. "I bought Ivaskin Violins because I fell in love with the place the moment I set foot in it."

"But you're not a violinist."

"I'm pretty good on the guitar," he said. He could

see that didn't impress her. "Think of it as an investment, if that makes it any easier for you to understand. I can afford it."

"You certainly can," she said. "The *Forbes* article I read on-line said your stock was valued at three hundred million."

"Sure, at its peak."

"You didn't wait until the bottom started to fall out to sell."

"Like I said, good timing."

Carter wasn't sure whether he should play up his wealth or continue to be his usual modest self. He wasn't overly impressed with himself. He had seen how fast and easily wealth could come and go. He had simply been in the right place at the right time and lucky to boot. Yet he wasn't too pure to pass up a chance to impress a woman he was interested in. The thing was, Maggie didn't seem like the sort of woman who was overly concerned with money. If she was, Carter wouldn't have been attracted to her.

"It's safe to say I won't ever have to worry about money," he said when it became obvious she was waiting for him to say something. "What's wrong with investing money in fine violins? I'd expect you to approve."

"I do, in principle."

"But . . . ?" Carter said, because he sensed there was more.

"It's just that I wonder . . ."

"Go ahead and say it, Maggie. You bought the coffee. We're here on your dime. You can be honest with me. You can always be honest with me."

"I was going to say I have been wondering about the

extent of your interests. Take the Angel violin, for instance."

"The Seven?"

She nodded. "Are you interested in acquiring it?"

Carter tried to recover the moment he realized he was gaping at Maggie with his mouth open.

"You don't want to sell it," he said, a statement, not a question.

"Of course not. But that doesn't mean you don't want to buy it."

"Ah," he said, leaning back in his chair.

"What I'm wondering, Carter, is this. We've spent time together in the past week. Is it me you are interested in or my violin?"

He chose his words carefully.

"The question is fair enough. Your violin is an extraordinary instrument. While there aren't a lot of people who could come up with the money to buy it, either to own it or in the hope of reselling it for profit, I have the means at my disposal to buy the Seven, if you wanted to sell it. But you don't want to sell the Seven. We both know that. Furthermore, it is impossible for me to imagine you without the Seven to play, or the Seven without you to play it. The two of you seem to be made for each other, a perfect match."

Carter slid his hand across the table and covered hers. She made no move to pull away from him.

"Which is a long way of saying, Maggie, that what I'm interested in is not the violin we're about to lock up for the night in a bank vault until you can move into a house where a security system can be installed. The true object of my hope and desire, Maggie, is you."

24

As chairman of the university's music school and conservatory, which operated as a semiautonomous entity within the greater department, it fell upon Dr. Jane Crittenden to preside at important official occasions. Jane liked being in charge, but it wasn't always pleasant. Part of the price of power was being the one who wielded the whip, or, when necessary, the executioner's ax.

Jane was in charge of the panel of judges that sat in deliberation during auditions to the music school's conservatory program. These sessions tended to be either extremely enjoyable or extremely painful, depending upon the applicant's talent. The auditions were a high-stakes high-wire act in which failure meant death—at least career death, so far as it applied to being welcomed into the conservatory's warm, professionally nurturing bosom.

A conservatory audition brought the aspiring performance major to a crossroads that could be reached only after a lifetime of study and preparation started in early childhood. The high road from this life intersection led into the conservatory and a program that would almost certainly assure a talented young player a career with a major symphony orchestra or, for the elite of an already elite group, opportunities to perform as a soloist. This road was open to only the best, the brightest, the most prepared. The alternate road led to the university music school's education program, which churned out graduates not to perform but to teach, in schools and stores.

Jane was thinking about this, as she invariably did, when she left her office and walked toward the main auditorium. Jane did not know why they used the great hall for the auditions. The practice predated her and had become part of a tradition people resisted changing. Conservatory auditions were nerve-racking enough for students in and of themselves, without making the applicants stand alone and naked, as it were, beneath a single white spotlight, before a panel of inquisitors who would determine whether their future would be a Madrid concert stage or a dissonant band room in a small-town junior high school.

Jane opened the door and stood for a moment at the top of the center aisle, letting her eyes adjust to the darkness. Heads turned toward her. She smiled. Dr. Eck was there, of course, for she was in charge of upper strings. There were other senior faculty members, the standing conservatory board. There was a smattering of students. They didn't have a vote, of course, but were present mainly because they were required to attend a given number of recitals.

While only the best students in the school were accepted into the conservatory program, they were not the crème de la crème of rising stars. Those students went to Juilliard and schools of the first rank. But Jane's conservatory was not far behind and was gaining. Maria Rainer had been highly complimentary of the program.

Everything turned on getting the best teachers. Jane had wheedled and cajoled the money out of the university to put together a first-rate faculty. Teachers of the highest caliber tended to be difficult, like Katarina Eck. Eck's authoritarian manner—the students called her "the Nazi" behind her back—was a frequent source of friction that Jane had to deal with, but she was worth it. Eck's students had gone on to play with some of the nation's best orchestras, and there was no better advertisement for the conservatory than that.

Jane had been dreading today's audition since setting the date. The only ray of hope had been that the student would back out, as she had repeatedly. But dreams die hard, and the girl apparently planned to go through with this audition, her last chance. Jane held no hope that the student would rise to the occasion, as sometimes happened. She had talent, Eck said, but had struggled since arriving at the university. Her talent was blocked, perhaps because of the personal issues Jane sensed whenever she looked into the girl's eyes. She was insecure and vulnerable in a profession that required almost megalomaniacal egotism and nerves of steel to survive. As selective as Jane was, she hated having to feed lives and dreams into a shredder that would spit them out labeled *not good enough*. Yet there was no other way. The conservatory existed to separated wheat from chaff. Not that it made it any easier.

Jane sat next to Eck and looked at her watch. It was two o'clock on the dot. There were footsteps from stage left. Maggie O'Hara walked onto the stage. She wore a long black dress; the conservatory recitals were formal. An accompanist, a young man from the conservatory, followed her, holding his piano music.

The judges and audience applauded politely. Jane happened to glance at one of the students, Nicole Hoffman, and saw the malicious glee in her smile. She smelled blood in the water and was looking forward to the spectacle of Maggie crashing and burning. Nicole was one of Eck's favorites and already admitted to the conservatory, but Jane had never liked the girl. Nicole Hoffman was too perfect. She was beautiful and wealthy and talented and had never had to work for anything.

Jane stood.

"Good afternoon, Ms. O'Hara."

"Good afternoon, Dr. Crittenden."

The girl sounded more sure of herself than usual. At least she had pluck, Jane thought.

"What would you like to play for us today?"

"Jean Sibelius's Violin Concerto in D minor, op. 47."

"Very good."

Jane shot a quick look at Eck, trying not to show too openly her fury at Eck for letting the O'Hara girl choose so difficult a piece for the audition. She could have just as easily failed with something easier. It would be a miracle if the child was able to get through the entire piece without breaking down and weeping with frustration, and failure, at the sonata's technical difficulty. But Eck ignored her. She was staring at Maggie O'Hara, or that was what Jane thought until Eck spoke.

"Is that a different instrument than the one you have brought to lessons?" Eck asked in an imperious voice.

Jane expected Maggie to wilt, but to her surprise the

girl smiled at Eck. Jane couldn't remember a student ever smiling at the violin professor. Eck clearly didn't like it.

"It's a violin my grandfather gave me. I thought it might bring me luck."

"Do you really think it wise to play an unfamiliar instrument for the recital that will decide whether you gain admission to the conservatory?" Eck said, her voice rising, her tone hectoring.

"Excuse me," Jane said, forcing a smile. She could not believe Eck's behavior. It was as if she were trying to unnerve her student. "I am sure Ms. O'Hara knows what she is doing. Shall we proceed?"

Eck gave the girl a curt nod, as if to tell her to hurry up, to quit wasting their time with her infernal delays.

Jane sat back in her chair and let out a slow breath. She looked around the small audience one last time. All eyes were on Maggie O'Hara. Eck was glaring at her with almost open hatred. Nicole Hoffman appeared almost giddy with delight. The others seemed respectful, but doubtful.

Maggie O'Hara lifted the violin to her chin and began to play.

25

FLUORESCENT BALLASTS SUSPENDED from the ceiling by chains illuminated the gas station's two service bays. A midnight-blue Ford Taurus was up on the hoist. The mechanic—his name was Jack, according to the red lettering stitched above the breast pocket of his shirt—stared at the car's exposed underside.

"Nothing hanging loose that I can see," Jack said. He pushed a screwdriver up under the car and wiggled it. "The universals look okay."

"Do you think you can repair the vehicle?"

"It's most likely the transmission, like Bobbie told you when he picked you up on the interstate. It starts but won't drive when you put it in gear?"

"That is correct," Dylan Glyndwr replied.

"There's nothing I can do on Sunday night," the mechanic said, wiping the screwdriver on his shirt. "It's a rental?"

Dylan nodded. "From the airport in Chicago."

"I'd call 'em up and tell them to bring you a new car."

It was an excellent suggestion. Using the pay phone next to the coffeemaker in the station, Dylan called the emergency-service number listed on the rental contract. The operator, speaking from a call center in another state, told Dylan the agency's local office was closed and wouldn't be able to supply him with another car until the morning. The company would pay for Dylan to spend the night in a hotel in the town where he was stranded.

Dylan slammed the receiver down.

"Got ya covered?" the mechanic asked, coming over to help himself to a cup of stale coffee.

A vein throbbed in Dylan's temple, always a sign he was dangerously angry. He could have killed the mechanic for asking so foolish a question, but there was no point in complicating things. Fortune had been cruel to him that day. He had endured the long flight across the Atlantic only to have his flight in Chicago canceled. Dylan hated driving himself, but he had little choice unless he wanted to be stranded at O'Hare, so he rented a car and headed west. Not long after crossing the Mississippi River, there was a noise somewhere in the vehicle's inner workings, and the automobile lost power and slowly coasted to a halt. His quest to possess another Angel violin, now into its second century, was pointlessly delayed a mere hundred kilometers from his destination.

The mechanic stared at Dylan, waiting for an answer. When none was forthcoming, he repeated the question, as if thinking he was not heard the first time. "They bringing you out a new car?"

"They cannot deliver a new vehicle until the morning."

Jack grinned. "You ain't from around here, are you, mister?"

Dylan felt his self-control beginning to slip.

"You sound like you're from England."

Struggling to maintain his composure, Dylan briefly closed his eyes, silently cursing Fate for the fickle bitch of a goddess she was.

"I am Welsh," Glyndwr said levelly.

"Really? What's the difference?"

Dylan felt himself beginning to shake.

"Bobbie can give you a ride to a motel. There are a couple on the street you came in on from the inter-state." The mechanic gestured with his disposable coffee cup, indicating the direction of the highway. "We also got us a new Marriott downtown, if that suits you. I hear it's expensive. I can settle up with Avis in the morning when they come for the Taurus."

"I think the walk will do me good," Dylan Glyndwr said. "I need to clear my head."

"Suit yourself," the mechanic said, and took a gulp of coffee.

"I almost always do, Jack."

The vampire walked past the mechanic and into the night.

Jack would never know how close he had come to drinking his last cup of bad coffee.

26

MAGGIE FELT A rush of freedom when she left Dr. Eck's office, as if escaping from the claustrophobia of a vault where there was not enough oxygen to freely breathe.

She pulled the door closed behind her, resisting the impulse to slam it shut. Lessons with Eck were to be endured, and even though Maggie had found her wings, she still had to be just a little in doubt that she would survive her weekly encounters with the demanding Katarina Eck.

A woman was standing against the wall opposite the office, her hands folded in front of her, as if waiting for the lesson posted on the schedule on Eck's door to conclude. She did not look much older than Maggie, but it was obvious from both her clothing and the way she held herself that she was not as young as she looked, and that she carried a certain authority. Her long hair was wound into a braid, which she wore pulled forward over her right shoulder. She was dressed with simple elegance: white blouse, black cashmere sweater worn over her shoulders, long skirt—a silky fabric, a gypsy print that was almost Oriental—and simple black slippers. She was small but gave off a vibrant sense of energy that would have been impossible to miss. She reminded Maggie of a yoga instructor—self-possessed, filled with quiet energy, not an ounce of fat on her supple body, and above all else, calm.

"Hello," Maggie said as the woman came toward her, stopping in front of her, managing to block her way without being the least bit threatening or presumptuous.

The woman smiled at her, and it was as if the sun had come out from behind a cloud to flood the music school hallway with radiant light. It was in that moment that Maggie recognized Maria Rainer, the guest conductor who had come from Berlin to direct the school's Mozart festival.

"Maestro Rainer." Maggie felt herself blush. "I recognize you from pictures in magazines. It is an honor to meet you."

"The honor is mine, Miss O'Hara."

Maggie was so stunned that the conductor knew her name that it was a moment before she realized Maria Rainer had extended her hand. It was small and firm and very warm.

"You may call me Maria, if you like. I rather like the informality of things in America. May I call you Maggie?"

"Of course." Maggie adjusted the shoulder strap on the violin case holding the Angel violin to give herself time to recover her bearings. "I'm a big fan of your work. Your recordings of the Fifth and Ninth are both amazing. They sound as if Beethoven had just written them."

"I wanted to free poor Ludwig and bring him back

to life. It is all in the approach. Most orchestras are un-adventurous and overly academic."

"Especially with Beethoven. His music is so passionate. On your recordings you can almost feel him bleed with emotion." Maggie felt her face beginning to burn again. "I'm sorry. I'm gushing."

"Not at all, my dear. Your critique is exactly right, if I may say so."

The German swept her eyes over Maggie, as if appraising her against what she'd heard—and God only knew what *that* was.

"I don't mean to keep you," Maggie said. "You must have an appointment with Dr. Eck."

"No, I was waiting for you."

Maggie just stared.

"I heard about your conservatory audition from Jane Crittenden, among others. People are talking about you."

"Oh, my."

"They are talking about you in a good way," Maria said. "Your performance is the talk of the school. You impressed a lot of people."

"But not Dr. Eck," Maggie said, and instantly regretted it.

"I would imagine she is as impressed as everybody else. Some teachers are from the old school and think it is their job to challenge their pupils."

Maria turned and began to walk with Maggie toward the exit.

"I did not see your name on the list of violinists who will audition with me to play the Mozart solo."

"I didn't sign up."

Maria stopped and Maggie stopped with her. The

conductor, who was a good five inches shorter than Maggie, reached up and put her hand lightly on Maggie's shoulder.

"Promise me you will at least think about auditioning for me."

Maria smiled good-bye before Maggie could respond, turning to head back down the hall, her silk skirt billowing out as she moved away in a brisk, purposeful stride.

27

MAGGIE O'HARA SAT on the bed cross-legged and bare-breasted with her eyes closed, like a Hindu goddess in meditation.

Carter, on his side, head propped up on one hand, admired her the way he would have admired a work of art or one of the eighteenth-century violins in his shop.

In the candlelight, Maggie's flawless skin appeared to have the color and texture of butter, smooth, silken, creamy. Pachelbel's *Canon* in D Major played softly, rich strings glancing over the bass figure, the music picking up tempo and taking flight as the principal violin lifted away from the baroque orchestra. Carter saw the fingers of her left hand move slightly, as though in her mind she were playing the part on the Angel violin.

It had been interesting to Carter, who had known his share of women, to see the change that had overtaken Maggie in the short time since she'd first brought the Seven to Ivaskin Violins. It was strange how an inanimate object could transform someone's life. Of course, the Seven was no ordinary violin, but still it had been extraordinary for Carter to witness the metamorphosis of what had only a short time ago been a timid, uncertain girl. The Angel violin had served as a kind of philosopher's stone, only instead of transforming lead into gold, as medieval alchemists tried to do, it had turned the dross of Maggie O'Hara's unrealized dreams into something alive and beautiful.

How wonderful it would be, Carter thought, to preserve her at this moment, the wings of her artistic powers spread fully open, and her physical beauty at that precious, short-lived intersection between the suppleness of youth and the concupiscence of feminine maturity. A violin like the Seven could be preserved indefinitely with careful conservatorship, but people began to decline almost from the moment of their fullest development. Maybe that was why he sometimes felt a twinge of sadness when he looked at a young woman beautiful enough to be a living work of art; there was no escaping decline and decay. Human beings were mortal. *We begin to die,* Carter thought, *the moment we are born.*

Maggie opened her eyes halfway and looked at Carter, her gaze flickering between the passion and languor of the Pachelbel.

"What are you looking at?" she asked softly.

"You. I was looking at you and thinking how perfectly beautiful you are."

A dreamy smile turned up the corner of her lips.

"And I was thinking how good it would be if I could play you the way you play the violin," Carter said.

He reached to find her hand where it rested on her knee. The music swelled as they again intertwined their bodies amid the tangle of sheets. The music of the canon flowed into them, setting the rhythm for their hearts, beating faster together to the hastening figure.

The Seven waited in its case beside the bed, quiescent, still, content—if an inanimate object, albeit a magical one, can be content—to exist completely in that present moment.

28

DYLAN GLYNDWR STARTED down the street with the strap of the small travel valise slung over his shoulder. Three females came out of a house in the middle of the block, walking away from him. Even in the dark he could see youth in the way they moved. Their laughter floated back to him.

He stopped on the street corner and closed his eyes while he drew in a slow, deep breath. Their scent came to him on the night breeze like the smell of three blossoms opening before the moon. And beneath the perfume of their young bodies, an aroma far sweeter still—the intoxicating aroma of young blood.

He followed after them without anything particular in mind beyond prolonging the thrill of a distant flirtation. The Angel violin was far too important to risk the sort of complications that might arise if he had to hastily abandon bodies.

Dylan reached out with his senses, focusing his hearing until he could listen to their conversation. They were talking about boys, of course. Such as it had always been, the same eternal conversation—of love, of dreams, of disappointment in love as well as delight in it—continuing endlessly in every tongue spoken on the planet. What would preoccupy the mortal race, if not for affairs of the heart? It was to humans as blood, and music, were to the vampire Dylan Glyndwr.

The girls left the sidewalk, angling north across a grassy park forested with old oaks whose sheltering shadows overreached the brick buildings of a college campus. A small private school, Catholic, judging from the statue of a saint whose outstretched arm appeared frozen in the act of blessing the trees and the street that lay beyond.

The girls went between two buildings.

To lose oneself in love—it was a foreign concept to Dylan, not in the abstract but as something that had happened, that could happen, to him. He had once loved a girl, but that had been a long time ago, before his exile from Wales, and he could hardly remember the maiden, whose bones had surely turned to dust in the long centuries since he had looked upon her fair cheek and sighed with longing. And there was the time, not long but ineffably sweet, with Maria, his little German contessa. He had given her the dark gift, changing her to be like him, thinking they would be together forever. But she did not love the blood with the same wanton abandon. The memory was bitter. It stung Dylan to think of it now, as he almost never did, the thing that she had called him.

Evil.

The last of the trio of girls disappeared around the corner just ahead.

Perhaps his heart had been poisoned at too young an age, Dylan thought, his mood darkening in equal proportion to his quickening desire for the girls he was following. To have your family slaughtered, your kingdom stolen, and your countrymen enslaved, while you are hardly more than a boy, is not the sort of experience that predisposes one to gambol merrily at the dance, bewitched by the fair graces of a comely young wench.

Dylan came around the corner in time to see girls in the lobby of a three-story building, a dormitory. His eyes scanned the upper windows, a crooked smile crossing his face as the dark aroma of blood, as rich as fine brandy, as powerful as the smell of burning opium, rolled over him. An entire building filled with young women, an almost irresistible concentration of the only thing on the planet besides music that gave him the pleasure to lift himself from the private hell he carried with him on his wanderings.

Glyndwr was at the door now. He rested his hand on the cool metal of the handle, letting the urge, the Hunger, draw him onward.

Perhaps if he was very careful and tried not to kill any of the girls . . .

He opened the door and went inside.

29

THE JAMES RECITAL Hall was part of the interconnected chain of university buildings on the west bank of the river toward the north end of the campus. The complex, built during the 1960s, was home for the college of music and included several recital halls, the largest of which was the James, along with the big auditorium used for the subscription concert series, traveling productions, and major events.

The music school buildings were an assemblage of stark white rectangles, giant concrete tissue boxes tethered to one another with enclosed walkways framed in black steel. The only glass in the complex was at the entry to the main auditorium, with a soaring parabolic window that leaked during heavy rainstorms. The buildings had a chilly, technological feel to them. The style of architecture diminished the people, as if the students and professors were an infestation marring the inorganic monolith's abstract geometry.

There were five students waiting in the recital hall's outer vestibule. The four who sat talking to one another on a bench were in the conservatory's graduate performance program, working on their master's degrees. They gave Maggie brief, curious glances and fell easily back into their conversation. She was almost invisible to them.

Nicole Hoffmann sat alone on another bench. She didn't look in Maggie's direction but acknowledged her arrival with a smirk and brief shake of the head, amazed Maggie had the chutzpah to show her face at the audition.

Maggie added her name to the list. She was number seven. The first violinist was already inside.

The audition was technically open to all violinists at the university, though the faculty had made it plain that only the most promising students would be asked to participate. By implication, if you were not asked to audition as the soloist for the Mozart concerto, you were not welcome to audition.

Maggie had been invited, just not by Dr. Eck.

Nicole's posture stiffened when Maggie turned toward her, so she went instead to sit alone against the far wall, beneath an abstract mural that seemed to depict a horse exploding.

Auditions typically filled Maggie with a cold, jagged dread. Nobody liked standing up alone at the front of a room to have their playing put under the microscope for scrutiny. But this time was different. Sitting with her back against the bench, her right hand resting upon the case that held the Seven, Maggie felt completely at ease. Instead of hanging by her fingernails above a precipice of total panic, she felt focused and in control. Her mind was calm, her heart open; her breath came with an easy, regular rhythm, like gentle waves coming up on the beach and then receding, back and forth, in and out.

It was almost a given that one of the graduate

students would be chosen as soloist for Mozart's Concerto No. 3 in G Major for Violin. Nicole Hoffman also had a chance. She was a good violinist, the first violinist and concertmaster in the undergraduate orchestra. And Nicole looked the part of an elegant soloist—model thin, with big, almond-shaped eyes and long blond hair. Every eye would stay with her whenever she was the featured soloist, watching her dip and sway with the music, playing as if she were making love to the violin.

Maggie was the dark horse, the unexpected long shot come out of nowhere, uninvited by Dr. Eck to test herself against the others in the competition. She smiled to herself to discover it was a role she enjoyed playing.

Nicole seemed to feel Maggie's eyes upon her and glared at her. The look ordinarily would have pinned Maggie to the wall, but she was immune to Nicole's hostility, floating in the warm currents of her strangely relaxed mood. Nicole was trying to make her nervous, hoping to rattle her so she would freeze up during her audition, maybe even hoping Maggie would lose her nerve and flee before the jury got to the seventh violinist on their list. But that could only mean Nicole was afraid Maggie might actually manage to pull off a miracle at the audition. But then Nicole had been at Maggie's conservatory recital. She knew what Maggie—and the Angel violin—could do. Instead of fueling Maggie's self-doubt, Nicole had succeeded only in making her feel more confident.

Nice try, Maggie said, mouthing the words silently.

Nicole looked away, dismissing her rival with a snap of her long, perfect hair.

One of the double doors to James Recital Hall opened. A violinist—a graduate student named Kiko—came out. She walked quickly across the entry, not looking at any of the others. Maggie sensed Kiko was about to start crying, and she knew exactly how she felt. Kiko hit the bar opening the door to the outside and went out, heading up the sidewalk toward the art department so quickly that if she'd gone any faster she would have been running.

The door to the hall opened again, a hollow whoosh that during previous auditions had made Maggie think of the trapdoor opening beneath the feet of someone about to be hanged. The five heads in the entry that had been locked onto the back of the fleeing Kiko swung in the opposite direction. Dr. Katarina Eck, Maggie's teacher and the head of the violin program, stood in the door, peering severely through half-moon reading glasses at the clipboard in her left hand.

"Anna Hemerich," she read. Then, looking up, in a slightly less prosecutorial voice she said, "Anna, we are ready for you."

It was only as Anna went past her into James Recital Hall that Eck seemed to notice Maggie. She glanced at the clipboard then back at Maggie, her mouth puckering as if to take a hard drag on a cigarette.

"Maggie? A word, if you please."

Maggie got up with her violin case, which only increased Eck's impatience. Maggie refused to let the violin out of her sight unless it was in the bank vault or, when she went to her classes away from the music school, locked in a cabinet at Carter's house, which had a new state-of-the-art security system.

Katarina Eck let the door swing shut behind them

once she was inside. James Recital Hall was dark except for the stage. Maggie could see Anna there, taking her violin out of its case. The silhouettes of three people sat in the center aisle five rows back from the front. Maggie recognized Joseph Genet, the Haitian student working on his doctorate in conducting who was in charge of the orchestra. She also knew Jane Crittenden, the dean of the music school, by her outline. Seated between them was Maria Rainer, the guest conductor from Germany.

"Maggie, what are you doing here today?" Eck asked in a furious whisper.

"I came to audition, Dr. Eck," Maggie said, keeping her voice low to avoid disturbing Anna's concentration as she turned onstage. "I signed up. My name is on the list outside."

"Are you sure you want to do this?"

Maggie nodded.

Eck put her hands on her hips and leaned forward at the waist until her face was inches from Maggie's.

"I don't mean to be cruel, but you have absolutely no chance to win the part. Your conservatory recital was good enough, but, frankly, I have never heard you play anywhere near that level. You had a good day, a lucky day. Isn't it enough to be satisfied with gaining entrance to the conservatory? Do not humiliate yourself here today."

The sound of murmuring voices came from down below. It was the usual audition chitchat: *What is your name? What would you like to play for us today?*

Dr. Eck didn't know Maria Rainer had invited her to audition. *Curious,* Maggie thought. But she decided not to use it as a trump card. She was there with Maestro Rainer's encouragement, but the real reason she had come to the audition was that she wanted to be there. The boundaries and limitations seemed to fall away whenever she picked up the Seven. Maggie wanted to know just how far they could go together, the little Irish fiddler and the Angel violin.

"I want to try," Maggie said. "My arm and back problems have vanished. I've been playing for hours every day without any discomfort. I've reached a new plateau."

"You are going to embarrass the school," Eck hissed. "You are going to embarrass Dr. Crittenden and your fellow students. And you are going to embarrass *me*. I want you to leave this building immediately."

The people seated near the stage turned, looking for Dr. Eck so the next audition could begin. From the stage Anna Hemerich squinted, trying to see who seemed to be defying the iron-willed Katarina Eck.

Maggie leaned very near to the violin teacher's angry face and said in a firm, calm voice, "No."

30

DYLAN'S FOOTSTEPS WERE uncertain as he wandered across the campus, his eyes unfocused, his expression distracted, intoxicated from the tremendous volume of blood he'd consumed.

He was alone and liked it.

Mortals felt lost unless supported by the comfort of a crowd. They were comfortable only when they were within the protective confines of the flock. And when they wondered about the truth—which happened rarely enough, so far as Dylan Glyndwr could remember—they turned to the shepherd for answers.

Vampires were the shadows of their human counterparts. The best vampires, in Dylan's experience, were monsters like him, souls mistreated by the world, who found it easy to break away and live within the scarlet shadows of their own dark desires. Vampires were solitary hunters by nature, wolves existing beyond society's stifling comforts, thinking and acting for themselves, taking pleasure when they wanted it and on their own terms.

The stylized drawing of a violin materialized out of the darkness. The poster taped to a lamppost beside the sidewalk was promoting a violin recital featuring

Mozart, Brahms, and Lekeu. The recital was scheduled for that night, in the campus chapel at eight.

Perhaps the girl would be there. And maybe, Dylan thought, his ancient heart quickening, Maggie O'Hara would have the Seven with her! He knew there was little chance, really no chance, that the girl would have traveled from her university to hear the recital, but his thinking was too disorganized for him to care.

Dylan had already spotted the chapel. It was on the north side of the campus, a square, modernistic building with a tower that looked as if it could have belonged to a nuclear power station. The vampire began to move across the deserted campus, walking quickly now, with a purpose and a destination. He took the stairs two at a time, went in through the bronze doors, up another short flight of stairs, and into the chapel.

The place was almost empty. Instead of a crowd, there were fewer than a dozen people awaiting the violinist.

Americans, he thought. They had no real appreciation of culture.

Dylan made his way to the front of the chapel, past most of the people who were clustered shyly back a third of the way from the raised apron leading to the altar. He scanned the minds of the ones who might have been Maggie, but she was not there. Frowning, he slid into the second pew from the front. Across the aisle from him, an elderly couple chatted in whispers. They were the sort who liked cultural events, especially ones that were free, Dylan thought.

His mind and body still hummed with intoxication so intense that the stone walls seemed to breathe with him in imitation of life. Dylan reached his arms over the back of the pew in an unconscious imitation of the crucifix suspended over the altar.

Christ looked down on the vampire and grinned, his ribs moving in and out as he breathed along with Dylan and the building, His hands straining against the iron spikes nailing Him to the cross, but maybe this was just the gravity pulling at Him.

Dylan was hallucinating. What was that modern word? *Stoned,* he thought.

The crucifix was an interesting interpretation of Christ, almost Orthodox in the way the hands, feet, and face were elongated. The wooden Christ was suspended from the ceiling in a circular molding that must have matched the tower Dylan had seen outside. It was like a well seen from the bottom looking up, with Christ suspended in the earthly realm but only temporarily, already being recalled to heaven. Or was it meant to depict the reverse, Jesus coming back into the world? Dylan couldn't work it out.

The chapel was far longer than it was wide, a narrow space with the ceiling high above. It had been built out of massive blocks of some composite material, concrete perhaps, though it looked almost like limestone in its porous whiteness. The floor was faux green marble ribbed with black veins that crawled like snakes if Dylan looked at them too long. It was an austere space for a Catholic chapel, no decorations on the walls, the altar made of plain, unadorned wood. The cross and chalice had been removed and the altar shoved back in the corner. The choir was farther on, beyond a head-high wrought-iron screen of the sort more common in an Orthodox church. The pews were made of simple oak with a light stain.

Dylan had lost his faith and his kingdom with the same arc of the English sword that lopped off his father's head. He had been in churches since then, but always for his own purposes, never God's. He had been wicked, more wicked than the worst mortal man could be in a lifetime, in a score of lifetimes. And yet he did not feel that the sacred space rejected him, wanted him gone. The church was for sinners, he had been taught as a child, and who could be a greater sinner than he? He had more right to be in the chapel that night than anyone.

But had he been "evil"? What was *evil,* anyway? Wasn't it anything that threatened the weak and took advantage away from the strong?

The suspended Christ's golden eyes sparkled, as if in confirmation that Dylan's keen mind had penetrated the truth.

Mortal law didn't apply to Dylan because he was not human. Did the laws of Turkey apply to the French? Was an American cowboy expected to obey the elaborate court rituals of the Imperial Japanese household? *Absurd!*

Dylan had lied, stolen, and seduced, and without the least sense of regret or remorse. And he had killed. He killed whenever the urge took him. He had no idea how many he had killed. To keep an accounting of the lives he had taken would have indicated it was an occurrence he considered worth noting. He did not pay attention to the number of beautiful young women he had drained dry of their blood for the same reason he had no clue how many glasses of wine he had swallowed over the centuries, as if mere alcohol had any power over his body.

What did a mortal life matter to Dylan Glyndwr? God might know when every sparrow fell to earth, but such things were of no consequence to the vampire.

But there was more. The look in Christ's eye hinted at it. The very chapel seemed to crouch down in anticipation of Dylan's stumbling onto the next great revelation.

The vampire, like the carving of Christ suspended over the altar, caught in limbo between heaven and earth, was almost a divine being. He was immortal, yet tethered to the earth. His only peers were angels and devils.

Go on, the crucified Christ seemed to urge.

Unless, he thought, he belonged to the family of angels—or devils.

Dylan slumped down in his pew. Angel or devil—he did not need to think about that very hard to know to which category he belonged. It did not occur to him that, like the man he had once been, the choice was his to make.

A girl came onto the altar, which would serve as the stage. The silence in the chapel seemed to swell, pregnant with hidden meaning. She introduced the violinist and her distinguished accompanist, who came onto the stage as she spoke. The girl sat in the straight-back chair beside the piano to turn pages for the accompanist.

They began with Mozart's Sonata in F Major for Violin and Piano.

"Ah," Dylan whispered to himself, his brooding instantly forgotten. He had known Wolfgang many, many years ago. The boy had been a remarkable violinist, as had his father, a famous pedagogue whose treatise on the violin was still respected. Mozart had once written a concerto for Dylan.

The violinist played expressively but with tasteful restraint. Dylan could hear the influence of Menuhin in her playing. She had studied with the great violinist. He could tell. And here she was, playing for no one. The piano was a little out of tune, but the accompanist did a good job, touching lightly on the problem notes, supporting the violinist as her playing moved from this realm into the transcendental realm of art.

The second selection was Brahms's Sonata in F Minor for Clarinet and Piano. It was, as Dylan had suspected, a transcription putting the violin in the lead voice. The arrangement's adagio movement dwelt mainly in the violin's low, darker register, the violinist playing with great emotion on the lower strings up on the neck, evoking a rich, mellow passion that touched Dylan.

Dylan blinked to clear his eyes during the Brahms adagio. He leaned back and shut his eyes, the music pouring over him like water. The blood high had started to fall away, leaving him feeling lost. Lost memories floated up in his mind, his father and his mother, with feelings of tenderness and mercy he had not known in centuries.

He opened his eyes to the face of Christ looking down on him. The solution seemed close at hand. It was as simple as a change of heart, a change of mind.

If only it were that simple!

The Angel violin was so near that Dylan could almost *feel* its sublime presence, though he knew that was only the blood playing with him.

There would be plenty of time for Dylan to look within his poisoned soul, once he possessed the Seven.

31

"THEY ARE REALLY very good."

"The first audition did not go so good, I think, Maestro."

"It was just a case of the nerves, Katarina," Maria replied with American-style informality, though it was evident the professor preferred to be called Dr. Eck. They were standing in a group at the edge of the stage: the guest conductor from the Berlin Philharmonic; Dr. Jane Crittenden, dean of the music school; Dr. Katarina Eck, the chairman of the violin and viola program; and Joseph Genet, a doctoral candidate in conducting from Port-au-Prince, Haiti.

"The first violinist, Kiko, should we invite her back and give her a second chance?"

Katarina and Joseph both looked toward their dean.

"That would hardly be fair," Jane said.

"What do you think, Joseph?" Maria pronounced his name the way they did in Haiti: *Jo-sway.*

"I think Dr. Crittenden is correct," he said. "If a second audition is given to Kiko, then a second chance must be given to exactly everybody."

"I suppose you are right," Maria said. "You are to be congratulated on your program here. Your students have exceeded my best expectations. You are so far from the coasts and major cities, I do not know how you have done it. Deciding on a soloist will require some thought."

"It's a good problem to have," Joseph said.

"I quite agree, *Jo-sway.*" Maria turned to Eck. "Are there any other auditions?"

"One more," Eck said, sounding not at all happy, but then she never did.

"I thought we were finished," Jane said, frowning.

"We had a late signup for the audition," Eck said. "Someone unexpected: Maggie O'Hara."

"Better call her in," the dean said, checking her watch. "Maria and I have reservations at the University Club." Then, to Maria, she said, "Maggie had a rather exceptional recital recently to get into the conservatory program."

"I heard," Maria said.

"I think it was a fluke," Eck said not at all kindly.

"Then we shall have to see for ourselves," Maria said. "Call her in and let her play. When it's over we can applaud her for her fortitude and ambition, if not for the eloquence of her playing."

Eck trudged up the aisle to collect the latecomer.

The door at the rear of James Recital Hall opened and closed. Maria heard two sets of footsteps descend the aisle sloping toward the stage. Maria looked over her shoulder and smiled. Maggie returned her smile, and Maria could see that she was focused and yet relaxed, qualities found in the best players but seldom in the inexperienced.

"This will be interesting," she whispered to Joseph.

Maggie took out her violin and got ready to perform,

attaching the shoulder rest to the instrument, tightening the bow, applying rosin to the horsehairs. She touched the bow to her strings to check her tuning. As the first notes rang out—the open G string, then the D, A, and E—a strange electricity moved up Maria Rainer's spine, as if a ghost from her past were calling to her. Maggie O'Hara played the G and D together, then the D and A, and A and E, pausing to adjust the E string.

Maria closed her eyes, her hands gripping the arms of the theater chair. Listening to those first sweet notes, floating down as if from heaven above, she momentarily forgot who she was. She had been so many different people in so many different places, all of them unique and yet essentially the same. Now it was as if she had broken free from the bonds of both identity and time and was simultaneously living in multiple places in the present but also in the past. Her lives telescoped away then fell back, light refracted by a prism then brought back sharply into focus. The shock of it all took her breath away, but then came the exhilaration as powerful as the first taste of blood after a long fast. There truly was a river, a hidden thread that the soul followed as it traveled through time and space. There was no other way to explain the uncanny coincidences that had visited her throughout her long life as a woman and a vampire.

"Sorry," Maggie O'Hara said from the stage, as if she needed to apologize for tuning.

Maria felt Jane leaning close to her. The other woman whispered in her ear, asking if she was all right.

Maria opened her eyes and saw, really saw, Maggie O'Hara for the first time. Young, good-looking though no great beauty, intelligent, anxious to please, and straining at the seams of her being with newly released talent. There was something magical about her eagerness, but Maria knew that was the violin's magic. She would have known it anywhere, even from a few notes played to adjust the Angel violin's tuning.

"Play a three-octave G scale for us, please," Jane asked. All of the candidates had been asked to begin this way.

Maggie O'Hara played the three-octave scale, the intonation spot-on perfect. She immediately went into the major and minor arpeggios that went with the scale, not to show off but out of habit, and, Maria knew, because the *violin* wanted to play them.

Such tone! Maria had waited a long time for this day, knowing it might never come but hoping beyond hope that the Seven would be found. Maggie's playing of the formal part of the audition was flawless. Some believed it was impossible to play an Angel poorly. Perhaps the proof of that was onstage for them. Maria leaned slightly forward in her chair, thinking that this must have been how Crusoe felt when he first found footsteps on the beach of the island where he had been marooned.

"What are you going to play for us today, Miss O'Hara?"

"I thought I would do some Bach for you. I have a new violin, and it seems to be especially fond of Bach. I hope you don't think it sounds silly for me to say that."

"Not in the least," Maria said, returning the girl's smile. "I know exactly what you mean."

She settled back into her seat to see what magic

Maggie O'Hara and her violin could work with each other, wondering, for the few seconds it took Maggie to put her bow to the strings, what became of the lover who so long ago addicted her to music _and_ blood in the same passionate embrace.

32

THE YOUNG MAN with the ponytail looked up from behind the counter when the door to the wine shop opened.

"I was wondering if you could be so good as to give me directions to this address," the visitor said, putting a card on the counter with an address written in elegant cursive.

"You're not from around here, are you?" the young man said, trying to be friendly.

"No," Dylan Glyndwr answered tightly, the muscles in his jaw tensing. "I am here for a brief visit. An errand really."

Curious, Dylan thought, how often he needed to restrain his temper recently. He credited it to the Seven's proximity. Angel violins were strange, magical instruments. He had not killed at all during the brief time he had possessed the previous Angel. All he had cared about for those happy weeks was playing music. Dylan had even come to regret, though only a little, his having murdered the instrument's previous owner, the old Italian luthier. It took him a moment to remember the man's name. It had been a long time ago.

Silvio.

"It's just a couple blocks from here," the young man said. He glanced up from the card, regarding Dylan closely. "Do you mind if I ask who you are looking for?"

Dylan held his opposite's stare, pushing past his eyes and into his mind. The young man's thoughts were discolored with a jealousy that tinted his mind an unpleasant shade of sickly green.

"Why do you ask, Peter?"

"I know a woman who has an apartment . . ." His eyes grew wide. "How did you know my name?"

"It's written on your name tag, as plain as the nose on your face: Peter Hill."

"I'm not wearing a name . . ."

Peter Hill looked down at his shirt as if to assure himself that he had not gone mad. The vampire was already on the other side of the counter, his hand on Peter Hill's shoulder, gripping him so hard that it hurt, forcing him down to the floor. The feeble resistance disappeared the instant Dylan placed his other hand upon the young man's forehead, plunging into his mind with such rude violence that Peter Hill began to shake with a seizure keyed by the rough disruption of his brain's electrical patterns.

Ten thousand bright images exploded in Dylan's mind as he tore through Peter Hill's memories. It was like watching a motion picture projected almost too fast to make out anything. Yet it was all there for the vampire to view in exquisite detail that not even Peter would have been able to recall—the tastes, the touches, the sounds, the smells—all as they had been originally experienced by the man Dylan held down on the floor.

It was odd luck that Dylan had happened upon Maggie O'Hara's old lover. Peter had not seen Maggie for weeks and knew nothing of the Seven. Still, his memories provided Dylan with information about the girl and her habits that could prove useful. The vampire knew which practice room Maggie liked best at the music school. Yellow roses were her favorite flowers. She did not care for perfume. She adored poetry and Mozart. That was something they had in common.

Peter Hill's body continued to shake after Dylan stood up to go, a film of frothy spittle coating the young man's lips.

The door opened.

Dylan looked over his shoulder, hoping to see Maggie. An overweight man came into the shop, his brow furrowed like a washboard as he looked around. *The manager,* Dylan thought. *No, the owner.*

"Can you help me?" Dylan asked. "The clerk seems to be having some kind of seizure. He's behind the counter."

The man peered over the counter, suspicious of a trick. He was not as stupid as he looked, Dylan observed.

"Does he have epilepsy?"

"If he does, I sure as hell didn't know it," the man said. He snatched the telephone off its cradle and dialed 911. Dylan slipped out while the owner was talking to the operator, asking for an ambulance to be sent.

Maggie O'Hara's second-floor apartment was only two blocks away. It was a big white frame house that had been converted into apartments. Through the front door, up the creaking stairs, was a wooden door on the right with a metal "4" fastened to it. He could see the one-room apartment as if he'd been there dozens of times—as Peter Hill had been. Dylan was familiar with the crowded table where they had studied, the chair where he always sat, the bed where he made love to Maggie.

The vampire took the stairs two at a time, excited by his faux memories of Maggie O'Hara's amorous charms. He had come thousands of miles for the Angel, but perhaps there would be time for him to pleasure himself with her before taking her blood— and her violin—and returning to Europe.

He rapped three times on the door, the sound sharp, insistent. He had hoped to come to her while she was practicing so that the sound of the Seven would entice him onward to an exquisite banquet of earthly delights.

But on the other side of the door to apartment number 4, there was only silence.

33

MAGGIE O'HARA AND Maria Rainer walked along the river toward the sculpture garden outside the college of art: two women, one dressed in an expensive yet simply tailored peasant's skirt, the other wearing jeans, a violin case slung over her shoulder. They found a bench overlooking the river and sat down. It was the end of an Indian-summer day, the warm sun and blue sky holding back the frosts and bitter winds that would arrive soon. The water was like glass, though leaves fallen from overhanging trees—brown, red, orange— floated slowly by, riding the lazy current.

"You have been given a special gift," Maria said.

Meaning talent, Maggie thought. But she had found that only because of an even greater gift: the Angel violin.

"You must use your gift wisely, Maggie. Treated with respect, it will take you anywhere you wish to go. If you fail to honor it, it will bring you only disappointment and grief."

"I promise to work hard," Maggie replied in a solemn voice. "I have dedicated my life to the violin. It *is* my life."

Maria's hand covered hers on the bench. As always

her touch was firm and warm almost to the point of being feverish. Maria Rainer's body seemed to burn with the passionate intensity she brought to conducting. The rehearsal they had just finished was unlike any Maggie had ever experienced. Driven by Maestro Rainer's precise conducting and vigorous encouragement, the orchestra had built together toward the climax like lovers locked together in passion. Maggie had improvised cadenzas so dazzling yet bright and pure that she felt as if her body had been possessed by the ghost of Mozart. She and the Seven had become one, playing, breathing, feeling, moving together: one heart, one soul, one love, one song. Maria had seen that. No, Maggie thought, correcting herself: Maria had *caused* it.

"I am going to suggest something to you, Maggie, that you may find shocking."

Maggie's look remained fastened on Maria's green eyes. The sense of friendship and intimacy between them had been as effortless as it was spontaneous. She did not think Maria would suggest anything improper—Maggie was entirely conventional in her ideas about love—yet she was not of a mind to reject anything the other woman might have suggested out of hand. Maria Rainer was an esteemed conductor who had reached down from the Olympian heights to pluck Maggie from obscurity and set her feet on the road to achieving everything she had ever dreamed. That alone made her want to kiss Maria Rainer, if only out of gratitude.

"I want you to think about quitting school."

Maggie blinked. "What?"

"Dr. Eck is an excellent teacher, if somewhat old-fashioned and unyielding in her methods," Maria said. "And Jane Crittenden has started an excellent conservatory program here. But neither Eck nor the level of training you'll get at the conservatory is nearly good enough for you, Maggie. You have something that needs special nurturing."

"And if I drop out, then what?" Maggie asked.

"You could come with me to Germany, where I will personally undertake to see you have everything you need to develop your playing to the fullest capacity of your talent."

The offer took words away from Maggie. Despite her relative youth, Maria Rainer was acknowledged to be the best of the youngest generation of conductors. Critics compared her favorably with Toscanini, Bernstein, Solti. Her offer to take Maggie under her wing was unimaginably generous—and fortunate. Which only made it all the more absurd that the image of Carter should pop into her head at that moment. She was more than a little fond of Carter, but it would be silly for her to reject the opportunity of a lifetime because of someone she'd gone to bed with a few times.

"I don't know what to say," Maggie said, stammering a little. "I feel like I should pinch myself to see if I'm awake and this is really happening."

"Do not say anything, my dear. Just think about it. You don't have to decide now."

"I'm incredibly flattered you would make such an offer."

"The honor would be mine," Maria said. "There have been only a few times I have heard someone play with so much expression and emotion. And the tone you get from your violin—it is like listening to an angel sing."

"I have to admit that some of the credit belongs to my violin."

Maria raised an eyebrow.

"It is a very rare old Italian violin my grandfather brought home after World War Two. It's funny the way you described it as like listening to an angel. That's supposed to be the thing about violins made by Archangelo Serafino. According to legend, they sound like angels. They call them 'Angel' violins."

"Yes, I know the story. I started in music as a violinist before I discovered that my real talent was conducting. Which one of the Angels do you have? They are known by the numbers designating the order in which they were made, I believe."

"I have the Seven. You look startled. Is something wrong?"

"It is only that I heard the Seven was lost in World War Two. I had heard it was either destroyed in the bombing or lost in some cave with other hidden Nazi loot."

"My grandfather bought it from a German officer. The details are sketchy. I don't have any papers for it, but I've researched it and there is no dispute over ownership. It had belonged to Hermann Göring, who was pretty notorious."

"I know," Maria said, looking away.

"How it got from Göring to the anonymous officer is not known, but there's nothing to indicate it was stolen. There was talk that Göring stole it, too, but that's never been more than a rumor. Nobody knows where or how he got it. To be completely honest, all of that makes me a little nervous. I'm afraid of being blindsided by something from out of the blue—some claim or bit of information. I honestly don't think I could live without the Seven."

"Then that's all the more reason you need a powerful patron behind you," Maria said. "I don't recall reading about the Seven being found. I would think the discovery would generate a good deal of interest."

"I've kept it quiet for now," Maggie said. "I'm not trying to hide it so much as avoid the distraction. Getting into the conservatory, auditioning to be your soloist—there's only a certain amount of stress I can cope with at one time."

"I understand perfectly. The Seven and its angelic sisters are akin to the Holy Grail for collectors. The announcement that one was found will be very big news indeed." She gave Maggie a shrewd look. "Partnering news about the Seven being found with the story of its young owner's debut in a major European concert series would make your name internationally known overnight at the start of your career."

"Oh, my," was all Maggie could say, feeling a little faint.

"But there is much work to be done before you are ready for that, my dear. I will not mislead you about that. However, under my tutelage you will be ready, and rest assured you will not begin your professional career before it is time for you to become one of the world's preeminent violinists."

Maggie forced herself to take a slow, deep breath. That was why she felt light-headed. She was starting to hyperventilate.

"It is a lot to think about, so do not try to wrap your

mind around it too quickly," Maria said, gently stroking Maggie's hair. "We will take it one step at a time. We will do it together: you, I, and your Angel violin."

Maggie closed her eyes as her friend and mentor continued to stroke her auburn hair. It was a soothing feeling, like being comforted by her mother, though she had been so young when her mother died that she didn't remember much more than what it was like to be a child and feel safe and protected.

"If you would like to play the Seven sometime . . ." Maggie said after a bit.

"Perhaps," Maria responded, "but not too soon. You play the Angel so well, my dear. I could make it sing, but never like you. Besides," she said after a pause, "I am afraid that once I played such an exquisite violin, I might not want to give it back."

34

IT WAS ELEVEN o'clock when Dylan Glyndwr returned to the house where Maggie O'Hara had an apartment. He stood in the street, looking up at her dark windows.

The front door was unlocked. Dylan went in and up the stairs. The smell of rice steaming came from the door opposite the O'Hara woman's apartment. He tried her door. It was locked. Dylan closed his eyes and focused his attention on the brass dead bolt, feeling the tumblers slowly start to move, using his mind to feel for places that needed to line up for the lock to release. After a few moments Dylan heard a muffled click. He turned the doorknob and went into the darkened apartment, closing the door quickly and silently behind himself.

The vampire looked around in the dark, taking the space in with a single sweeping glance. The humbleness of the room, decorated in worn, secondhand furniture, bordered on the pathetic. Its owner's only indulgence—and hint of personality—was a framed poster of a violin from the series Dylan had seen advertised in *Strad* magazine.

He moved slowly through the room, touching his fingertips to the bedspread, the tabletop, breathing in

Maggie O'Hara's essence. The vampire's senses were acute enough that he would be able to pick her out even in a crowd.

The bathroom was obviously a converted closet. Dylan shook his head. It was difficult to imagine a human living in such reduced circumstances, even if she was a poor student. He picked up the hairbrush sitting on the sink. Even in the darkness his preternatural eyes picked out the ruby glint of the few strands of auburn hair trapped within the bristles. He brought the brush to his nose and breathed in, filling himself with the delicate scent of her skin and the faint but distinctive perfume of Maggie O'Hara's blood wafting faintly before him, all but undetectable.

Dylan touched the bar of soap in the dish on the sink. It was dry and firm. He did not see a toothbrush. He opened the medicine cabinet on the wall, a cheap metal box. It lacked some of the objects he would have expected to find in a young woman's bathroom, conspicuous gaps among the cotton balls and other beautification accoutrements that indicated Maggie O'Hara had gone away.

With a groan, he returned to the cramped living room that represented the total of Maggie O'Hara's meager personal space in the world. He knew better than to expect to find the Angel violin left unguarded, but he forced himself to look. Dylan opened the door to the half-size refrigerator last, and simply so that he could assure himself that he had not overlooked a potential hiding place. The only thing inside were two containers of yogurt and a small container of milk. Dylan opened the carton and smelled. The milk was sour, indicating the girl had probably not been home for days. He threw the milk back into the refrigerator and slammed the door.

"Why do you constantly deny me!" Dylan cried, shaking his fists at the ceiling.

The question, addressed to God, went unanswered.

Dylan left the apartment, no longer concerned with being quiet. He rapped on the door across the hall. An Asian man answered.

"Excuse me, but I have an urgent need to contact Maggie O'Hara, the woman who lives across the hall. A family emergency, you understand. Could you tell me where to find her?"

Though he had trouble understanding the man's English, it was plain the Asian had only a nodding acquaintance with Miss O'Hara and knew, from an off-hand comment from the landlord, that she was a music student. He suggested Dylan inquire at the school in the morning, and gave him vague directions about finding it.

Dylan had no intention of waiting until morning. He should have already had the Seven in his hands, but instead he could almost feel it slipping away from him to the sound of mocking laughter from the powers that rule the universe.

It was late and the streets deserted as Dylan went through the neighborhood and down the hill toward the pedestrian bridge crossing the river. The night had become chilly, but he scarcely noticed; what was cold to a vampire? He hurried past a garden filled with modern sculpture—incomprehensible objects that spoke to Dylan only of the chaos in the world.

He expected the doors to the music school to be locked at that hour, but strangely enough they were open. Dylan went in, feeling that the place was nearly deserted. From the distance came the sound of someone rehearsing Debussy on the piano. Dylan started down the hall, his chin slightly lifted, his eyes sharp with alertness.

A janitor came out of one of the rehearsal rooms, pushing a cart filled with trash—paper, soda cans, cardboard coffee cups from a vending machine. Dylan could smell the vodka on the man despite the wad of spearmint gum in his mouth. It was impressive that he could even stand up considering the amount of alcohol he'd consumed.

Dylan continued down the corridor, past the darkened practice studios, until he sensed something that made him stop. He put his hand on the door handle, feeling the trances of a faint psychic buzz. Definitely female. If it was not Miss O'Hara, it was someone very much like her.

He opened the door and flipped the switch, squinting against the sudden glare of fluorescent light. It was a claustrophobic space, even more claustrophobic than Maggie O'Hara's apartment. Into the tiny room, the walls lined with acoustic tile to absorb the noise, were jammed a studio upright piano of undistinguished vintage, a piano bench, two folding metal chairs, a music stand, and a small table whose top was marred with coffee stains.

Dylan closed his eyes and drew a slow, deep breath in through his nose.

She had been there, Maggie O'Hara, her scent lingering in the air like the scent of vanilla in a kitchen after baking.

The vampire turned off the lights and stood in the

darkness, his eyes closed. The tip of his tongue poked out of his mouth, like a viper sampling the air for the electromagnetic emanations of its prey.

The intoxicating perfume of the girl's blood was still quite strong in the airless, poorly ventilated room. It was spicier than what he'd sampled in her apartment.

He held his hands extended before him, the fingers splayed wide, receptive to the most ephemeral remnant of presence.

And though it was infinitesimally faint, he was sure he could feel it: the lingering psychic imprint left behind after the Angel violin's eternally exquisite song.

35

THE HOUSES ON McClellan Street were dark by the time Maggie O'Hara drove home. A flickering blue glow could be seen through the upstairs windows of a few houses, the final minutes of *The Tonight Show* or *Letterman* playing for people who had fallen asleep with the TV still on.

The evening's rehearsal started at seven and was supposed to end at nine, but Maria Rainer kept them over until half-past. Student musicians tended to look at their watches and shuffle when practices ran long, but nobody minded putting in the extra time that night. The guest conductor seemed to possess a magic key for unlocking the nuances in Mozart's music. Maggie had heard the violin concerto hundreds of times, but never played as well as the university orchestra had done it that night in rehearsal.

Afterward, Maggie retreated to her favorite practice studio at the music school to work on the passages where Maria had asked the string players to breathe together. Maggie had never put much conscious effort into coordinating breathing and bowing—it seemed an issue more for woodwinds and brass than a violinist—but she was amazed at the difference it made in her phrasing. She spent two hours with the music before remembering she'd promised to meet Carter by ten for a glass of wine. For once she wasn't the last to go home, she thought, hearing someone practicing Debussy on the piano. She stopped at Romanov's to make sure Carter wasn't still waiting for her, but he had already gone. Hoping he wasn't too upset with her, Maggie carried her violin case back to the car and headed toward the leafy subdivision and the house she'd been sharing with Carter since they became lovers. She liked Carter a lot, and the state-of-the-art alarm system he'd installed in his home allowed her to keep the Seven with her.

McClellan wound its way among a series of rolling hills above the river, the lots large and wooded. The people in the neighborhood had a lot of money, not as much as Carter, of course, but plenty, the houses all costing at least a half million dollars. In summer, when the trees filled out, it was almost impossible to see the large houses with their three- and four-car garages from the street. The house where Maggie was staying was a big step up from her one-bedroom apartment, and from her late grandfather's brick-faced 1950s Elmhurst split-level. Not that it was *her* house, of course, though Carter was plainly interested in a long-term commitment. And so was Maggie, though Maria's invitation for her to come to Berlin to study was a huge complication.

Maggie pulled into the long drive that curved around to the left, following the arc of a small creek running along the boundary of Carter's property. She still had to work that out—whether she would go to Berlin. The opportunity seemed too much to pass up.

But on the other hand, there was something special developing between her and Carter.

The outline of the house, set halfway up a hill beyond an expanse of sloping lawn and naturalistic landscaping, emerged from the copse of oak trees. The lights were out. Carter was already in bed, although Maggie guessed he was still up reading, waiting for her. She was not too tired to make love, if he wasn't mad she'd stood him up. Carter was understanding about her obsessive practice habits. If he wasn't, he wouldn't have been able to tolerate her for even the short time they'd been together.

Maggie pressed the button on the garage-door opener clipped to the visor. Nothing happened. *The battery must be dead,* she thought. She'd have to park in the drive. There was a bite to the night air. *It might get cold enough to frost,* she thought, heading for the front door with her keys in hand. An owl cried somewhere in the night. Another owl replied from the distance, a wild haunting sound, as if the raptors were exulting over their nightly kills.

The porch light was dark. It must have burned out, since Carter always left it on for her. She briefly considered whether he was truly angry at her and if she should have gone to her apartment, where she hadn't been for days. But Carter wasn't like that. He didn't get mad. She'd never seen him upset. She would have to be careful not to take advantage of his good disposition.

She was halfway to the door when she realized someone was standing next to it, leaning against the wall between the house and one of the pillars holding up the overhang, hidden in the shadows.

The breath caught in her throat so that she gave a startled gasp as she wrapped her arms around the case that cradled the Angel violin.

He moved into view. He was about Carter's height, but it obviously wasn't Carter. His hair fell to his shoulders and he wore a suit. Carter wore his hair in a short, athletic crop; he certainly owned some suits, but Maggie had never seen him wear one.

"Do not be afraid," the man said, standing squarely in front of the door. He spoke with a British accent. He had a strong, pleasant voice, like an actor in a PBS drama, but what was he doing standing in the dark outside the door at midnight?

Maggie could scream, but who would hear her? Probably not Carter, on the other side of the house in the master bedroom, the windows closed against the chill, music playing softly in the background—assuming he hadn't had a few drinks waiting for Maggie to show up at the bar and gone to sleep. The neighborhood's seclusion no longer seemed to be anything but a menace.

She took a step backward, wondering if she could beat the man to her car. She remembered the outline of a car parked back on McClellan. That had struck her as odd—there were never cars parked on McClellan—but not to the degree that she had thought about it. The intruder had parked there, short of the drive, and walked up to the house unnoticed.

"Please, Maggie, I will not hurt you."

There was just enough light for her to see him smile. He had very white teeth.

But his voice . . . it had a soothing, almost hypnotic quality. Maggie felt the alarm begin to run out of her.

He knew her name, was well dressed, friendly, and good-looking, as she saw when he came toward her. She was overreacting, too much big-city paranoia in her for her own good. There wasn't anything menacing about the man, whoever he was. There was even something familiar about him, as if they were old friends and she was simply having trouble remembering. That was the way it was sometimes even with people you knew well: remove them from a familiar context and you had to look at them twice to gain a sense of recognition.

A car came down the street, traveling very fast for McClellan from the sound of it. It turned into the drive behind them, the tires chirping when they hit the curb too fast. The headlights lit the front of the house as the car came around the curve, making the stranger squint and look away, holding up one hand to shield his eyes. Now that Maggie could really see him, she thought of Hugh Grant, but with long hair and a bit of an edge to him. It was strange to see such quantities of culture and physical strength embodied in the same person. From her limited experience with men, they tended to be either strong and rugged or intelligent and sophisticated but soft. Carter came close to combining the two types, but even he had a lot more sailor and mountain climber in him than violin aficionado and poetry junkie.

The car door slammed.

Maggie looked over her shoulder, expecting to see Carter arriving home late, which would have explained the dark house. But it was Maria whom she saw coming around the front end of the sleek black BMW sedan, hurrying as if Maggie and the handsome man would explode if allowed to come into personal contact. Still, there was no anxiety in Maria's voice when she spoke, talking in a bantering tone to the man suddenly standing behind Maggie. How had he gotten so close so quickly? she wondered.

"Call it a woman's intuition, but I thought I might find you here," Maria said.

"Is it really you?" he said, sounding as if he was having trouble believing his eyes.

"Yes, it is. It has been a long time, a very long time indeed."

The oddness of the moment intruded upon the curiously dreamy mood possessing Maggie's mind.

"Excuse me, Maria," Maggie said, shaking her head as if to clear the cobwebs. "Am I in the middle of something?"

"Not at all, my dear. I would like to introduce you to an old friend who happens to be one of the world's finest living violinists, though he keeps a rather low profile."

"Oh?" Maggie smiled as she turned back toward the man. He looked like a violinist. She was surprised she hadn't noticed it before: passionate eyes set into the intelligent face, fierce and sensitive at the same time. And he had an artist's hands—long, slender fingers that surrendered nothing in the way of strength and power for their evident gracefulness. Maggie was unable to read the man's expression. It was probably just the famous British reserve coming to the fore, but he seemed remote and even momentarily hostile, although she could not imagine why, when he had just been speaking to her in such a kind, almost seductive tone.

Maria stood beside Maggie and rested her hand

gently on the young woman's shoulder the way one would with someone young and inexperienced and in need of friendship and protection.

"Maggie O'Hara," Maria said, "I would like you to meet Dylan Glyndwr."

36

A MAN APPEARED in the kitchen doorway wearing black Nike running shorts, pulling a T-shirt over his head. He was tanned and well muscled although not overly developed, a perfect body, like a mountain climber, yoga instructor, or ballet dancer, Maria thought. A body like that *and* money—little wonder Maggie was smitten.

"Hi, Carter," Maggie was saying. "I hope we didn't wake you up."

"I was reading." He gave them all an easy smile. He meant it. Maggie went to him and they exchanged a light kiss.

"I hope you don't mind, Carter. I thought we'd all have a nightcap."

"Great idea." Carter went to the man, who was closest, his hand extended. "I'm Carter Dunne."

"Dylan Glyndwr."

"Great to meet you, Dylan." He turned to Maria. "You must be Maria Rainer. It's an honor."

"It is a delight to meet you, Carter. Maggie has told me how supportive you've been of her and the unusual trust that has been given her."

Maria nodded toward the table where Maggie had

set the violin case. Dylan Glyndwr's eyes were fixed upon it the way a hungry wolf would regard a lamb. As long as Maria was there, he would not dare to make a move on the violin—or to harm Maggie and Carter.

"I'm happy to do what I can," Carter said. "It's a pretty big honor to have anything to do with such an important instrument."

His hand was much larger than Maria's, his grip firm and strong, his skin cool and dry. Maria felt the strong surge of vitality flow into her where their auras joined. There was an extraordinary amount of life force in each of the mortals; to drink of their blood would be to share the thrill of the distilled elixir of life's purest essence. Maria was too disciplined a vampire to be tempted, but she could see the same was hardly true of her Welsh counterpart. Given the opportunity, Dylan Glyndwr would likely drain them both dry and be gone—taking the Angel violin with him.

"You are all coming from the orchestra rehearsal?"

"We finished about nine-thirty," Maggie said, a blush coming into her fair cheeks that Maria found quite becoming. "I stopped off at the music school to go over some of the parts we worked on tonight. I'm afraid I completely lost track of the time. I'm sorry I didn't meet you, Carter."

"It doesn't matter," he said with a wave of a hand.

"Dylan is an old friend," Maria said, glancing at him briefly out of the corner of her eye. "Someone at the music school told him I might have come back here with Maggie after the rehearsal. It was really just dumb luck that I ran into the same student and arrived here about the same time as Maggie and Dylan."

Maria gave Maggie and Carter her most innocent-looking smile. She was lying, but they accepted the claim at face value.

Maria had felt vaguely ill at ease all day, but it was not until the rehearsal that she realized the source of her discomfiture was the presence of another vampire in the small city on the prairie. Vampires could always tell when another of their kind was nearby. Maria's sensitivity for other *vampiri* had grown increasingly acute over the years, yet she had not known it was Dylan Glyndwr. She never would have guessed it would be Dylan.

"I just bought a case of Ravenswood merlot," Carter said, slipping effortlessly into the role of host, gracious though they'd turned up uninvited on his doorstep at the witching hour. "I could open a bottle. Or there's some chardonnay in the fridge downstairs."

"It's too chilly for that," Maggie said. "Open the merlot."

"I could get you a brandy or something else."

"The Ravenswood sounds lovely," Maria said.

Carter looked to the other vampire, who continued to stare at the violin case. "Dylan?" he asked.

"Yes? Excuse me. I do apologize." He shot Maria a sidelong glance, realizing she must know what he was thinking, although she had made no effort to intrude into the privacy of his thoughts. "It has been a long day for me. Anything would be fine. Whatever you are having, Carter."

Maria continued to stare at Dylan, a half smile on her face to disguise her concern. It had taken her more than a mortal lifetime to recover from her previous encounter with Glyndwr. He was brilliant, of course, but deeply troubled and ultimately dangerous. That made him a bit of an anomaly. Vampires attracted to the darker side of the blood's song tended not to survive long. Maria wished she could tell herself he'd changed his ways, but she knew from her first look into his eyes that he hadn't. Dylan Glyndwr was a killer.

Maria had expected something like this to happen from the moment she realized Maggie O'Hara had the Seven. It was part of the Angel violins' uncanny power that they attracted both the best and the worst of mortals and vampires. The paradox for Maria was that objects representing the greatest good proved irresistible to the most evil and degenerate souls. How else to explain something like Hermann Göring's passion to collect the world's greatest art treasures, including the Seven?

Dylan had gone back to staring at the violin case, an object of almost palpable lust for him. He either did not know or did not care that the Seven could find its fullest voice only in the possession of someone innocent and pure. That was why the Angel sang so sweetly in Maggie O'Hara's hands, Maria thought. You could walk the earth for a long time before you would find anyone as humble and good at heart as Maggie, who had dedicated her life to the violin with the same simple devotion of a young woman giving herself to God. It was ironic but fitting that the Seven came to her only after a long period of pain and struggle. But in this, too, there was meaning, Maria thought, for one could not truly become an artist without knowing suffering.

"Dylan," Maggie said—he looked up at her, startled, as if caught in the midst of an illicit act—"is one of the world's leading violinists and an old friend of Maria's."

"I thought the name was familiar," Carter said, but it was evident to Maria, and also to the other vampire, that he was just being polite. "Do you have a specialty?"

"I mainly play baroque chamber music," he answered. "It is not extremely popular with the public, though I find it artistically rewarding."

"Carter owns the violin shop in town. He has an excellent luthier on the staff, so if you have any repair needs or are in the market for a violin, talk to Carter."

"Thanks for the marketing help, Mag," Carter said teasingly as he fitted the corkscrew into the top of a bottle from the wine rack on the counter that divided the kitchen from the airy great room, with its high peaked windows overlooking the creek running by somewhere in the darkness. "Gianni Felici is a topnotch luthier. If you need any work done while you're in town, Dylan, I'll be happy to fix you up gratis."

"Your offer is kind. As a matter of fact, I had Gianni work on one of my instruments. He is a master."

"Really," Carter said, and grinned. There was a soft pop as the cork came out of the bottle. "It's a small world."

The vampire looked at Maria and nodded.

"When was that?"

"Long ago," Dylan said. "I doubt he would remember."

"I'm lucky to have him. He came with the shop when I bought it as an investment. The only reason he didn't buy it is because he's thinking about retiring. To tell you the truth, I don't think he'll ever hang it up. Gianni loves the work too much."

His eyes were on the glasses as he poured the wine.

He did it carefully, paying attention, as if it mattered. Maria admired that. If pouring a glass of wine correctly didn't matter, what did?

"And I guess I understand it," Carter went on as he served the wine. "I've really gotten bitten by the bug myself. I guess that's what happens when you learn to appreciate good violins." His eyes moved to Maggie and softened. "And when you meet some really good violinists."

Carter raised his glass in the girl's direction. "To you, Maggie, and your debut as soloist in the Mozart concerto with Maestro Rainer."

"We should be toasting Maria," Maggie said as they clinked glasses.

"Actually, I am in the market for a new violin," Dylan said.

Maria gave the other vampire a sharp look. He returned her stare, his eyes sparkling with malice.

"Of course, I do not mean a *new* violin but rather a new old one."

"Are you looking for something in particular?"

"A fine old instrument," Dylan said, smiling now. "But not just any will do. I am looking for something special."

"I recently inherited a Serafino."

"Did you really?" Dylan said with mock seriousness. "It was my understanding the Angel violins have all been lost."

"My grandfather brought one back from Germany after World War Two. He knew it was valuable, but he didn't really know what it was."

"Is it in the case on the table?"

Maggie nodded. "Would you like to see it?"

"But of course!" the vampire cried. "Why, I would have come all the way from Europe for such an opportunity."

Maggie was already opening the case, her face beaming with pride. But it was Dylan Glyndwr's expression that Maria stayed focused on. The vampire teetered on the verge of almost religious ecstasy when he saw the violin nestled in the velvet suspension case. Maria knew then that she had to contrive a way to keep Dylan from playing the Seven. If Dylan Glyndwr got the violin in his hands, even Maria might not be able to get it away from him, and to keep Maggie O'Hara and Carter Dunne alive.

37

DYLAN GLYNDWR GOT out of the BMW at the stoplight. "You will have to talk to me about it sooner or later," Maria called after him.

He did not respond but continued to walk away.

Maria reached across the seat and pulled the passenger door shut. There was no traffic downtown at that time, but she waited until the light was green, then went around to Washington Street, where there were plenty of parking spaces now that the bars were closed and the college town had shut down for the night. She did not have to watch Dylan to know where he was headed; she could feel his presence moving into the parklike area called the Pentacrest. Dylan was not trying very hard to flee her. He was not even trying to mask his presence. He was simply being difficult.

Maria crossed the street toward the ersatz-Greek buildings, their facades illuminated by floodlights. She went up the steps to the former state capitol building two at a time, passing between the huge pillars holding up the portico. The main entry was ajar. The other vampire had used his mind to disable the alarm system and unlock the door.

Maria went in and stood in the cool darkness. She

felt him standing over her on the next floor. He was smiling to himself, as if he'd won a private victory by forcing her to follow him if she wanted to talk.

"You are acting like a child," she called out.

Dylan did not answer. The sound of wood rubbing against wood came down from upstairs—a window opening. Maria climbed the spiral staircase in the middle of the building. At the top, the colder air from outside showed her the window. Dylan, however, was nowhere to be seen.

"Dylan," she said, her temper getting short.

She put her head out the window. The places his fingers had gripped the mortar spaces between the stone blocks pulsed with a faint infrared glow easily visible to vampire eyes. She detested these games, but she had no choice but to follow.

Dylan was sitting on the ledge that ran around the base of the Old Cap's golden dome, resting his back against the upward curve. She sat down, swinging her legs into the air next to him. Below them and away into the distance was the sleeping town.

"You have come for the violin," she said.

"What else would bring me to the middle of the steppes?"

"They call it the prairie in America. There are other violins, Dylan."

"But there is no other Angel violin," Dylan said. "I know. I have searched for two centuries."

"There could be others."

Dylan sniffed.

"There is the Seven. You did not know about the Seven until recently, Dylan."

"No, I did not," he said, looking down past his feet

to the sidewalk below. "Everyone thought it was lost in the war."

"Yes, lost, but not destroyed," Maria said.

"And now that it has been found, I know exactly where it is."

"I have a hunch other Angels will be found. I heard a rumor about the violin Orloff owned, the one supposedly destroyed when the Nazis bombed Warsaw."

"I heard the same rumor several years ago and tracked it to earth," Dylan said. "There was no substance to it, I discovered, though not until I paid a great deal of money to some Russian gangsters. They did not know who they were trifling with, but they learned well enough before our business together concluded," he added with a cold smile.

"There will be other Angels for you, Dylan. Leave the Seven and Maggie alone. Wait for another."

But Maria knew his answer before he spoke.

"You must be joking," he said. "I intend to have this one. And I shall."

"Then be patient and wait a little longer for it, Dylan. You have an eternity to possess the Seven. The girl is mortal. What are fifty or sixty years to one of us? Let her have her moment. The violin is not going anywhere."

"If it is the girl you are worried about, I will not touch her. There are other pretty young things here to satisfy my Hunger." He waved his hand in an arc, indicating the town, dark and quiet with sleep, its inhabitants innocent of the danger dwelling among them.

"Do not touch the girl," Maria warned.

"Then we have an understanding. You get the girl; I get the violin."

"We have *nothing*," Maria said, her temper briefly getting the better of her, something that almost never happened. "If the Seven belongs to anyone other than Maggie O'Hara, it is me."

"By what right?"

"I bought it, didn't I?"

"When?" Dylan said, turning toward her with such violence that it was a wonder he didn't lose his balance and fall.

"In 1760. I had an agent buy it for me in Vienna. The owner was in ill health. He was a violinist named—"

"Janklincz," Dylan said in a sepulchral voice.

"How did you know?" Maria asked, but it was easy enough to guess. "You were looking for Janklincz yourself."

The other vampire nodded. "Except you got there first. Why would you have wanted the Seven?"

"To play it, of course. Why else?"

Dylan Glyndwr regarded her skeptically.

"I try to keep a rather low profile in the world—we all do—yet I am a little surprised, even hurt, you have not heard something about me and recognized your old lover. It is not every day that a woman is put in charge of one of the world's best orchestras."

"I keep to myself," Dylan said. "I have little interest in the world and its affairs."

"Wise policy for a vampire. I will have to be anonymous for a century after my appointment in Berlin, but it is worth it. It is such a good orchestra, Dylan. You must hear it."

"You weren't interested in music when I knew you before."

"The seed was there. Why else would I have invited

a traveling Welsh troubadour into my castle? But perhaps you did infect me with some of your love of music when you repaid my hospitality by seducing me and sinking your teeth thrice into my neck, so that our blood intermingled and we became as one in the Hunger."

"I gave you the change because I loved you, Baroness."

"Then why did you leave me?"

"I was ashamed of what I had done to you," Dylan said and looked away. "It usually ends badly, as you certainly know for yourself by now, for mortals who make the change. The combination of Hunger and power leads to madness or the sort of excess that leads terrified crowds to tear vampires to shreds and burn the pieces."

"I found that all out for myself," Maria said. "It was cruel to leave me to suffer the agonies of the Change alone. You must remember the horror of waking up to the Hunger for the first time and not knowing how to quiet its raving need. I nearly killed a poor serving girl. Thank God she was strong enough to survive my clumsy attack on her."

"Why would you care?"

"Because I am not like you, Dylan. I am not a killer. I am your polar opposite. I love people, all people."

"You are a proper Christian nobleman, Baroness," Dylan said, his voice thick with sarcasm.

"I simply try to be good," Maria replied in a quiet voice. "If we are not put on the Earth to help others and celebrate music, beauty, and the ennobling things that make life worth living, then what's the point?"

"What indeed?" Dylan said.

"You have allowed cynicism to poison your heart. I have known that for a long time. That is why when I first realized you were still alive, in Paris in 1902, I made no effort to contact you."

Dylan had nothing to say to that. It seemed nothing of the passion they had shared remained for him.

"Did you ever think about me?" she asked.

"Sometimes, but not for a very long time. I did not realize you were alive."

There was an ardent light in his eyes when he turned his face to look at her. She thought he was going to say something about the time they spent together many centuries before, in a castle overlooking the Rhine.

"If you had the Seven, how did that pig Göring come to have it?"

Maria felt like crying—or slapping Dylan Glyndwr. Either would have been amazing, for she was very much in control of her emotions. Now, however, it was a struggle to contain herself. Dylan cared about nothing but his idée fixe. The only reason he would be interested in Maria would be if she would agree to supply him with the Angel violin.

"I would have taken the Seven from Göring," Dylan went on, oblivious to Maria's emotions, "but even I could not get within ten kilometers of Karinhall. It was guarded like a fortress."

"I gave the Seven to Göring," Maria said.

Dylan's mouth fell open.

"To be more precise, I gave it to him in barter."

"What could have been worth trading away the Seven?" Dylan demanded, almost shouting.

"Two hundred women and children."

It should have been obvious enough, but Dylan was

so obsessed with himself, with music, with possessing an Angel violin, that he was completely devoid of the usual social frame of reference.

"I was living in Poland when the Wermacht invaded in 1939. It was well known that I was sympathetic to the plight of those poor people. It wasn't long before I had two hundred guests staying with me, people displaced by the war, and by the Nazi's policies. Mostly they were women and children. There were a few gypsies, but mainly Jews.

"My estate was in a remote enough place that it took a while for the Nazis to get around to noticing me. But the Germans are thorough and methodical. One day an S.S. officer showed up to inform me trucks were on the way to haul my guests away. They weren't even taking them to the camps in Poland. They hauled their victims into the woods, lined them up at the edge of pits, and shot them with machine guns. Imagine doing that to children—to *children*. I don't imagine even you have ever harmed a child."

Dylan shook his head. Not as long as there were beautiful women.

"It occurred to me the easiest thing would be to buy them off. The Nazis were magnificently corrupt. I used one of my paintings by Titian to buy access to one of Göring's adjutants. When Göring learned that I had one of Serafino's incomparably rare violins in my possession, a bargain was quickly struck. The Seven went to Karinhall to be added to the field marshal's collection. In return, my guests were allowed to board a ship in the Baltic and escape to Scandinavia, where I made arrangements for them to stay until the end of the war. I went to London."

"You gave up the Seven to save some refugees?"

"I thought it was a fair bargain," Maria said.

Dylan was quiet a long moment, thinking over what she'd told him.

"Are you going to take back your violin from the girl?" he asked finally, still trying to understand her thinking.

"It's not mine anymore. I traded it away to Göring. Maggie's grandfather bought it from a German officer. God only knows who he was or how he got it, but there is no proof, legal or otherwise, that he did not come by it honestly. The Seven belongs to Maggie now. Wait until you hear her play it and you will see for yourself that the right person has it."

"It belongs to her only until someone takes it."

Maria gave Dylan a level look. She could feel the strength of his thoughts beginning to push against her. She pushed back with her mind, the two forces canceling each other. It would be interesting to learn who had the greater power—Maria believed good vampires were inherently stronger than the killers—but she did not intend to force the issue unless there were no other choices. Maria could not afford to make a mistake. She was the only thing standing between Dylan Glyndwr and Maggie O'Hara and her violin.

"No one is going to take the Seven from Maggie," Maria said. "I will not allow it."

Dylan favored her with another one of his chilly smiles.

"We shall have to see about that," he said.

38

MAGGIE STOPPED AND looked around, her expression dazed, like a sleepwalker awakening without conscious recollection of where she was or how she got there. She was on Burlington Street, two and a half blocks past where she should have turned to enter the downtown pedestrian mall.

What is the matter with me? Maggie thought, her self-irritation bordering on despair. She needed to stay mentally focused, not be wandering down the street like a moonstruck teenager. Maggie's first major performance as a soloist was the next night. If she managed to pull it off, she would be transformed from one of countless semianonymous musical drudges to respected soloist. And if she crashed and burned before the sold-out audience that had come to hear Maria Rainer conduct the opening concert for the annual Mozart festival . . . The mere thought was enough to send a shiver through Maggie's body. She could no more survive humiliation on that scale than she could fall from a hundred-story building and live.

But there was more on her mind than the concert, as if that weren't enough to preoccupy her. She had been walking across campus thinking about Carter, and

Maria, and the choice she would be unable to postpone much longer.

Earlier in the day, on her way to get coffee between classes, Maggie had spotted Carter through the window of Johannson's Jewelers. He was leaning over a glass case, talking to a female clerk. Although she didn't really have any way of knowing, Maggie's intuition told her he was looking at engagement rings.

Maggie liked Carter a lot, but did she love him? She wasn't sure. Love was a big word. Even so, it was easy enough to imagine spending the rest of her life with Carter. He was supportive of her music and understanding about her obsessive practice habits. Carter's fascination with violins provided a convenient intersection of interest between the two of them, but without creating the possibility for rivalry or jealousy. Maggie never would have been able to maintain a relationship with another violinist, which was why she always said no when someone from the orchestra asked for a date. First there would be comparison, then competition, and ultimately one career would have to take precedence over the other. It was impossible to imagine such a thing could work. But with Carter, it wasn't like that. Everything was easy. What Maggie wanted was important. Her rehearsal time took precedence. There were no arguments with Carter about how she spent her time, as there had been with Peter Hill and Maggie's other boyfriends. They both agreed: her career came first.

Which brought Maggie's thinking around again to Maria Rainer.

The chance to study in Berlin with a top-level conductor as her personal mentor was an opportunity so great that Maggie had never even imagined such a thing might one day happen.

And so which would it be: Carter or Maria?

What about Carter *and* Maria?

Perhaps, Maggie thought, standing in the same spot on Burlington Street as if rooted to the pavement, she could maintain a long-distance relationship with Carter while she was in Germany. Or maybe Carter would go with her. He had enough money to do whatever he wanted. Maggie began to frown, realizing that would almost certainly be a disaster. The work would become all-consuming once Maggie was under Maria Rainer's wing. Carter would be in Germany because of Maggie and Maggie alone, whereas for her Carter would be reduced to someone wanting her to take time away from the violin. Besides, when Maggie's playing burned brightest, it consumed her emotional oxygen and left little but ashes behind. Carter deserved better than that.

Maggie played it all through her head again, still at a loss to know what her heart was telling her to do. It was almost enough to make her want to run away from it all—Carter, Maria, the Mozart concerto. What a relief it would be to flee to a faraway land, taking the Seven to sweetly sing to her in the night. Maggie imagined herself in an old French colonial plantation house in Cambodia. In her mind's eye she saw herself standing on the veranda, looking out past the tea plants to the ruined temples. She lifted the Angel violin and began to play Bach to the moon rising over the jungle. But she was not in fact alone. Her lover was there—not Carter, not Maria, but someone else. As she played she could feel him moving toward her through the darkened house, a presence filled with tightly coiled power, like a tiger emerging in a silent crouch from behind a banyan tree.

A campus bus honked at a car hesitating at the stoplight, startling Maggie from her waking dream.

"This is ridiculous," Maggie said out loud. It wasn't like her to daydream.

The car moved and the bus followed, spewing diesel exhaust when the driver punched the accelerator.

The entry to the new Sheraton was just a little farther on. Maggie could cut through the lobby to get to the downtown pedestrian mall, where she needed to pick up some blank music paper at North Music.

The automatic doors swooshed open. The hotel, packed to bursting for home football games, was deserted during the middle of the weekday afternoon. The clerk behind the desk didn't look up. Maggie was halfway to the opposite side of the lobby when someone called out to her.

"Miss O'Hara!"

Maggie recognized the voice immediately from its accent. It was Maria's friend Dylan Glyndwr, the Welsh violinist.

She looked left, then right, then behind. Where was he?

The lobby seemed deserted except for the clerk, apparently impervious to distraction as she concentrated on her paperwork.

There was a sunken conversation space off to one side of the lobby, a secluded place almost completely walled off from the reception area by a series of planters and Oriental-looking folding screens. A hand came up from behind a wing-backed chair. Maggie could not see the face that went with it, but it had to be Dylan Glyndwr.

Maggie descended into the lounge, an intimate space of leather chairs and couches arranged around low cocktail tables, the dim glow of reading lamps fading in and out of comfortable shadows.

Dylan sat with both feet flat on the floor, his hands resting on the arms of the chair. He was elegantly dressed in a black Armani suit, a white collarless dress shirt buttoned at the neck, his long, rich hair brushed back away from his face and falling to his shoulders. Maggie had noticed how handsome he was when they met at Carter's, but somehow it hadn't touched her the same way—or in the same place.

"Hello," she said, feeling herself begin to blush.

"This is a rare pleasure for me, Miss O'Hara," Dylan said, standing up and extending his hand.

Maggie let him take her hand in his as if to kiss it, but he held it instead. His grip was firm, dry, warm, almost feverish. It reminded her of someone else. *Maria,* Maggie realized in the next moment. Her hand had felt hot. Was there something about Europeans that made their metabolisms burn more fiercely than Americans'?

Dylan Glyndwr's eyes narrowed. Maggie had the strange sense that he knew she was thinking of Maria and for some reason didn't like it. But that was impossible. How could he know what was going on within her mind?

"You have the Seven with you?" Dylan said.

Maggie's free hand rested upon the case slung over her left shoulder. She pressed the case against her side even as she wondered why she instinctively moved to protect the Angel violin. What did she have to worry about? Dylan Glyndwr was Maria Rainer's friend. Certainly Maggie had nothing to fear from him. Maggie felt herself relax—first the arm around the violin, then her shoulder, then her entire body. Her mind was telling her to relax, and as if commanded to respond to a hypnotic suggestion, she felt herself sink into a calm, almost sleepy ease.

"What brings you to the hotel, Miss O'Hara?" Dylan asked in his sonorous voice. "I wish I could flatter myself by thinking it was to pay me the honor of a visit."

"It's a little embarrassing, actually," Maggie replied. "I was walking down the street so completely caught up in my thoughts that I missed my turn. I was taking a shortcut through the hotel lobby to the other side of the block."

"Then it is my good fortune, for I have been wanting to have a few words with you in private. Please sit down, Miss O'Hara, if you have a moment."

Maggie sat on the couch across from where Dylan Glyndwr had been; instead of returning to his chair, he sat down on the couch facing her, the violin case beside her on the opposite side.

"I had intended to order tea, but they do not serve it in this hotel."

"Welcome to Iowa," Maggie said, and laughed.

"Teatime is one of England's few ennobling contributions to the culture of the world. When one is used to dining late, as we do on the Continent, a light repast around four in the afternoon helps keep one's hunger in check."

"England isn't as bad as all that, is it?" Maggie

asked. "I was in London last summer with the school orchestra. I liked it a lot, though it was pretty expensive."

"London is a charming city," Dylan Glyndwr agreed, "but more European than English, if you ask me."

He leaned forward slightly, and his deep-set eyes seemed to look straight into Maggie's soul, releasing a flock of butterflies in the pit of her stomach.

"You remind me of someone I used to know," he said. "You have the same beautiful auburn hair."

"A girlfriend?" Maggie asked.

"Yes, but that was a long time ago in Wales. She was killed. Otherwise, who knows what might have been?"

"I'm sorry," Maggie said.

Dylan nodded and looked down at the floor.

"Maria says you are one of Europe's best baroque violinists," Maggie said, intentionally changing the subject.

"Modesty is not among my virtues, Miss O'Hara. I am the best baroque violinist, and not only in Europe."

"I'm surprised I don't have any of your CDs. I don't think I've seen them anywhere. Can I order one from Amazon?"

"I have chosen not to record," Dylan said.

The way Maggie looked at Dylan Glyndwr saved her from having to ask him to explain.

"Baroque chamber music is meant to be experienced as the musicians play it. You can no more put baroque music down on a recording and have it breathe than you can embalm a human body and pretend that it is alive."

"That strikes me as an extreme position, Mr. Glyndwr, if I may say so."

"We are free to speak our minds. As for extreme, it does not matter to me whether it is or not. I know what I believe. I will not compromise."

He rearranged himself on the couch, turning so that he was just a little closer to Maggie. "I heard you perform at the dress rehearsal for the Mozart concerto," he said.

"Oh?" Maggie said, feigning nonchalance. She was anxious to hear Dylan's critique of her playing—but at the same time she dreaded being judged and found inadequate.

Dylan leaned closer, his eyes on her eyes, and spoke in a low voice filled with emotion.

"I have never heard anyone play the Mozart violin concerto the way you did. The cadenzas were brilliant. I can see why Maria is so enthralled with your playing. I was myself deeply touched." He brought his hand to his breast and touched the area over his heart.

Maria.

The word echoed in Maggie's mind.

Carter.

The second name was more distant still in Maggie's mind. Both were forgotten in the next instant. Dylan Glyndwr's face was now close to hers. She smelled the faint perfume of expensive cologne released by his body's warmth. What integrity he had, refusing to record because of the way it degraded the experience for the listener! Music needed more people like Dylan Glyndwr, who stood up for what they believed.

"I have a proposition for you, Miss O'Hara."

She could feel the breath of each word, moving from his lips to hers. She kept her eyes on his, her eyelids half lowered, her own lips moist and parted.

The curious feeling of being in a dream reclaimed her. She made no effort to resist but allowed herself to float along on the warm, blissful current.

"Call me Maggie," she said.

"Come back with me to Amsterdam, Maggie. I will teach you to reach places in your soul with your playing that you scarcely imagine exist."

His hand was on her shoulder. Maggie did not pull away from him. It was as if some strange gravity had a hold of her, pulling her into the dark, bottomless pools of his eyes.

"I hardly know you," she whispered.

"You know me. Look into my eyes, Maggie O'Hara, and you will know everything you need to know, and see everything that I can give to you."

Maggie continued to match Dylan Glyndwr's ardent gaze, while a hundred images flashed past her vision as if she were seeing the land behind his eyes— battlements in flames, fleeing through the forest on horseback, loneliness so tender that it made her heart feel as if it were breaking, until everything changed with a kiss deeper than any mere kiss could be.

Her lips were on his, and his on hers.

Music filled Maggie's mind, music she could feel in her blood. It was the song of two violins playing together in perfect harmony, fulfilling every desire, erasing every disappointment, making Maggie feel complete in a way she never knew she could be.

Dylan Glyndwr's lips were against her neck now, his teeth slipping into her skin effortlessly, painlessly.

Maggie heard herself gasp and she held Dylan to her more tightly still as he swallowed the blood—*her blood!*—rushing out through the tiny punctures in her neck with each beat of her racing pulse.

The fear came into her then: fear of dying; fear of the unknown; fear of the unnatural; fear of the creature who posed as an ordinary man but was not a man, a being who lived beyond the laws of men, subject only to the governance of his own desires.

But overtaking the fear was the almost simultaneous rush of pleasure beyond any Maggie had ever known. No sensation could match the soft explosion unfolding within, no words define the limitless waves of electric delight dancing through each cell of her body.

Maggie felt a weakening, almost like falling, with each heartbeat. At the same time, a strange sense of power more mental than physical came into her through Dylan's kiss. The meaning of the music playing in her mind was instantaneously unlocked, like Egyptian hieroglyphics upon the discovery of the Rosetta stone. The melody in her heart, the intervals between notes, the harmony and counterpart being played in Dylan's heart—Maggie understood it perfectly and with the same sense of revelation she would have felt if she'd casually looked into a microscope and gained instant recognition of the structure and meaning of all existence. Her mind became faster, smarter, more nimble with each swallow of blood Dylan took from her. Maggie discovered she could reach out with her senses and know things that were impossible to know according to the limitations of ordinary logic. She could *see,* for the few brief seconds she could concentrate, the hotel clerk on the other side of a locked office door, bending over a line of white powder on the desk with a straw.

Dylan had not lied. He could teach Maggie things she had never imagined it possible to know.

Maggie surrendered completely to the embrace, her body against Dylan's, flesh to flesh, muscle to muscle, bone to bone, blood to blood. Maggie ceased to care whether she lived or died. Even the Angel violin was forgotten as Maggie was carried away on the rising tide of ecstasy. Not even the glorious Seven could compete with the song of blood.

39

"MAGGIE?"

The girl was in a straight-backed wooden chair with her back to the green-room door. She wore the dress Maria had helped her pick out for her debut as a violin soloist, a black formal, with a long skirt and an elegantly scooped back. Maggie had piled her thick auburn tresses high upon her head so that even from behind Maria could see the single strand of pearls against the lightly downed skin on her neck. The pearls were Maria's; she had lent them to her new protégée for luck. The violin case, closed, sat on the table in front of Maggie before a dressing mirror encircled with lights.

"Maggie? It is nearly time."

The girl did not respond or even indicate she'd heard. Maria could see Maggie's face in the mirror—Maria's own face, bright with expectation, above the girl's and behind her. Maggie was looking down toward the floor, her eyes hooded. The girl's fair complexion, all the whiter still due to the days she spent sequestered indoors, practicing the violin, was a lighter shade of its usual pale.

It was at that moment Maria knew.

"My dear girl," she said, and rushed to Maggie's side. She gently lifted Maggie's chin with the edge of her hand. Maggie's skin was feverish. There was a wounded look in her distant eyes when she finally looked at Maria, as if she had been touched by something that left her with a sadness that would resonate within forever.

"I cannot begin to tell you how sorry I am, child," Maria said, and touched her fingertips to the side of Maggie's bare neck. No sign of the wounds remained; those would have healed quickly, the normal mortal healing rate greatly accelerated by the enzymes vampires carry within their saliva. But Maria could see easily enough where Maggie had been bitten. The skin where the holes had been was warmer than the surrounding tissue and displayed the distinctive glow of newly regenerated flesh.

"Do you remember?" Maria asked.

Maggie nodded.

"We shall discuss this in detail, my dear, but later," Maria said. "I have to leave you now to conduct. You plainly are in no condition to join the orchestra. I will have someone find Nicole Hoffman and tell her I need her to stand in as soloist."

Maggie's body stiffened at the other violinist's name. It was unfortunate that the understudy happened to be Maggie O'Hara's rival, but there was no helping it now.

"No," Maggie said, pulling away from Maria and getting to her feet. Her balance was a little uncertain, and she was obviously struggling to overcome the lethargy enveloping her within a cocoon of numbness.

"It is not your fault, Maggie," Maria said gently. "If

anyone is to blame, it is I. He told me he would leave you alone. I should have known better than to trust Dylan Glyndwr. Wait here for me until after the concert. You will be safe, I assure you."

Maggie held up her open hand to stop Maria.

"I want to play," she insisted.

"But Maggie, in your weakened condition do you really think it wise?"

Maggie closed her eyes a moment before answering. "I must."

Maria took her hands, holding them in hers, and looked deep into the girl's eyes. Determination was there, burning almost as intensely as the talent.

"I could help you," Maria offered. "A few drops of my blood would serve as a tonic to your system, although we would have to be careful not to overstimulate you."

Maggie's eyes grew wide.

"You, too?" she asked, taking her hands away from Maria's and moving a step backward.

Maria neither confirmed nor denied it. It was unnecessary to say more. Maggie knew the truth about her.

"I must warn you first of the risk," Maria said. "If you share yourself too many times with one of us, the exposure will initiate a change that cannot be reversed."

"I want to do it on my own," Maggie said, her voice a little steadier. She stood up straight and looked directly at Maria with an expression that was almost fierce. "I can do it," she said. "I *will* do it."

"Very well then, Maggie, if you insist. I wish you luck."

There was a light tapping on the door. "Five min-utes," a voice called from the other side.

"You must get ready," Maria said. "Is your violin in tune?"

A jolt of recognition went through the girl. She had done this many times—getting ready for a concert. She knew what to do. And if her instinct and her train-ing held up, maybe she would regain enough of her senses to get through more than a perfunctory remem-brance of the notes when she was standing in front of the orchestra with the Seven.

Maggie's fingers had no trouble opening the case, but she went no further.

"It is not too late to change your mind, my dear," Maria said, seeing her stricken face in the mirror. "There will be no dishonor. You are not well. I will look forward to you coming with me to Berlin no mat-ter what happens tonight."

Still Maggie didn't move. If was as if she had turned to a pillar of salt, like Lot's wife.

Maria put her arm around the girl and only then re-alized the reason she had frozen. The expensive sus-pension case lined with green velvet, a gift from Carter Dunne that had cradled the Seven since Gianni Felici's repairs, was empty.

The Angel violin was gone.

PRESTO

40

CARTER MADE IT back to the house in half the time it usually took, pushing the Porsche as hard as he dared around corners, going as fast as seventy miles per hour down darkened residential streets, gritting his teeth when the little 911 flew through intersections without slowing. Maggie's other violin—the one she'd played before the Seven—was in an upstairs closet. Carter grabbed it and raced back to his running car, slamming the front door so hard on his way out that a picture fell off the wall. The sound of breaking glass did not slow him as he jumped down the steps two and three at a time.

He found Maggie waiting where he'd left her, standing in the wings, watching the orchestra finish the overture to *The Magic Flute,* the first performance on the night's program.

The audience exploded with applause as the overture ended.

"Carter," Maggie said, and smiled, taking the violin. "You have saved the day. Thank you."

She kissed him, not on the lips but the cheek. She felt hot against his skin. There was something strange about her behavior—composed and relaxed even to the point of exuding an almost palpable sense of inner calm. Maggie O'Hara was a lot of things—intense, serious, passionate—but never *calm*.

Maria Rainer had turned away from the podium and was bowing to the audience. The applause grew louder. From the back of the hall came cheers and whistles. Maria motioned for the strings to rise to acknowledge the response. It was a good beginning for the festival, and for its guest conductor from Berlin, but it added to the already enormous pressure for Maggie to perform well. And, Carter thought with a new flush of anxiety, she would have to do it using an inferior violin she had not touched in a long time. He was amazed that she seemed to be handling the crisis so well.

Maria was walking toward them, coming off the stage. The conductor came offstage after every part of the program, part of the ritual of classical performance.

Maggie looked at Carter as the conductor approached. Maybe she was sedated, he thought. Some performers took tranquilizers to help them overcome stage fright. He wouldn't have blamed her for cadging some off another musician in the orchestra. Had he been in her position, he probably would have been so upset that the invaluable Angel violin had been stolen that he would have found it impossible to carry through with the performance.

"Maggie," Maria said. "Are you ready, dear?"

"Just about," she said, putting the violin case on a chair and opening it.

But what if the other violin wasn't in its case? Carter thought with a sudden spike of anxiety. It was, however, in the case, along with two bows that even to Carter's relatively inexperienced eye looked undistinguished.

Maria gave Carter a perfunctory smile. She hid it well but she was nervous, too, he thought.

From the stage came the lonely sound of a single oboe playing an A. The lower strings began tuning to it. Maggie had the violin to her chin, tuning along with the players onstage. Carter had never heard her play the instrument before, but it sounded like exactly what Maggie had described to him: a middling-quality Chinese violin built for a serious high school player. There was a galaxy of tonal difference between the Seven and the student violin Maggie was about to play. Carter, his shirt already damp from running to and from his car, felt a fresh flush of perspiration across the small of his back. How in the world could she play the Mozart cadenzas on *that* violin?

"Ready?"

Maggie looked at Maria and nodded.

"Play from your heart, my dear," Maria Rainer said, then turned and headed back toward the stage. The audience applauded as she climbed onto the podium before the orchestra, the musicians tapping bows against music stands or lightly clapping their hands against their legs.

Maggie continued to adjust the tuning pegs. The violin didn't even have new strings, Carter realized with a greasy feeling in his stomach.

Maria was looking toward them from the podium. The audience couldn't see them off to the side, hidden by the long black curtains, but Maria and the musicians nearest the wings looked toward Maggie with a combination of anticipation and curiosity. Carter was trying to think of the appropriate words of encouragement when Maggie walked past him toward the stage.

Bravely walking to her execution, Carter thought grimly.

Carter could see his seat—three rows back on the center aisle—empty, waiting for him, but there was no time to get to it now. Maggie nodded to Maria, and the conductor lifted her bow. Carter would have to listen to the concerto from where he stood. At least he would be the first to congratulate Maggie when she came off the stage afterward, or to comfort her if it went badly.

As Maggie struck the first chord to key the concerto's start, Carter wondered how something could begin with so much promise only to go so disastrously wrong.

41

"WHO ARE YOU?" Maggie asked.

It was late and the pub had started to clear out. The remaining symphony members were behaving with considerably more looseness than they had earlier, immediately after the concert. Carter was at the bar, arguing politics with one of the cello players, who were in main a rowdy crew, leaving Maggie alone at the table with Maria—if that was her name.

"Who are you really?" Maggie repeated, a note of disagreeableness in her voice.

"Maria Rainer," the woman opposite her replied. "*Baroness* Rainer, if you want to stand on protocol. I no longer use my title. Nobility is more of an encumbrance than anything else these days. And besides, the last Baroness Rainer has been dead a long time, at least as far as the people whose job it is to keep track of such things know."

"How long is that?"

Maria hesitated, as if considering whether to answer. "Four hundred years," she said finally.

"My God." Maggie gasped. "I don't know whether to be amazed or scream."

"I would prefer that you not scream," Maria said with a small smile.

"And you're a . . ."

"You know very well what I am, Maggie."

"You are a vampire." Maggie fell back against the chair. "I feel as if I'm losing my mind. Is this really happening?"

"You must never doubt yourself, my dear. Self-doubt is the root of the problems you have had mastering the violin."

But Maggie was shaking her head even before Maria finished. "There is no such thing as vampires. They're Eastern European folktales."

"Actually, Maggie, if you survey the literature of many cultures, you will find references to vampires from ancient Babylon to the Bible."

"But myths are not real."

"Do not be so sure, Maggie. There is at least a grain of truth to most myths."

"But you go out in the sunlight," Maggie said, her tone argumentative. "I've seen you during the day dozens of times. And the cross I sometimes wear around my neck—it never seemed to bother you."

Maria reached into the top of her dress and pulled out a gold crucifix. "That's an old wives' tale. I have worn this for long time. Do you like it? The detail is exquisite."

Maggie nodded.

"Michelangelo made this to prove he could work in miniature. It is a lost-wax casting. He carved the original in wax, which was then lost in the process of making the mold. I've always found that fascinating: the artist must destroy the original to create an art object that will last an eternity. It is not unlike what is involved in creating a vampire."

"But you do need to drink . . ." Maggie's voice trailed off.

"Yes, my dear. We must drink the living blood of a mortal to satisfy one peculiar need. We do not require much—no more than the amount you would pour for a small glass of port after a good meal."

"Do you . . . kill?"

"Of course not," Maria said quickly. Then, after a beat, she added, "I do not."

"But others do."

"I will not lie to you, Maggie. There are lawless renegades among my kind as there are among yours."

"Like Dylan Glyndwr."

"He is dangerous, Maggie. You must stay away from him."

"Your warning is a little late," Maggie said, her voice shaking. "He *bit* me. He drank *my* blood."

"He finds you almost as irresistible as the Angel violin. Did you see the way he looked at you during the dress rehearsal? I did not believe he would dare touch someone under my protection. I underestimated the degree to which evil has him in its dread grip. I again apologize to you for that."

Maggie's hand was at her throat. The terror she had known in Dylan Glyndwr's embrace—and the pleasure—would stay with her as long as she lived. But the tears that began to roll down her cheeks were not for what was past, but what was yet to come.

"Will I change now? Will I become like you and Dylan, one of the undead?"

"Calm yourself," Maria said, her tone so reassuring

that it was as if the vampire had the power to command Maggie's emotions. "You have nothing to fear. It takes repeated episodes for the Change to take hold. And please, as a favor to me, do not use that unfortunate term, the *undead*. It is absurdly melodramatic. There is nothing dead about me."

"How many times does it have to happen?" Maggie demanded. "Two bites? Three?"

"It is not good for you to know too much about us, my dear."

"I already know too much."

Maria gave Maggie a look of appraisal. "Perhaps. There are ways of dealing with it, if it becomes a problem."

"How?" Maggie said, her emotions taking over again. "By killing me?"

"Do not be hysterical," Maria said a little shortly. "It can be arranged for you to forget; that is all. You would not be harmed. You would not know a thing about it. It could happen like that." She snapped her fingers.

"How? Using telepathy?"

"Something like that."

"Can you read my mind?"

"If I wish. I find it distasteful to pry into someone's private thoughts. If I want to know what you are thinking, I can ask you."

"If you can read my thoughts, tell me what am I thinking now."

Maria looked at her and sighed. Maggie thought Maria wasn't going to do it, but she felt a moment of dreaminess that reminded her of how she'd felt outside the hotel earlier, when Dylan Glyndwr seduced her, drank her blood, and stole the Seven from her without her even realizing it.

"You were wondering if I want you to take the Change, and if becoming a vampire would unleash your talent. Then you were thinking about how you felt outside the hotel, before your assignation with Dylan."

"You *can* read my mind."

"I should be hurt that you think me capable of lying."

"What have you been doing ever since we met if not lying? Your whole life is a lie, isn't it? Everything you do and say is part of one big act of deception."

"You wound me, my dear, but you are not entirely mistaken," the vampire said. "But you must consider this: it is sometimes necessary to lie. There are times when a lie is the kindest thing you can tell to a person, or persons, or even all of mortal society. How well would most human beings sleep, knowing we were out there in the night with the power to take their blood, their bodies, their property, even their lives, as it suited us to do so?"

"Not very well," Maggie meekly answered. "I don't know if I will ever sleep again."

"Nonsense. This is just another fact you will learn to accept. If not, I will help you forget."

"I don't want to forget," Maggie said softly.

"Then be reasonable," Maria said. "As for unleashing your talent, you proved well enough on your own tonight that you do not require much assistance. You did not even need the Angel violin to lift you with its wings."

"I would have played better if I'd had the Seven."

"True enough. But you played extraordinarily well

without it. That is why I have invited you to study with me in Berlin. I can help you, not in any of the ways you fear or secretly covet, but by being your teacher. What we accomplished tonight—what you accomplished— is only the beginning."

"Do you think I will ever see it again, Maria—the Angel violin?"

"I would not expect it. Dylan has been searching for one of Archangelo Serafino's miraculous violins for two hundred years. He will use every bit of his power to disappear now that he has it. I pity him. He will lock himself up in a room in some remote corner of the world, like a drug addict with an endless supply of opium, and exist alone, in a sickly-sweet cloud of delirious pleasure."

"Then you don't think he'll come after me?"

The question seemed to startle Maria. "Did he give you reason to think he might?"

"He asked me to go away with him to study violin, the same as you have. And he already has my violin."

Maria gave Maggie a level look that made her feel as if she were pinned against her chair.

"Listen to me very carefully, Maggie O'Hara," Maria warned. "You must stay away from Dylan Glyndwr. If he reappears in your life sometime in the future, do not talk to him, and by all means you must not believe anything he has to tell you. Glyndwr is a creature of darkness. There is no one on the planet, mortal or vampire, more dangerous for you now than Dylan Glyndwr. Promise me?"

"You don't have to ask, Maria. He attacked me and he stole my violin. I would just as soon sell my soul to the devil as have anything to do with Dylan Glyndwr."

"It would be tantamount to the same thing," Maria said. "This is another reason I want you to come with me to Berlin. You will be under my protection. Dylan will not be able to harm you. Have you made up your mind? I am flying back to Germany after the festival in a friend's business jet. There is room for you. If you do not have a passport, I can arrange that, too. I have many friends in important places."

"I haven't decided," Maggie said.

"Meaning Carter," Maria said.

Maggie nodded.

"I appreciate the trouble you are having deciding."

"What do you think is more important, Maria: music or love?"

"That is something you must decide for yourself," Maria said. "But you will have to choose. There isn't going to be room in your life for both music and love for a long time to come, unless . . ."

"Unless what?" Maggie asked, looking closely at the other woman.

"I misspoke," Maria replied. "The time has come, my dear, for you to decide what you want most out of life."

42

EITHER ALCOHOL OR sex tended to relax Maggie O'Hara and put her to sleep, and the rare combination was usually doubly effective. But Maggie had too much to think about to sleep. In the small hours of the morning, she lay awake in bed next to Carter, watching him sleep, unable to sleep herself.

Carter or Maria: the choice had become simpler without getting any easier.

The numbers on the digital alarm clock said three in the morning. One of the bad things about insomnia, at least for Maggie, was that the later it got, the more desperate she was to fall asleep, which in turn made it all the more unlikely she would drift off.

She slid out of bed and went downstairs in the dark, not turning on any lights. She didn't want to wake up Carter just because she couldn't sleep.

Maggie opened the refrigerator, squinting against the light, her eyes used to the darkness. She reached for the milk jug. She was turning away, the door swinging shut, when she saw Dylan Glyndwr in the vanishing glow, leaning against the far counter.

The refrigerator door closed with a soft pneumatic sound.

Dylan was still there, Maggie knew, but her pupils had contracted from the now-disappeared light and her eyes were unable to see in the dark. Maggie did not cry out. That would have brought Carter at a run, and it required no imagination to guess the confrontation that would follow, and the result. The danger, the horror, that had been called into the darkened house was there on Maggie's account. She would have to deal with it as best she could. Maggie would charm Dylan, flatter him, lie to him—she would do whatever it took. She would even give him her body and her blood, if that was the only way to save Carter.

"What do you want?" she said, somehow managing to keep her tone neutral, as if it did not surprise her to find a vampire standing in the dark in her kitchen.

"I came to talk to you."

"I thought there might something else you wanted to steal from me, the way you stole my violin."

"The Seven . . ." She could hear the reverence in his voice. "Actually, the Angel violin is what I want to talk to you about."

"So talk," Maggie replied.

"I cannot begin to tell you how long I have yearned to get my hands on an Angel violin. They are incomparable instruments."

"I know," Maggie said dryly. "I used to have one."

"I had one once, too, a long time ago. Such an instrument! It sang so sweetly that I forgot the pain that had surrounded me after the English killed my family and stole my country."

"Is that why you hate the English—they killed your family?"

Dylan ran his hands through his long hair and

looked up at the ceiling. His breath came out in a long, ragged, emotional sigh. Maggie was afraid she'd triggered a memory that would send the vampire careening into psychotic violence, but he pulled himself back from the edge with an effort she could see even in the gray-toned night shadows.

"My father was King of Wales before the English came. They murdered my clan. The girl I was betrothed to was raped and drowned in a stream. She was the sweetest maiden. She had hair just like yours."

Maggie stood and listened because she had no choice, though Dylan Glyndwr's grief was so extreme it seemed likely to spill over into madness at any moment.

"Today," he said, "people look to the Balkans, to Africa, to Eastern Europe, and shudder at the brutality. They don't realize that there has never been a more brutal race than the bloody English. Civilization is only a veneer that exists to hide their monstrous savagery. Pray that the world never again knows such cruelty."

"I didn't know," Maggie said.

"After the English, I was doomed to wander from country to country, forever without a home. But no matter what country I was in, music was always my refuge. It eased my burden and made it easier to bear the pain. When I obtained an Angel violin, it was as though a miracle had happened. When I played the Angel, it was as if the evil that I had suffered—and the evil that I had inflicted on the world—had been erased by God. It was not just forgetting, but absolution. My soul was untroubled and pure. Though it lasted only as long as I played the violin, it was enough to free my soul. When I played the Angel, I was home in my country, my father was alive, and life was still good for me."

Dylan's head fell forward, the thick locks of his hair coming down like curtains on his face.

"I had the Angel with me on a ship attacked by a British man-of-war. The ship sank. The Angel was lost. Somewhere, in the ancient book where our fates were written down in aeons past, it was determined that the English and I were to be immortal antagonists, enemies that can give neither peace nor quarter for so long as the other still breathes."

He looked up at Maggie.

"For two hundred years I have searched for another Angel violin. And now I have found one. What could I do but take it? In my heart even I know it was wrong. I am a despicable wretch—evil, poisonous, foul, my soul damned for all eternity. I am not fit to clean the bottom of your shoes, Maggie O'Hara. And yet, when the Seven reappeared in the world, there was nothing I could do but take it for my own. Can you see that?"

Maggie looked back into his eyes—not eyes so much as black holes in the shadows arranged in the shape of his face—for a long time before answering.

"I want you to have the Seven," she said. "Consider the violin yours. Had I known your story, I would have given it to you. I want you to keep it. I forgive you for taking it without my permission. Only make me one promise in return."

His chin came up.

"Promise me you will let the Seven heal you. Let the peace it gives you go into your soul and change you. There are far worse things you can do than steal an old

violin from a girl too naïve to understand the otherworldly power it possesses."

"I have done far worse things than steal." Dylan
groaned. "I have killed without remorse, harvesting
lives like the reaper moving quickly through a field of
golden grain with a sharp scythe."

"You do not need to hurt people," Maggie said,
thinking of Carter but trying not to, knowing the vampire might read it in her mind. "Let the Seven teach
you compassion and mercy."

"Perhaps I could—and perhaps it could—if it were
not for my other problem."

Maggie held her breath as she waited for the other
shoe to drop. His eyes glittered back at her in the darkness. It was not the way he looked at her that unnerved
her as much as it was knowing a predator was standing
close enough for her to see his breast rise and fall in the
darkness. His instinct was to kill. He enjoyed killing.
And if he now made a move on her—or Carter—there
would be absolutely nothing she could do.

"I wish to God I had never heard you play the Seven,
Maggie O'Hara," the vampire said. "If I had stayed at
the hotel instead of attending the final rehearsal for the
concerto, I would be on my way to Amsterdam now
with the Angel by my side. But I did not. I made a mistake, a deadly mistake."

Maggie's heart was racing and her palms began to
sweat. There was a set of butcher knives angled into a
butcher-block holder on the counter beside the stove.
Even if she could manage to grab one and plunge it up
to the handle into Dylan Glyndwr's breast, would that
be enough to stop a vampire?

"After I stole your violin," he said, "I repaired to a

hotel in a nearby city. I could scarcely wait. I brought a bow with me, a baroque bow, as I prefer. I picked up the Seven. What a thrill it was to hold it at last! The Angel violin, the object of my quest—finding the Holy Grail could not have brought me as much satisfaction. I held it to my chin and began to play Vivaldi. The Seven sounded fantastic, of course. What else would one expect? And yet something was missing. Something was wrong. It did not sound the way it did when *you* played it, Maggie O'Hara."

He stopped and looked at her with significance.

"Thank you," she said simply, not knowing what else to say.

"But don't you see? The Seven knows it belongs to you. Do not ask me how that is; I only know that there is no disputing it. It is part of the miracle of the Angel violins. The Seven was meant for you from the first. For so long as you are alive, Miss O'Hara, the Seven belongs to you and you to it. It will not sound so good in the hands of another player, even as you will not play as well on any other instrument."

She was looking down, but she could feel Dylan Glyndwr's eyes on her.

"Though I deeply regret it—and it pains my soul more than I can tell you—there is only one thing I can do."

Maggie closed her eyes. The vampire was going to kill her, breaking the spell between her and the Seven, and freeing him to possess the soul of the violin that had already taken possession of his heart. Maggie did not want to die, but there was a small part of her that welcomed the vampire's lethal embrace. The recollection of the pleasure Dylan had given her the last time was so powerful that death—or spending eternity as a vampire—seemed a fair price for such ecstasy.

But Dylan Glyndwr did not gather Maggie O'Hara up into his arms. She did not feel the warm, almost feverish heat of his body pressed against hers, the tenderness of his kisses, or the explosion of bliss as he plunged his teeth deep into her neck.

Dylan was standing near her when she opened her eyes, not moving, not threatening, neither about to embrace her nor waiting for her to embrace him.

"You belong to each other," Dylan said. He lifted his right arm. In his hand, gripped by the neck, was the Seven.

Maggie took the violin from the vampire, too surprised and stunned to say anything.

"I have no right to ask anything of you but I cannot stop myself."

Maggie looked up at him, waiting.

"I am the only one who can help you develop your talent to its fullest. Return with me to Amsterdam. I will share everything I have with you. I will make you immortal in the world of the violin. And, if you so desire it, I will also make you immortal in body."

The offer took Maggie's breath away. The idea repulsed and sickened her, and yet, she knew, it was something she had been secretly considering since the moment she understood that Dylan Glyndwr was no ordinary mortal.

"As you are, Maggie O'Hara, the Seven will be yours for fifty or sixty years, if you are lucky," Dylan Glyndwr said. "But the Angel violin will be yours to play forever, if you become a vampire."

43

C ARTER WOKE UP late—he knew that from the angle of the sun on the wall. He slid into a pair of New Balance running shorts and went downstairs in bare feet, feeling the worse for the Irish whiskey he'd drank the night before.

Maggie was sitting at the breakfast bar, staring into a cup of coffee.

"Good morning, sweetie," he said, sounding more cheerful than he felt.

"Morning."

Carter went to Maggie and kissed her on the forehead.

"You were fantastic last night. At the concert, I mean. You were fantastic in bed, too. You're always fantastic in bed."

Maggie blushed. "Carter."

"The audience adored you. How many standing ovations did they give you? Four? Dr. Crittenden told me she was revising the orchestra's performance schedule for the rest of the season to spotlight the university's brilliant young virtuoso. Even Katarina Eck praised you. And I noticed Nicole Hoffman talking to you after the concert, instead of being her usual snotty self. A complete triumph."

"I did do okay, didn't I?" Maggie said. There was sadness in her smile. She was thinking of the Seven, Carter thought. It was too bad that the violin's theft cast a pall over what should have been a moment of purest exultation.

"You did more than okay, Maggie. Your playing was perfectly dazzling. And to think you did it playing a second-rate fiddle. You are finished paying dues in this town, Maggie. Things are going to change in your favor. You're too good for the university, and they all know it. The butterfly has emerged from her cocoon," Carter said with a mock bow that made his head throb.

"I need some of that coffee," he said, moving to get a mug. "I think I may have had just one whiskey too many last night."

"You were funny," Maggie said with a grin. "Everybody thought your imitation of Dr. Eck was hilarious."

"Oh. I'd forgotten about that. I hope she wasn't in the pub to see that."

"She wasn't, and lucky for you."

"What was that Irish thing you did in one of the cadenzas? That took everybody by surprise. I don't think I've ever heard people start to clap and cheer in the *middle* of a classical concert."

"It was a bit of 'Drowsy Maggie.' It's an old Irish fiddle song I used to play for my grandfather before he died," Maggie said, her voice breaking.

"He would have been proud of you, darling."

Carter put his cup down next to Maggie's and wrapped his arms around her. He held her close, her head under his chin, so that he could smell the perfume of herbal shampoo in her thick hair.

"I know you didn't want to deal with it last night, but we need to call the police this morning about the Seven being stolen. We'll have to fill out a report. There will be a lot of questions, especially when we notify the insurance company. I don't imagine they'll be very happy at the prospect of paying out millions of dollars, assuming the police don't recover the Angel violin."

"We don't need to tell the police."

"Maggie—"

"I got it back."

Carter backed away to see her eyes.

"Really?"

"There it is. See for yourself."

The violin was in its case, on the sofa in the great room.

"That's fantastic! But how? And when? This morning?"

"It was returned," Maggie said vaguely.

"By the thief?"

She nodded.

"Why? Guilt?"

"Yes, that was part of it."

"We should call the police anyway. This is serious. That violin is worth millions, and it's a cultural treasure to boot. The police ought to know about anybody who would steal something so valuable, even if they gave it back."

"The violin was returned anonymously," she said, and looked away from him.

"Maggie?"

He waited until she met his eyes.

"Are you leveling with me?"

It took Maggie a while to answer. "I need you to trust me on this, Carter. I know what I'm doing."

Carter picked up his coffee and walked to the window. There was not a cloud in the sky, but the bright sunlight shone down on the earth with little warmth. In places still untouched by its light, there were silver touches of frost. Summer was gone. Winter was not far off.

"Are you sure about this?" he said, still looking out the window.

"Yes, I am," Maggie replied without hesitation. "There is nothing to gain by pursuing the matter, and much to lose."

Carter looked over his shoulder at Maggie. Her face was set in resolve.

"All right," he said, releasing the tension in his body with his breath. "It's your decision to make."

She nodded.

"And speaking of decisions, there's one I wanted to ask you to make last night, but with all the excitement it didn't seem the right moment. I'll be right back."

When Carter returned to the kitchen, he was carrying a small box in his hand. When he gave it to Maggie, she looked as if she was about to start crying.

"Go ahead. Open it."

"My God, Carter," she said in a breathy voice. "It's beautiful!"

"I liked it," he said, pleased with her reaction to the ring.

"It's huge."

"The diamond is two carats. You deserve no less, Maggie. In fact, more."

"Carter . . ."

"You know how much I love you."

Maggie swiped at a tear with the back of her free hand.

"I want to spend the rest of my life with you, Maggie. Will you marry me? I promise to never ask you to make compromises with your music for my sake. I know that music and the Angel violin are the first two priorities in your life. I am more than happy to be third, if you will have me. That's how much I love you."

"Carter," she said, smiling and crying at the same time, "I don't know what to say."

"Then don't say anything; just put the ring on your finger. If you can't say yes now, at least don't say no. I want you to have it regardless. If you don't want the man who goes along with the ring, I can have the stone reset in a necklace. Then maybe you can wear it sometimes, when you stand in front of an audience in New York or Paris and play your Angel violin."

"Carter, you are the sweetest man on Earth," Maggie said, her voice shaking, as she slipped the ring onto her finger.

"If that's true," Carter said, leaning forward to kiss away her tears, "you don't want to be the one who lets me get away."

44

DYLAN GLYNDWR STOOD outside Ivaskin Violins, leaning on the fender of his rental car. The shop was not what he would have expected of Carter Dunne. He had taken Maggie O'Hara's lover to be a typical nouveau riche American, yet Dunne's establishment was a pleasant little cottage, not some modern abortion of prefabricated metal and smoked glass. Much to the vampire's surprise, the place was thoroughly inoffensive to his refined sensibilities. He could see the outline of violins through the front windows, a shape that pleased him more than anything except the female form in sidelong odalisque repose.

Dylan went up the walk and entered. The business seemed deserted, although the selection of old violins and bows was welcoming enough to the vampire.

"Well, hello, Dylan."

Carter appeared in a doorway holding a demitasse cup in his hand—not dreadful American coffee, Dylan could tell, but espresso brewed from freshly ground French-roast beans.

Dylan had completely underestimated Carter Dunne, he decided.

"This is a surprise," Carter said, putting down the coffee to shake hands.

"I must apologize again for the late-night intrusion at your house. The hour was ungodly."

The vampire didn't specify *which* intrusion. Maggie must not have told her lover about Dylan returning the Seven after stealing it from her. The mortal's manner wouldn't be so friendly otherwise.

"Don't mention it," Carter said. "What can I do for you, Dylan? Are you looking for a violin? This morning we took delivery on several lovely eighteenth-century violins from the auction in Boston—two French, three Italians, and a German violin."

"Actually, I was hoping you could help me locate Miss O'Hara," Dylan said.

The American tried not to react, but the prickly spike of jealousy was easy enough to see. Dylan did not blame Carter Dunne. Maggie O'Hara was the sort of woman any man would be jealous about, were she sharing his bed.

"I don't mean to sound unfriendly," Carter said, "but I would have guessed you were more interested in Maggie's violin than in Maggie."

Dylan held Carter's stare, both men reflecting the same smile stretched to the limit that divided civil behavior from open hostility.

"I will not insult your intelligence by denying that I would like to possess the Seven for myself," Dylan confessed. "What violinist wouldn't? But by the same token and with all due respect, who could hear Miss O'Hara play the Angel violin and not be smitten to the depths of the soul?"

"Is that why you are here, Dylan—because you have been *smitten?*"

"Only in a manner of speaking that is perhaps too old-fashioned in its gallantry for the American vernacular."

Carter gave a short, mirthless laugh. "We are as capable of gallantry in this country as anybody."

"No doubt you are, sir. But the fact is I had a certain matter of mutual professional interest to discuss with Miss O'Hara."

"Oh, really?" Carter asked with more doubt than it was polite to express.

"Really," Dylan replied. He wondered if the man was going to attempt to punch him. Dylan hoped not, because he really did like Carter's violin shop and wasn't anxious to kill him where he stood.

"Maggie's violin was stolen," Carter said, looking at Dylan closely as if to gauge his reaction to the information. "She got it back, though."

"I heard something to that effect. Miss O'Hara was very fortunate. I would have expected anyone bold enough to steal such an invaluable instrument to spirit it out of the country with all the dispatch they could muster. Its return to Miss O'Hara is, perhaps, another in the series of miracles attributed to the Angel violins."

"The thing I can't understand," Carter said, "is why someone would go to the trouble to steal it and then turn around and give it back."

"Perhaps the thief heard Maggie play the Seven and realized the two belonged together."

"They certainly do," Carter Dunne said. For whatever reason, the air had suddenly gone out of the plucky mortal. He looked away, a sour expression on his face that held as he drank from his coffee, as though the drink had become cold and bitter in those brief moments.

"I'm afraid you're out of luck on all accounts—both the girl and the violin," the American said. "Maggie has gone away. She has taken the Seven with her."

It was Dylan's turn to stare. He turned his penetrating eyes on Carter Dunne and quickly saw within the man's mind enough to render unnecessary any further discussion with Maggie's lover.

"She went with Maria Rainer," Dylan said.

"They flew to Germany aboard a private jet owned by one of Maria's patrons."

"You are attached to the girl."

"Yes, I am," Carter said.

"Is she coming back?"

"I honestly don't know."

Dylan nodded, looking down at the floor.

Something strange and disturbing was happening inside the vampire: he was feeling compassion for Carter Dunne. Dylan did not experience emotions, at least not for others, and certainly never for mortals. Yet hearing Maggie O'Hara play the Angel violin in the dress rehearsal had melted an invisible barrier in his ancient heart. Dylan felt for the girl, and he felt for the man who loved her. He knew the pain Carter Dunne was suffering because he—Dylan Glyndwr, deposed Prince of Wales, virtuoso violinist, and vampire whose lust for blood could never be fully satisfied—had fallen in love with Maggie O'Hara, too. Why else would he have given her back the Angel violin? What did it matter that the Seven and Maggie were joined soul to soul? Had that stopped the vampire from killing Serafino's superannuated apprentice and stealing *his* Angel violin?

No!

But poor Carter. He would be lost without the girl.

At least Dylan could play his music when he needed to forget. And there were plenty of other women in the world whose blood would help drown the flame trying to ignite in his heart after so many centuries of darkness. Besides, he and Maggie would both be performing in Europe. Berlin was not so far from Amsterdam, he thought, feeling almost cheerful.

"Maybe it will keep this from being a completely unhappy visit if I confess that I am, in fact, looking for a violin."

Carter looked up.

"I was naïve about my chances to obtain the Seven. But I still am, as I think you say in America, 'looking.' "

"Well," Carter said.

Dylan could see the wheels turning in Carter's mind. Maybe Maggie wouldn't forget about him entirely. And he was, after all, in the business of selling high-end violins to wealthy players, when the opportunity afforded itself.

"Could I show you one of our new violins—our new old violins, that is? One of the French instruments is already set up for baroque playing."

"Yes," Dylan said. "I think it would be an excellent idea."

For a moment they stood looking at each other, the vampire and the man, both with the same sad smile. They had more than a little in common: they both wanted the same woman, and they both had lost her, at least for the present, to Maria Rainer and the Angel violin.

"I'll just be a few minutes. I have to go downstairs to get the violin."

"No hurry," the vampire said. "I have all the time in the world."

Above his head, Dylan heard the sound of a stool scraping on the wood flooring. Footsteps moved toward the stairs and began to descend. An elderly man with an apron over his white shirt and tie came down. He was carrying a viola.

"You can only be Gianni Felici," Dylan said.

"*Buon giorno*," Felici said, and bowed his head.

"You repaired Maggie O'Hara's violin. It is an honor to meet the only living luthier to have worked on an Angel."

The vampire shook hands with the old man. Felici's skin was cold to the touch, his circulation poor. Dylan introduced himself, and asked Felici if he made violins.

"I used to, years ago, but for a long time I have confined myself to repairs," Gianni Felici answered, looking back at the vampire with watery, red-rimmed eyes. "Violinmaking is an art for younger men. I no longer have the energy or patience."

"Archangelo Serafino was old and blind when he made the miraculous Angel violins," Dylan countered.

"God blessed him with talents I do not possess." The old man held up his hands, the knuckles swollen, the fingers ribbed with blue veins. "I am getting arthritis. I will be forced to retire soon. I should have quit before now, but I love the work. Even my eyes are beginning to fail. But I am afraid that, unlike the case of Archangelo Serafino, there will be no miracle violins in my future."

"What would you say, Signor Felici, if I told you I could cure the problems with your hands and eyes," the vampire said, his voice dropping to a lyrical purr.

"The Fountain of Youth exists only in fairy tales, Signor Glyndwr."

"But if you were a young man again, would you use the knowledge you gained working on the Seven to build me a replica Angel violin?"

"If I were young again," the elderly luthier said with a thin smile, "I would do my best to fulfill your wish."

Dylan draped his arm around the old man's bony shoulders and spoke lowly into Felici's ears, like one conspirator whispering to another.

"Signor Felici," the vampire said, "have you ever puzzled long and hard over a difficult problem, only to discover the solution could be staring you straight in the face?"

**When the sun finally sets on
the British Empire...*Beware!***

THE LONDON
VAMPIRE PANIC
Michael Romkey

A killer is loose on the streets of Victorian
London—a fiend who thrives on darkness...
and blood. The murders are indiscriminate,
ruthless, and linked by the same hideous
calling card: the torn throats and bloodless
bodies of the victims. Led by the famous
vampire hunter Dr. Abraham Van Helsing, six
men set out to track down the maniac, and
bring the nightmare gripping the city to a
blessed end. If they can stay alive....

Another unforgettable tale of the undead, by
the author of *Vampire Hunter.*

**Published by Ballantine Books.
Available wherever books are sold.**

Visit www.delreydigital.com— the portal to all the information and resources available from Del Rey Online.

- Read sample chapters of every new book, special features on selected authors and books, news and announcements, readers' reviews, browse Del Rey's complete online catalog, and more.

- Sign up for the Del Rey Internet Newsletter (DRIN), a free monthly publication e-mailed to subscribers, featuring descriptions of new and upcoming books, essays and interviews with authors and editors, announcements and news, special promotional offers, signing/convention calendar for our authors and editors, and much more.

To subscribe to the DRIN: send a blank e-mail to join-ibd-dist@list.randomhouse.com or sign up at www.delreydigital.com

The DRIN is also available at no charge for your PDA devices—go to www.randomhouse.com/partners/avantgo for more information, or visit www.avantgo.com and search for the Books@Random channel.

Questions? E-mail us at delrey@randomhouse.com

 www.delreydigital.com